Praise for *The Good Girls*

"This clever thriller lures you in, then hits you where it hurts—with shocking power."
—Dylan Farrow, #MeToo activist and author of *Hush*

"Brimming with suspense, along with a compelling cast of suspects, Bartlett's latest offers up a gripping, page-turning mystery about small-town secrets and the reasons girls keep them."
—Stephanie Kuehn, Morris Award–winning author of *Charm & Strange*

"Beautiful and powerful, *The Good Girls* is a revelation. I couldn't stop until the breathless end, and it's been haunting me in the days since I finished. Full of dark secrets and twists you won't see coming, this one will keep you in its grip long after the last page."
—Sarah Lyu, author of *The Best Lies*

The Good Girls

CLAIRE ELIZA BARTLETT

HARPER TEEN
An Imprint of HarperCollinsPublishers

For all the girls who couldn't speak up, for the girls who were ignored, denied, and punished for being themselves. I will always believe you.

PROLOGUE
THE DEAD GIRL

The end of my life starts here.

A rainy, sodden autumn has turned the river below into a roaring monster. Rocks jut out like jagged teeth, jet black against frothy white. My blood sings as the weathered wood sags behind me—someone has followed me onto the tiny bridge over Anna's Run.

I've been running. Running for so long, I forgot what it feels like to stop. My whole body is still poised to flee.

But it's too late for that now. Legends say Anna's Run takes one unlucky sacrifice every year. The wind wraps around my neck like a cord.

The figure at the end of the bridge moves closer. I try to turn, but the world around me rushes and I can't keep up. The water, my blood. Even my vision spins, moving too fast for the rest of me.

And then everything crystallizes to a point: One image, the hand stretched toward my chest. One sound, the crash of water around a body. One feeling: cold that knocks out thought, knocks out even the memory of your own name. Cold that steals the breath from your lungs.

Everything has been stolen from me. My future, my life— and now my body, swallowed whole by the nightmares that make up Anna's Run. Even my story isn't mine anymore.

That's the thing about being dead. You no longer get to say what happens next.

1

THE LOUDMOUTH SLUT

MUÑEZ: The date is Thursday, December 6, 2018, the time is seven fifty-five. Detective Muñez interviewing Claude Vanderly. Thank you for joining us, Miss Vanderly. You must be wondering why we've—

CLAUDE: It's the dead girl, isn't it?

Oh, sorry. Emma. But that *is* why you wanted to talk to me, right? Because I'm the person most likely to know something? Because I'm the person most likely to have something to do with it?

MUÑEZ: We just have a few questions.

CLAUDE: Sure. You *randomly* selected the girl who gets into the most trouble at Jefferson-Lorne. Well, I wasn't involved, so let's start there. I mean I'm, like, a feminist. I don't go around killing girls. And I can't give you much help with the investigation either. I didn't really know Emma. She was a bit of a loner, but she hung out with Avery sometimes. You should ask Avery Cross why Emma would be at Anna's Run last night. Or what sorts of enemies she might have made.

MUÑEZ: Miss Vanderly, we're talking to you right now, not Miss Cross.

CLAUDE: I'm just trying not to waste your time. It's your call. Sadly for you, I have a solid alibi. You know Jamie Schill? Principal Mendoza does, don't you, sir? Jamie goes here. And we're friends.

Friends with benefits, actually. So yeah. You can guess what I was doing last night.

MUÑEZ: No accusation is being made toward you. This is simply standard procedure. We're trying to establish a timeline. And due to the nature of the ... emerging evidence, most of the student body has been involved now. Can you tell us how, exactly, you first heard about Emma?

CLAUDE: Fine. Okay, so when I first heard ... It was this morning. At Jamie's house.

I woke up with Jamie's nose pressed into my back. Yes, his nose, you perverts. He burrows down in the night when he's cold, and it's the closest we get to cuddling. For a moment I thought I'd beat the alarm and I had a few glorious warm moments to myself. Then Jamie's mom knocked, and he woke with a twitch and a snort. It was 6:45. The alarm went off fifteen minutes ago. Oops.

Mrs. Schill didn't know I was over. She's one of those clueless moms who think their son is going to stay a virgin until he's married. Nothing inspires terror in a boy like trying to keep his friend with benefits a secret from the woman who pushed him out of her vagina, and Jamie went from comatose to panicked and kicking in about a tenth of a second. I thumped onto the floor in a tangle of limbs and comforter. "Hide," he hissed.

"Good morning to you, too," I grumbled, which wasn't entirely fair. We've never done that whole boyfriend-girlfriend thing. He knows it freaks me out, which is part of why I actually spend time with him outside of parties and school.

"Shut up," Jamie pleaded, half pushing, half rolling me toward his closet while simultaneously retrieving my jeans, T-shirt, and phone. With his puppy eyes he gave me one last, imploring glance. I gotta give it to him, he has those eyes. They're brown, with a ring of green in them, and wide, and framed by insane lashes that I would sort of kill for. He stared back at me, obviously distracted from the task at hand. "You're beautiful," he sighed, which he always says right before he kisses me.

Early-morning makeouts are fine with me. I had his night-shirt in my fist and was leaning forward when the knock came again. "Bear? Are you all right in there?" Jamie's mom has this cutesy voice that makes me want to vomit in my mouth.

We froze. "I'm just getting dressed." Jamie uses that trick a lot when I'm around. It usually works.

This morning was anything but usual. "I need to talk to you."

Jamie looked like *he* wanted to vomit in his mouth. "Sorry," he whispered, then disentangled my hand from his shirt and slammed the closet door in my face. I was in the dark, half giddy and half asleep. My eyes felt packed with sand; I must've forgotten to take my contacts out in the night. My knees were jammed up against the door. And then I noticed the smell. Most boys' rooms smell like a cold gym. Jamie's smelled like his deodorant, clean and fresh and soft somehow.

Since I couldn't get dressed without kicking open the door and saying a not-so-nice good morning to Mrs. Schill, I unlocked my phone.

That was when I started to realize: this was going to be a weird day.

First off, I had like a gazillion messages from my mom. Mom isn't like the Mrs. Schills of the world. She doesn't give a shit if I'm sleeping over with a guy. She doesn't text me every five minutes if I'm nearing curfew. She doesn't even *give* me a curfew. But the messages were piled on top of one another, a mountain of worry. The thought of climbing it made me want to flop back onto the ground—but that would have resulted in the aforementioned door kicking, and baring my goods to Jamie's mom. So I took a deep breath, steeled myself for the worst, and clicked.

Just checking in to see if u r ok? Mssg back pls xxx

Hon I know I don't normally do this but pls text

Please call.

Something happened at Anna's Run.

". . . Anna's Run," Mrs. Schill said at the same time. I fumbled the phone as it slipped in my hands.

"I don't know anything about it," Jamie said. "What's going on?"

"I have to get to work. There'll probably be a lot of rumors going around school today. Just remember, don't believe everything you hear." I stifled my snort against my knee. I bet Mrs. Schill believes everything she hears about *me*. "And if you need to call us, call us. Okay?"

"Okay," came Jamie's voice, muffled by what was undoubtedly a bear hug. She looks like a strong wind would snap her in half, but that woman could break bones if she wanted to.

Jamie waited ages before deciding it was okay to let me out of the closet. By that time my legs had woken up *and* gone back to sleep. I wobbled to my feet, using his closet wall as support. "Mom's on her way out, so we should be in the clear. I gotta shower. Then we'll go."

"What about *my* shower?"

The side of his mouth cocked up. "You don't need one. You smell good."

"Liar," I accused, but smiled back. As Jamie went to shower I took an experimental sniff under my arm. Thank the Universe for spray deodorant.

His shower, at least, gave me time to call mom. She picked up on the first ring. "Claude?"

"No, Darth Vader."

"That's not funny," she snapped, but I could sense her relief. Some of the tension seemed to unwind from her voice as she said, "Are you all right? Where are you?"

Like I said, Mom never asks me that sort of thing. "I stayed over at Jamie's. I'm fine, everything's fine. What's going on?"

Mom took a steeling breath. "Someone's been calling around. There was an incident at Anna's Run last night."

An Incident. Sounds ominous, but honestly? Jefferson-Lorne is the sort of town that invents drama for shits and giggles. And Jefferson-Lorne is rife with rumors. I should know, I'm at the center of practically every rumor I hear.

"Don't panic," I told her. "It was probably a prank. People do stupid shit all the time."

"People also die at Anna's Run all the time," Mom said.

Anna's Run is our resident one-stop shop for urban legends. The little bend in the river seems harmless, even picturesque—but the calm drift of the water hides a wicked current that carved out the bank below. If you go in, you get sucked under and pushed downstream before you even realize that things have gone wrong. The pressure of the water makes it impossible to break free—that's what the legends say. I mean, they also say that the river sprang from nowhere after the hanging of Anna's witch coven, and that the current feels like dead girls' fingers pulling you down. If you're not from around here, you don't realize. Anna's like a god in this town. A god of nature who has to be appeased. Everyone else in Colorado is worried about blizzards and pine beetles and forest fires, but for us it's the river. And people mess around with it. They think they can control it, or themselves, be safe next to a natural phenomenon that could kill you in thirty seconds. I mean, I'd never fuck with that place, or its reputation. But people lack general intelligence. Another nugget of wisdom brought to you by My Experience in High School.

MUÑEZ: So you're familiar with Anna's Run?
CLAUDE: *Everyone's* familiar with Anna's Run. I started

going there when I was ten. Back then my friends and I dared each other to call out for the ghost—you know, the ghost of Anna? She steals silver, like forks and spoons and shit, and ties it to the trees around the run. People climb the trees to get it back, and they fall into the water and don't come out again. Anna drags them down, holds them under so that they can't swim up and out. I took a bottle of wine once and threw it in the river. It came up downstream, empty. Guess Anna doesn't get a lot of merlot in her life.

MUÑEZ: The local police report shows that you were arrested at Anna's Run.

CLAUDE: Yeah, maybe.

MUÑEZ: Maybe?

CLAUDE: I mean, I don't remember any incident in particular.

MUÑEZ: You don't remember being arrested for suspicious activity and disorderly conduct? Those were the charges.

CLAUDE: Look, Officer, the police hate me, and the police hate my mom. I've never done anything my peers haven't done at Anna's Run. Are we going through my record or my alibi?

As I slithered into my clothes one-handed, Mom sighed. Her voice softened. "I don't mean to lose it on you. It's been a rough night. And you didn't text back. . . ."

"Sorry," I said as Jamie returned in a cloud of body spray. "Out like a light."

"Okay." She sighed again. "I love you, sweetheart. Have a good day at school and don't do anything I wouldn't do."

That's an old joke in the Vanderly home. Mom was the biggest terror in high school. Some of my teachers talk about her with awe.

Jamie and I walked the block and a half to my car. I park by the playground when I go to Jamie's so that Mrs. Schill doesn't see the Devil Incarnate's car sitting in her driveway each morning. Jamie slouched into the passenger side as I slung my backpack into the trunk. "Don't you get tired of sneaking around all the time?"

"Nope." For the record, I'm not a sneak. But I like boys— so sue me. *Don't you get tired* is the textbook beginning to a boy wanting to be exclusive. In my experience, boys only want to be exclusive if I'm getting laid more than they are.

So I revved up Janine—that's my six-speed Honda, 2014 model, charcoal gray, in case you're taking notes. "So what was your mom saying about Anna's Run?"

Jamie shrugged. "Weird things, blah blah." He looked at me sidelong, quirking one eyebrow up. "Someone probably heard a coyote in the night and panicked."

I slid into the game. "Someone fell asleep after too much weed and had a weird dream." Jamie's the best person to riff off. Also, doing this meant he couldn't stumble through the let's-be-exclusive proposal he'd so clearly rehearsed.

"Sex cult covering for their loud noises," he said.

I guffawed as I pulled away from the park. "Oh my Universe, who would even be in a sex cult in this town?"

"It's always the ones you think are most respectable." Jamie wiggled his fingers theatrically. "My money's on Mr. Cross."

"Ew." Mr. Cross owns most of the construction companies

here. He's the kind of guy who wears sunglasses indoors, who rubs elbows with the mayor and the governor, who invites all the teens over for a pool party, who has a yacht parked in front of his house even though we live in friggin' *Colorado*.

"Where are we going?" Jamie asked as I turned off the main road.

"We're taking the scenic route," I said.

"Claude," he groaned.

But I wanted to see Anna's Run.

"We won't actually see anything. And we'll miss breakfast burritos." Jamie's voice took on a suspicious tint. He saw me skip lunch once and now he's terrified I might be anorexic. "At least have some of my shake." He held up the protein shake his mom leaves him every morning.

"No thanks. Cement has more flavor." I held up a hand to stop his protest. "I brought lunch—I'll eat it for breakfast. Calm down."

"We could still be getting burritos," he grumbled, sliding low in his seat. Poor guy. He's used to having his way.

Sadly for him, I'm also used to having mine. We drove to Anna's Run.

Ordinarily I'd have liked the drive. The smell of the woods out that way is crisp and clean. We get a view of the mountains from the road, rising blue-gray and capped with snow almost year-round. The road is dotted with turnoffs that lead to dozens of hiking trails, going farther into the Rockies or up to Diamondback Ridge (great place for parties, by the way). And, of course, Anna's Run.

The water was high. I could hear that from the car, even

though I couldn't see the river through the trees; I've been out there enough to picture it. Squeaking bridge, rocks as sharp as blades.

Jamie was right: we weren't going to see anything. The cutoff to Anna's Run was blocked by three police cars. More cars were parked by the side of the road where the asphalt met prairie grass. I slowed Janine to a crawl. Over the rush of the river, I heard men's voices calling back and forth as they moved through the woods.

"They're looking for something," Jamie said.

I didn't have much time to think about it. We'd been spotted by a cop, and he was on his way over. And it wasn't just any cop. It was Deputy Chief Bryson, my personal nemesis in the Jefferson-Lorne PD. That man has it in for me, and he has since before he caught me stuffed in the coat check with his son at homecoming. I stifled the urge to roll the window up and speed away.

Bryson leaned on the windowsill. "Can I help you fine folks?" he said, giving me an impressive stink eye.

Jamie tried to be my white knight. "We're just driving to school, sir."

Bryson's eyes never left my face. "Don't you live on the other side of town, Miss Vanderly?"

"I'm giving my fine friend a ride." I batted my eyes. "We're stopping for breakfast burritos. Want to come?"

Bryson glared at me a moment longer. I was sure he'd ask us to pull over so he could check the car for weed—don't have any, by the way. But someone shouted to him, and he stepped away instead. "Drive on. And don't come back this way. You don't have business here, Miss Vanderly."

All in all, not the worst encounter with Bryson. As I put Janine in first, Jamie slumped over and let his head thump against the dash. "Why did we do that?" he moaned. "What if he tells Mom you drove me to school?"

"Relax," I said, patting his knee. "He's obviously got more to worry about than your personal life." I watched the scene as it receded in the rearview mirror. More cars were pulling up to the side of the road, disgorging adults in suits and uniforms. It looked like the beginnings of a search party. Or a manhunt. "Is that the FBI? Ooh, I bet they're looking for the sex cult."

Jamie wasn't in the mood anymore. "We shouldn't make assumptions about anything. Starting a bunch of rumors at school isn't going to help."

I just laughed. "Okay, Mom."

Jamie busied himself on his phone as I drove. Resentment hung heavy in the air around him. "What are you reading?" I asked, to change the mood.

"More Lily Fransen stuff. Can't they just move on already?"

"No," I said shortly, earning another weird look from Jamie. "Let's face it, the only justice she'll ever get is Senator Hunterton's name being dragged through the mud as long as possible. I don't want to let it go."

"But what if he's innocent?" Jamie said.

Classic. The first question is always *But what if he's innocent?* It's never *But what if he's guilty and she spent the last twenty-five years living with the trauma of being molested as a teen, with no recourse to justice?*

I guess that sentence doesn't fit well on a bumper sticker.

"Jamie, don't make me explain to you what a fuckwit you're being," I said. He slid down in his chair and kept scrolling.

Then he gasped. "Holy shit."

"What?" I checked the rearview reflexively. No cops following us, no deer waiting to jump into the road.

"Have you seen this?" He practically shoved his phone in my face.

"Jamie, hon. Driving."

I thought it was, like, a cat video. Or another meme of Lily Fransen's ugly crying face at the Senator Hunterton hearings.

I never expected *that* video.

We pulled into the Jefferson-Lorne parking lot and I finally grabbed the phone. That was when I realized the serious size of this shitstorm.

I couldn't identify anyone from it. It was super grainy, obviously shot in the middle of the night on a crappy camera. And I couldn't hear anything, either. The river's roar filled the speakers. But I could make out the two figures—one light, one dark. One short, one tall. Standing on the bridge over Anna's Run.

Then the dark one moved, and suddenly only one person stood on the bridge. The light one was gone in a flash of pale hair. The railing leaned, splintered, over the water. The frame froze.

"Holy shit," I repeated.

"Right?"

I would have been happy to turn Janine around and drive right back out of the school lot. But Jamie put a hand on my arm, and that hand somehow found a way down to *my* hand and squeezed. "It'll be okay," he said. Like I said, he's the sweetest liar. And it got me out of the car.

A Fort Collins PD car was parked at the curb by the foot of the stairs. You guys sure don't waste any time. As soon as I laid eyes on it, I knew that the dead girl was someone from here. And I knew that *you all* would want to talk to me.

The Loudmouth Slut always has something to answer for, right?

2

THE WOLVES

The hall is still, noiseless, like the reservoir before a storm. The air is thick with grief and shock. Three students push through the fog of it, their movements muted, their heels silent on the linoleum floor.

Still, everyone knows. The wolves are coming.

The office door opens and Claude Vanderly stomps out. She looks like she wants to break this storm, smash the quiet at the top of her lungs. Shatter the fragile shell that has encased everyone and let the rage out. She runs her bitten fingernails through box-black hair and slings her backpack over one shoulder. Then she turns and slams into the three girls. Their books and phones smash to the ground. Claude crouches and grabs for her things without looking up.

"If it isn't Vampirella." One of the girls smiles. "Lurking in broad daylight."

The girls couldn't be more her opposite: Short and petite, where Claude is tall and lanky. Their cuteness belies a sharpness in how they move together, as if in sync, as if everything they do in life is part of a cheer routine.

The two on the outside are dressed in black, but not like Claude—they're dressed for mourning, not making a statement. The girl in the middle, their leader, sports a pink sweater over her dark skirt and leggings.

This is Avery Cross. The queen of the wolves—in sheep's clothing, of course. Her blond hair is pulled into its customary high ponytail on her head.

"So. You're next." Claude rises, looking Avery up and down.

"You talked to them?" Avery asks.

Claude shrugs one shoulder. "Talked, fielded questions about my lifestyle—whatever."

The two girls to either side of Avery close in, ready to protect their own. Claude's expression turns momentarily to derision as she gives them a cursory glance.

"I think—I think it's nice that you're helping with the investigation."

Claude's snort is more angry than amused. "Helping? Nobody helps the pigs, Aves. At least, nobody smart."

Avery lifts her chin. "I'm helping." She bounces on the balls of her feet.

Claude's eyebrows go up. She smiles and cocks her head. "Like I said."

The girls to either side of Avery bristle. "And what did they want you for, Supergoth? Are you a prime suspect?" asks a girl with a brown ponytail to match Avery's.

"Lyla," Avery whispers. She turns pleading eyes up toward Claude. "What do they know? I mean, what are they saying about her? Do they think she's okay?"

"Who's okay after Anna's Run? She's dead, and everyone knows it." Claude doesn't see Avery flinch—or maybe she does, and it's why she continues. "They're never going to find out what happened to her, just like all the other girls who died there."

"Shut up, Claude," Lyla snaps. She tucks her arm through Avery's. "Ignore her. It's going to be okay."

Claude rolls her eyes. "Sure. It's going to be fairies and rainbows and unicorn kisses. And if you just wish hard enough, Anna will pop out of the water and give Emma back." She knocks one Doc Marten against the other. "Just keep clicking your heels, Dorothy."

Color rises in Avery's cheeks. Her feet bounce and her hands tighten around the straps of her backpack. The hardness in her voice makes even her friends lean away. "Just because I'm not bitter doesn't mean I don't live in the real world."

Claude leans forward. "Emma's *dead*. Everyone thinks so. And the police are going to do the same thing they've always done—blunder around for a while, then forget about her."

"That's not true," Avery half shouts. She's breathing hard, jostling on her heels like she wants to take off in a sprint. She takes a deep breath and lowers her voice. "They *will* find out what happened. And when they prove you wrong, I won't be surprised if they prove you're a liar, too."

The office door opens again, and two men come out. One still looks fresh out of his teaching internship, baby-faced and blond, too eager to smile. Mr. Pendler, English and journalism teacher, and Emma's academic adviser. The other has silver in his brown hair and beard, and wears a coach's whistle around

18

his neck. Mr. Garson, school counselor, head coach of the lacrosse team and cheerleading squad, and three-time winner of the Best Educator award for the county.

"You know the rules about noise in the hall, girls," Mr. Garson says.

Claude's Martens touch together again. *Click, click, click.* "Wouldn't want to break the rules, would we, *Aves*?"

Lyla steps in front, ponytail swinging. "At least Avery's trying to help. Everyone's going to know that you got called in because you hang around Anna's Run, doing who knows what. You probably know *all* the sketchy stuff that goes down there, don't you? Whatever you haven't done yourself."

"Ladies." Mr. Pendler puts a hand on Lyla's shoulder. She tenses, but he guides her back. "This is an awful time for everyone. I don't expect you to be able to concentrate, but believe me—the routine of class will be good for you."

Mr. Garson clears his throat. Mr. Pendler withdraws his hand from Lyla's shoulder. Garson says, "Miss Vanderly? I believe you have precalc?"

Claude's sneer is award worthy. "Good luck, Dorothy," she mutters, making sure to knock Lyla with her shoulder as she stalks by.

"Witch," Avery replies under her breath. Her eyelashes are heavy with unshed tears.

"Lyla? Natalie? Do you have hall passes?" Mr. Pendler asks.

Lyla and Natalie can't quite meet his eyes. Lyla pulls Avery closer. "We're emotional support. Aves needs us."

Avery's eyes are still on the ground. Pendler teeters on the edge, uncertain. But Mr. Garson shakes his head. "I know it's difficult, but they'll want to meet with you alone. Can you do that?" She nods. "Ladies, back to your classes. And Avery"—he fishes a tissue out of his pocket—"come on in."

Avery moves toward the open door but stops when she reaches the threshold. The look she casts back isn't toward Lyla and Natalie but at the long figure, moving down the hall, soon eclipsed by the sunlight. Then she pulls out her phone and begins to type.

3

THE CHEER CAPTAIN

CLINE: The date is Thursday, December 6, 2018, the time is eight forty-nine. This is Detective Cline interviewing Avery Amelia Cross, correct?

AVERY: Yes.

CLINE: Thank you for agreeing to meet with us. Please, take your time. I can only imagine how difficult this must be for you.

AVERY: It's—it's okay. I mean, of course it's not okay. Emma, oh my god. It's just—unbelievable, you know? I haven't been able to stop thinking about it since I found out. And I haven't been able to stop crying. God. My makeup must be raccooning right now.

I'm so sorry, that's an awful thing to think about at a time like this. It's just like Mom says: I can't keep my head screwed on straight for anything. But I just— Emma was here *yesterday*. We talked about our cheer routine. It was like another day, and now—

I'm sorry, do you have another tissue?

21

CLINE: Can you tell us how you found out about Emma?

AVERY: It was this morning. I know that . . . video's been going around since the middle of the night, but I don't look at Facebook after nine. I was working on my cheer routine all last night, with my best friend, Lyla. She's on the cheer team, too, and I sleep over a lot so we can practice. Then I drove us to school this morning.

I started to think something weird was going on when I saw the police car. We don't usually get them, you know. But even then, I just figured someone got busted for weed, right? Claude Vanderly's the type to get escorted out for having something special in her locker.

We were kind of joking about it when we went into homeroom. Usually we have a few minutes to ourselves, since we're earlier than everyone else.

Not today.

Homeroom was crammed, and loud. But the chatter stopped as I came in.

For a moment, I was sure it was about me. I know people talk about me. Going over my every move at competitions, counting the calories I put on my plate at lunch. Fear swelled up from my stomach, and for a second I thought I was going to be sick. *They'll think you're pregnant.* I swallowed.

The cheer team had set up in the corner. They were all crying. Walking to my seat felt like walking down the world's worst catwalk. Everyone was staring at me, and not in the good way. A ripple of whispers broke out. I checked the curves of my belly, the jut of my hip.

Natalie leaped out of her chair and gave us both a huge hug. "I'm so sorry, Aves," she said thickly. Tears streamed down her face, running a track through her makeup. "How are you holding up?"

"A-about what?" I stammered. I could still feel the pressure of every stare in homeroom.

She took in the look on our blank faces and her red-rimmed eyes widened. "Oh my god. You guys saw the video, right?"

"What video?"

"Oh my god. Ohmygod." Natalie leaned over. "Shay, your phone."

"The Ham confiscated it," Shay said, dabbing at her eyes with a tissue. "Just like yours."

I unzipped my bag and grabbed my phone. I don't usually take my phone out during class, but I had to know. What had reduced the team to tears? What had all of homeroom in their seats before 7:45?

Natalie took the phone from me. By the time she handed it back, a crowd of students had piled behind us. They pressed in, pushing against my shoulders, breathing down the back of my neck. My skin started to crawl.

"It's so creepy," said Kyle Landry, the lacrosse captain. He sounded *gleeful*. I wanted to tell him that if he thought it was so creepy, he could stop shoving his crotch up against my shoulder and go back to his desk, but—well. I'm not that kind of girl.

The video was super grainy, but I knew as soon as I saw the willowy shape of her, the ice-blond hair. Emma. The roar of Anna's Run filled the speakers.

And then, the push.

I couldn't breathe. As soon as the video stopped, the whispers rushed in, building around me. They erupted in rapid-fire guessing as the video began an automatic replay.

"It had to have been someone strong."

"Definitely a dude."

"And at least six inches taller than Emma."

A shadow fell over us. The other students scattered like autumn leaves in the flood. I looked up at the less-than-ecstatic form of Mrs. Willingham.

"Good morning, Miss Cross. I'm sorry, I know this must be a shock. Phones are confiscated for the duration of the day." The Ham held out her hand and I gave up the phone without a fight. It wasn't like I wanted to watch the video again. I wish I'd never watched it in the first place.

The Ham raised her voice. "That goes for everyone. No phones, no backup phones. Your parents can call the office if they need to get in touch with you. I have to step out for a moment, and I expect you all to act cordially." As she spoke, her eye drifted over to the door, as though she knew who was about to come through.

A moment later, Claude Vanderly slouched in, wearing the same clothes she was wearing yesterday. Her thick Goth eyeliner was smeared, like she just emerged from the closet with some other girl's boyfriend. As usual.

The Ham spoke to her for a moment. Claude looked pissed. Then she scanned the room.

She and I realized at the same time. There were two empty seats left in the room—one right in front of Kyle and his cronies, and one next to me.

The seat next to me should've been Emma's seat. She should've respected that. But Claude folded her long limbs under the desk and let her bag thump between us.

I was ready to ignore the challenge. Claude needs to be at the center of at least one drama a day, and I don't fuel her fire. But Lyla, bestie that she is, wasn't about to let Claude think she could get away with anything. And Lyla's never forgiven Claude for trying to seduce my boyfriend at homecoming last year, or for spreading the rumor that she succeeded. Lyla put a hand on my arm as if to say, *I've got this.* She raised her voice in Claude's direction. "I have a cross in my bag, if you finally want that exorcism."

Claude turned her head slowly, like she'd just noticed we were there. Like I said, she manufactures drama. "I'm sure it makes a great accessory for your preppy antifeminism." She looked at me and yawned. "Morning, Little Miss Prozac."

"Misandrist Barbie," I muttered back. I couldn't help myself. I try, but honestly. Claude can't act like her life has changed even though a girl is dead? She can't acknowledge that the world doesn't revolve around her and her weird agendas?

All the same, I instantly regretted it. I'd been up late—extra cheer practice with Lyla—and I was exhausted. It felt like I had swum the length of Anna's Run myself. And now this . . . I just don't have the energy to deal with Claude. Not today.

CLINE: Do Claude and Emma have a history?
AVERY: I don't know. Is Claude a suspect?
CLINE: Why don't we stick to talking about Emma?
AVERY: Because, I mean—if Emma was out on Anna's Run,

why *wouldn't* Claude have something to do with it? Claude's out there all the time. Not that I've seen her. Anna's Run is the sketchiest place in town, so I don't even like to hear about it, much less go there, you know? But—well, Claude was arrested for vandalism last year. Vandalizing Anna's Run. That's what Emma said, and her dad's the cop who made the arrest.

You must know him. Officer Baines, chief of police?

Anyway, I heard from Emma that it wasn't actually vandalism. It was *witchcraft*. Like, weird sacrifices and stuff. Claude's mom is a lawyer, so she got the paperwork changed, but Claude talks about Anna like she's a real person. Like she can— commune with her or something.

CLINE: What do *you* think about Anna's Run?

AVERY: There's loads of ghost stories about Anna. In middle school, we used to tell them at sleepovers to scare each other. We'd say that the river was cursed there. But once we got into high school, we realized it's just a place where kids go when they want to do something bad without their parents catching them. Like smoke weed, or drink. Or, you know, other things with each other. Stuff that Claude Vanderly is . . . kind of good at.

But Emma wouldn't hang out there. Emma's as good as they come. Not to mention her dad would *flip* if he found out. I don't know why she'd be at Anna's Run last night, but it must have been a good reason. Maybe she was running from whoever—whoever . . .

CLINE: Do you have any idea who would want to hurt Emma?

AVERY: Not at all.

CLINE: No one here, or in her personal life?

AVERY: Emma didn't have any enemies—well, I guess Gwen Sayer. Sort of. I mean, they were competitors for the Devino Scholarship. But Emma didn't have, like, *real* enemies. She was always busy with her studies, but nice to everyone. She didn't have a boyfriend, and she spent so much time on extracurriculars, it was like she didn't have any left over for making friends or foes. She was good friends with Lizzy Sayer, before . . . and then when Lizzy died, Emma's dad said he didn't want her hanging around with people like that. So if she wasn't at cheer, or the school newspaper, or speech and debate club, she was at home. And even though she was totally normal and awesome, she got a reputation after the Lizzy Sayer thing.

Lizzy died near Anna's Run. Do you think it's a coincidence?

I know it happened two years ago, but Emma was, like, *really* interested in Lizzy's death. It was super awkward, since Gwen is in the same grade as us and she doesn't want to talk about it. It was an accident, right? What else is there to say?

Emma was convinced it wasn't accidental at all. The more she looked into it, the worse it got. She was . . . obsessed. I don't like using that word, but she was. She kept going back, over and over. She started being late to cheer practice, taking extra shifts at the paper . . . We were all worried, but nobody could stop her from doing the research, right? It wasn't illegal or anything.

But then the incident happened.

CLINE: Tell me about this incident.

AVERY: It was a mandatory antidrug seminar at the beginning of the year. I think Principal Mendoza and Mr. Garson set it up, so we'd connect to each other? Like instead of getting drop-down drunk and stumbling along the ravine near Anna's Run, we'd . . . hug it out? I don't know. The presenter was really nice, and trying so hard. But then Emma raised her hand, and stood up, and said, "Lizzy Sayer didn't kill herself. And she didn't die by accidental overdose." Like she was announcing lunch. "Lizzy was murdered."

The whole school went wild. A bunch of people booed—they thought Emma was stirring up trouble, or trying to get attention. Some of the others shouted facts from the case, like she had two empty bottles of Jack in the back of her car, and enough alcohol in her system to make her blackout drunk. The poor seminar lady didn't know what to do. Principal Mendoza and Counselor Garson led Emma away, and the next time I saw her, she was back to not talking about it.

And who knows how her dad reacted when he found out what she'd done. I know my parents would flip, and her dad is *super* strict.

CLINE: Would this strictness have affected Emma's relationship with anybody?

AVERY: It affected her relationship with everybody. She went straight home after school or extras, and at home she wasn't allowed online. Ever. Like, her dad's convinced that every girl on the internet wants to bully Emma to death, and every boy on the internet wants to send a . . . you know. A *dick pic.* It annoyed me, because I put our routine videos on YouTube and I expect my girls to practice. But I started to feel sad for her. I don't even know what she did when her dad was on shift and she was home. But she never wanted to make him mad. He knew everything she ate, he knew where everything was in her room . . .

CLINE: Could Emma have sneaked out of the house to meet someone last night?

AVERY: Like, the guy who pushed her over the edge? I guess. I don't know who it would be, though. And she wouldn't have any record of it, in case her dad found it.

No, wait. She had a journal. I think she only wrote in it when she was here, but she wrote in it daily for sure.

CLINE: You've seen this journal? Do you know where she kept it?

AVERY: Um, her locker maybe? I never saw her take it out or put it away, now that you mention it.

CLINE: This has been very helpful, Miss Cross. Really. Thank you for your time.

AVERY: It's nothing. I want to help, and I want justice for Emma. Really, I'll do anything. Just let me know.

Okay?

4

THOSE LEFT BEHIND

The Sayer house is quiet this morning, as it always is now. Even the neighbor's dogs don't bark when they get too close to the dividing fence. The windows are covered in spots, and shingles hang loose from the roof. The rosebushes in the garden have gone to seed and their dry brown stems spill over the postage-stamp yard, filling the drain and coiling around the fence posts. Brown on brown in the crisp, cold December day.

A delivery kid tosses the morning paper on the stoop, then pedals quickly past. Senator Hunterton's face, full of righteous rage, crunches on dead foliage. The headline reads: HUNTERTON: I DON'T TOUCH LITTLE GIRLS.

Inside the house the air is stuffy, like a window hasn't been cracked since Lizzy Sayer died. The round table still has four cheap folding chairs covered in pleather. They split at the seams, pushing out plastic foam. Only one is currently occupied—Gwen sits with a cup of coffee and a square of toast. Her food is forgotten as her fingers fly over a battered iPhone she got from Heather Halifax at school. She doesn't even look

30

up as her father comes in, though when he kisses the top of her head, she mutters, "Morning," and tilts her screen toward the table.

"All right? You're dressed for work today," says Mrs. Sayer. Her voice lilts in the Welsh Valleys tones she moved here with twenty-one years ago. She pours a thin stream of batter into a pan in their prefabricated corner kitchen, all white laminate turned beige after years of stains and burns and general use. She still doesn't know how to make fluffy pancakes. Next to the pan the electric kettle boils; two cups sit ready with second-round teabags inside.

"I thought I'd take a half day. You know how Mecklin is."

They do know. Mr. Mecklin was the first to offer any help he could give when Lizzy died. The last to pass judgment on her blood alcohol content and what that meant for Mr. and Mrs. Sayer as parents. The only to offer to pay for family counseling.

But it's easier to pretend that Gwen's father has a hard-ass boss, and ignore the truth—that Mr. Sayer hates this house as much as they do, and he's running away from it.

"I'm making pancakes," Mrs. Sayer says softly.

Her husband kisses her on the cheek. "I'm jealous. I'll bet they're delicious. Gwen, take it easy today, okay?"

Gwen's still glued to her phone. "Why?" She never takes it easy. It's a point of pride.

Her parents hesitate in the kitchen, glancing between her and each other. Their looks are full of things they don't know how to say. Finally, her mother pours steaming water into the teacups, adding a dollop of UHT milk to each. "We think you ought to stay home from school."

The phone falls to the table with a thud. "I definitely don't." Gwen's voice is iron and thunder.

"You . . . With everything happening, you might need some . . . time to process."

"No." Gwen's hands turn to fists on the table. Her mother's eyes fly to them immediately. Gwen forces her fingers open, laying them flat on the plastic rose-print tablecloth. "I don't need time. The Devino Scholarship is being announced today. I can't be truant. What if that affects my chances?"

"It won't. The decision's probably been made for weeks. We've already called the school and told them that you can't make it in."

"I can't just *skip school*. I can't go the whole day without knowing." Gwen glares from parent to parent. Her hands tremble.

Her father's lips thin. "This isn't an option, Gwen. I spoke to Principal Mendoza early this morning, and the school's a powder keg—half the students are staying home, no one's letting their kid take the bus, limited activities after dark. You'll be able to focus better if you study at home."

Gwen's breathing like she's ready to charge. "You can't be serious."

"We'll ground you if we have to," Mrs. Sayer says.

"For going to school? Jeez, Mum, I'm not Lizzy."

Everything in the room stills for one terrible moment. Mrs. Sayer's face drains of blood. Her hand clenches around the spatula. The electric kettle pops.

Gwen tries to salvage the situation. "I'm not hiding booze and pills under my bed. I just want to go to school. Like it's a normal day."

Mrs. Sayer folds her arms. "It's not a normal day. You're not going."

Emma Baines—Friday, June 16, 2017

I've been dying to get home and put this into words. Uneasiness has been balling in my stomach and dragging me down. I couldn't eat lunch. Dad drove me home 'cause he thought I was sick. And now that he's back at the office, I can finally try to untangle this strange, queasy feeling that's making my hands shake.

The summer internship's been boring up to this point. I thought I'd watch the police fight drunken hobos or take statements from rich ski wives about how some vandal keyed their husband's Audi. I sort of hoped Dad would take me out on patrol. Instead I've been in the filing room the past two weeks, sneezing dust. I'll probably be the only girl in Colorado who comes back from summer break paler than I was before.

I've been reorganizing recent cases by number. The guys at the JLPD don't understand correct filing. I'm not supposed to read the files, and I'm normally not interested—does it really matter that Claude Vanderly was caught out past curfew at Anna's Run, again? Does it really matter that Mrs. Cross made sixteen noise complaints this year?

But then I saw her file. Lizzy's file.

It felt like someone had socked me in the stomach. I sat—more like collapsed—on the crappy rolling chair. Her file was heavy in my hands, thick with statements, photographs, reports . . . a whole ream of paper and months of investigation, all of which came down to a simple statement: Lizzy Sayer committed suicide.

Lizzy was like a big sister to me. And if she'd been *my big sister, I'd never have been the little troglodyte that Gwen is. I'd never have let her change the way she did after freshman year. I'd never have let her take her own life. And I'd always, always wondered . . . how did it happen? How did Lizzy go from being the brightest girl at school to showing up to homeroom drunk at 8 a.m.?*

The redacted report has been passed around the school like a dirty magazine. Of course I've seen it. But today, I held the unredacted file in my hands.

Don't open it, *my warning voice said. My warning voice is my voice of reason, or at least of practicality. My warning voice reminds me what Dad would do if he caught me, what would make me look bad for the Devino Scholarship, what would get me in trouble with Principal Mendoza or make the wolf pack look at me funny.*

What if Dad comes in to get something? What if he checks the security cameras? *My pulse began to beat double.*

But I always knew that Lizzy's truth must be different than the redacted report paints it. I always wanted to talk to her one last time. And this file was as close as I'd ever get. I flipped it open.

A lot of the redacted stuff is personal details, and stuff that my dad would term a "moral danger" to give to the public. Like, there was a torn condom wrapper on the back seat of Lizzy's car, and fluids showed up under UV light that the police never tested, deeming them "too old" to be of significance to the investigation.

And there were footprints.

It rained the night Lizzy died, a brief thundering that made Anna roar and set all the wind chimes in Lorne clattering and clamoring. The storm was over by the time Gwen reports Lizzy left the house. So the dirt would have been fresh and wet, unusual for Colorado. Boot prints are clear in the photos, and from big feet. The police don't really talk about them in the report. Maybe they're from before Lizzy parked her car and stumbled down the ravine. It's a well-used trail, after all.

Or maybe someone was with her the night she died. Someone who was never found.

THE LORNE EXAMINER ONLINE
December 6, 2018, 11:00 A.M.
Investigation Formally Opened
in the Disappearance of Emma Baines

Police are officially declaring Emma Baines a missing person as of this morning. The teen girl, a dedicated student at Jefferson-Lorne High School, was last seen by her father, the chief of the police force, before he left for his evening shift on Monday.

"She's a good girl," Chief Baines told the Examiner. *"She doesn't mess around with drugs or drinking. She was going to go for a scholarship at Boulder." Baines further asserted, in claims substantiated by Emma's fellow students, that Emma spent most of her time at home, studying, or at school-sponsored extracurriculars. She was a finalist for the Devino Scholarship, a full undergraduate scholarship given to students of academic and moral excellence in financial need.*

The entire Jefferson-Lorne community has become involved in the search, and police from as far as Westminster have driven up to take part. A video showing a physically similar girl being pushed over the edge of the bridge at Anna's Run, posted to Emma's Facebook profile early this morning, is undergoing thorough investigation.

Emma Baines is 5'4", described as slender, with pale skin and pale blond hair cut at shoulder length. She is seventeen years of age.

Any members of the public with information regarding Emma Baines are encouraged to immediately contact the Jefferson-Lorne Police Department.

5

THE OVERACHIEVER

Gwen goes to school anyway.

She waits until her mother's hanging the laundry on the line out back, then sneaks out the front door. It's a forty-five-minute walk in the chill air and biting wind. She sends a quick text.

This side of Jefferson-Lorne is a step down from the mobile home park. The houses are long and thin, propped on cinder blocks, with paint curling back from the rotting boards to reveal all the shades that came before, back when people were proud enough to care what the outside of their house looked like. It's the kind of neighborhood where you nail a board over broken glass and cover it with plastic wrap because you can't afford a new window. It's the kind of neighborhood where all the fathers go around with shovels after a snowstorm, because half the mothers are single and working. It's the neighborhood where all the miners lived, before the yuppies sank their claws into Lorne, and demonstrated, and lobbied their representatives, and got the mines shut down. Now the lucky ones among those men, people like Gwen's father, have gone into construction, tearing down the little houses and replacing them with enormous ski lodges, winter homes of the wealthy white people that are ten times the size of the only home Gwen will ever get. If she stays in Lorne, she'll slowly watch her neighborhood get bulldozed and replaced with carefully cultivated McMansions that loom empty three-quarters of the year. If she's lucky, she'll get a job as a housekeeper or a gardener in one of them. Trimming hedges while the Avery Crosses of the world sip spiced caramel lattes that cost an hour's wage.

But that's not going to be her. That's the mantra she recites as she walks. She pulls her shoulders back and walks as though she owns the road, as though the cutting December wind can't even touch her through her threadbare coat.

Her face and hands are red by the time she gets to the front office of Jefferson-Lorne, and she can't feel her nose. She hands over a forged tardy note to the secretary in the attendance office. Through the thin walls, muffled conversation occasionally rises in volume. "Is Principal Mendoza in?" she asks.

"He's at a meeting." The secretary offers her a smile. "Thanks for coming in, dear." She doesn't even check the note.

Gwen hesitates as she leaves the office. The hall is silent—it's the middle of second period. She leans against the wall outside the principal's office, tilting her head toward the door.

". . . Give us a few more days, at least," Mendoza says.

"The Fund needs confirmation, the name of the college,

and to verify credentials. We can't sit on this. There are a lot of deserving applicants, and if it needs to go to somebody else—"

"She's *missing*, for god's sake."

"We do understand the tragedy of the situation. But remember, a lot of other people are waiting on an answer from us until they decide where they can afford to go to school. We need to be sensitive to their lives, too."

Chairs scrape and there's a thump as someone gets to their feet. Gwen starts, and before she can chicken out, knocks.

There's a pause. A few seconds later, the door is wrenched open. A man in a suit pushes his way past Gwen and down the hall. Gwen turns to Principal Mendoza, a lean man with his shirtsleeves rolled up. He wears the kind of face that makes students cry. "What can I do for you?"

Gwen does not shrink back. If anything, she straightens. Flips her dark ponytail over her shoulder. "I was just wondering. About the scholarship. Will the announcement go out today?" Nerves lend her voice a Welsh lilt, like her mother's.

Mendoza stares at her for a long moment. "How . . . ? Never mind. The announcement has been postponed until further notice."

He tries to close the door, but it bounces off of Gwen's faded red sneakers. "How long?" she asks.

Mendoza takes a deep breath. "Unfortunately, Miss Sayer, there are more important things to be concerned about. Please go to class."

He shuts the door more forcefully this time, but Gwen's already stepped back. The door bangs shut. She whirls around—

And slams right into Lyla.

"Oh," Lyla says. She wears a black skirt, black tights, and a shirt that falls off one shoulder. A black choker wraps around her neck, and heavy eyeliner and mascara complete the look. Her eyes widen as she sees Gwen. "Gwendolyn Sayer, as I live and breathe. Are you coming in late?"

Gwen shifts from foot to foot. "So?"

A wicked smile touches the corner of her mouth. "You broke a perfect attendance record. What were *you* doing last night?"

Gwen just sighs. "Shut up, Lyla." She heads toward gym class.

"Touchy," Lyla calls after her. "I guess it wasn't sleeping."

Gwen doesn't reply.

DISPATCHER: 911, what is the nature of your emergency?

MAN: There was a girl. A girl in the water.

DISPATCHER: Where was this girl?

MAN: Just downstream of Anna's Run. . . . She was floating. No, she was being dragged. The current wouldn't let her go.

DISPATCHER: Sir, could you please tell us your name and where you are right now?

MAN: I was fishing, see, and my phone got turned off last month, so I—I didn't have no phone. I came here as soon as I saw her, but I don't think you'll find—

DISPATCHER: Sir, could you tell us where you are?

MAN: I'm at the OK gas station on Forty-Ninth. Just off Wallis. But it's half a mile to Anna's Run from here. You won't find nothing. She's gone now. She's gone.

DISPATCHER: Sir, have you been drinking? Sir. Sir?

6

THE SKIRMISH

Shoes squeak on the gym floor, the fitness equivalent of nails on a chalkboard. A semi-flat soccer ball thuds along with little enthusiasm. Otherwise the only sounds are the slapping of feet and twenty students huffing in air that smells like cold sweat and disinfectant. Their gym uniforms, green shorts and white tees with the Jefferson-Lorne wolf mascot, are barely sweaty. Most of the students aren't even trying to play. Avery Cross just shimmied up the climbing rope like it's what she was born to do and now she's over in the corner, doing crunches. Two other students play hacky sack. A lot of people stand around.

Mr. Darrow sits at the bottom of the bleachers. Occasionally he shouts something like "Eyes on the ball, Mr. Fairbanks," or "Push yourselves!" Then he runs a hand through his thick hair, like he's trying to tear it out.

There is only one person who keeps an eye on the ball. There is only one person who pushes herself. Her dark brown ponytail bounces just above her shoulder blades as she runs. She seems to slide between her classmates as if they were ghosts. Her face is pinched, the same way it is when she's taking notes or working on a quiz. Gwen Sayer puts 100 percent into everything, whether it's SAT prep or mandatory indoor soccer practice. Some students make a half-hearted attempt to steal the ball, but the smarter ones get out of her way. And Gwen just keeps running, circling back, snagging the ball from whoever the goalie tosses it to.

The gym door opens, and everyone turns away from the game. With a baring of teeth and a savage kick, Gwen sends the ball spinning into the goal. Then she turns to see two detectives enter, a man and a woman. Their soles leave black rubber streaks on the gym floor. Mr. Darrow hurries over to them.

Twenty pairs of eyes focus on the two suits. The soccer ball bounces off a corner.

The male detective gestures at the door. Mr. Darrow nods. Turning to the silent class, he says, "Keep playing. And remember the *participation* part of your grade. Keep up the good work, Miss Sayer."

As soon as the door closes behind Mr. Darrow and the detectives, all pretense drops. The goalie, a small girl named Riley, sits on the floor. Friends begin to clump together, whispers passing between them, building up like rain at the start of a flash flood. Others are silent. Eyes flicker toward Gwen, then away. Gwen tucks a strand of damp hair behind her ear and straightens her T-shirt. She goes to retrieve the ball, ignoring her classmates.

One of the cheerleaders, Natalie, sits on the bottom of

the aluminum bleachers. "I can't believe Darrow thinks we're going to do class today. Like it's just a normal day."

"I know." Lyla stretches one long leg. She braided her hair for gym class, pinning it to her head in a crown. She plays with the rose-gold pendant hanging beneath the black ribbon choker. "He's totally ignoring the tragedy."

Gwen rolls her eyes from half a gym away. "Sure. You're so devastated you had to make sure you remembered your water-proof eyeliner this morning."

Her words carry through the hall. Someone snorts. Natalie leans away, but Lyla's eyes flash and she straightens, face flushing. "Excuse me?"

Lyla and Gwen haven't been friendly since Lyla asked Gwen if she was poor because of her sister's coke addiction. The fact that the whole cheer squad was on Team Emma for the scholarship hasn't helped.

Gwen folds her arms. "Cut the fake mourning. Nobody's fooled. If you really thought this was a tragedy, you'd stop trying to capitalize on it by complaining about having to actually do work."

Lyla lifts her chin. "Capitalizing? I was her *friend*."

"No one was her friend," Gwen snaps. Her words fall into an ugly well of silence. Students shift, trying to ignore the truth. Two red blotches appear on Gwen's cheeks. She rubs one side of her face as if she could wipe off the blush. "You weren't exactly there for her in life, and pretending you were all BFFs now doesn't make you a better person. You might as well be honest about it."

Lyla moves forward, catlike, stalking. "Well, *honestly*, I'm not surprised to see you dry-eyed. Isn't it convenient that Emma disappeared right before the scholarship announcement? Wasn't that announcement today?" Her words dig in, full of hurt. "Nobody else stood a chance against you except Emma. So *honestly*, you've got a lot to gain by her disappearance."

"I'm not going to be fake about this. I respected Emma that much, at least," Gwen says.

"Okay, guys." Jamie Schill steps in. He's half a foot taller than either of them, but the nervous tremor in his voice does anything but lend authority. "Maybe we should just get back to the game."

Lyla says past him, "If anyone's being fake, it's you. Why don't you drop the act and skip through the halls? You need that scholarship for college, don't you?" The blush on Gwen's cheeks spreads. "How badly?"

Gwen lunges forward—right into Jamie's hand. His open palm presses against her abdomen and she grimaces. Jamie puts another hand on Lyla's shoulder. "Guys," he says. His big eyes are pleading.

Gwen and Lyla glare for a moment. Then Gwen pulls away. "Fine," she says. "Let's get back to the game."

Someone tosses the ball. Gwen moves forward to catch it. But Lyla intercepts gracefully, catching the ball with the toe of her shoe. For a moment everything is still. A tipping point. Then Gwen lunges, and Lyla sidesteps, taking the ball with her. They're off across the floor, pacing each other with ease.

Gwen steals the ball, turns back toward Riley's goal—then Lyla nudges her with a hip, making her stumble, and takes the ball back.

Somebody shouts, "Foul!" and a few people let out uncomfortable laughs. No one steps in. Gwen spins on her feet, and behind the determined set of her face, rage burns. She sprints across the floor, shoving against Lyla with her shoulder. Her hair whips into Lyla's face. Lyla's dainty, smug expression cracks. A snarl breaks through. Their legs tangle, angling for control. Their fingers convulse like claws.

Lyla elbows Gwen, just as Gwen goes for the ball. Gwen stumbles over the ball and falls with a curse and a thump. She holds her shoulder, face twisted in agony. Lyla bends over her.

Their eyes meet. "Whatever you did, we'll find out," Lyla hisses.

The gym door bangs open and everyone jumps. Gwen sits up; her whole face burns. She stares at the floor, breathing hard through her nose, clenching her hands to keep them from shaking.

"Miss Sayer." Mr. Darrow comes back in. He jabs one thumb over his shoulder. "You're up for an interview." The space around Gwen seems to grow. She pushes herself to her feet, setting her jaw, rolling her shoulder gingerly. Mr. Darrow frowns. "What happened to your shoulder?"

"I fell over the ball," she says, still staring at the floor. Tears swim in her eyes.

"Go see Mr. Garson when you're done. He'll take a look at it."

She nods, and when she looks up again, she's back in control. She takes a few more steps, stopping in front of Lyla.

Lyla lifts her pointed chin, glaring. Sweat has beaded on her face. She wipes her forehead, smearing her smoky eye. Gwen's mouth twists in a bitter smile. "Looks like your eyeliner's not waterproof after all."

AVERY: hey <3 study night? My place? Parents are out till 11

STUDY BUDDY: I can't, the Emma stuff has my parents freaking

AVERY: shoot yea. But im gonna need my hoodie back at some point

STUDY BUDDY: ?

AVERY: hoodie. U better remember taking it off me!!!

STUDY BUDDY: oh I do. ;)

STUDY BUDDY: but I also remember giving it back?

AVERY: ummmm but I don't have it??

STUDY BUDDY: (. . .)

AVERY: ?????

THE SCHOLAR

MUÑEZ: The date is Thursday, December 6, 2018, the time is eleven twenty-seven. This is Detective Muñez interviewing Miss Gwen Sayer. Thank you for coming to see us. We'd like to talk to you about—

GWEN: Emma?

MUÑEZ: Emma Baines . . . and your sister.

GWEN: . . . Why?

MUÑEZ: Due to the similarities of the incidents, we thought it might be wise to take a second look. Could you tell us about your sister?

GWEN: No, actually. I don't see what this has to do with Lizzy, if I'm being honest. Our family doesn't need to talk about this again; we need to put the fake sympathy behind us and get our lives back on track.

MUÑEZ: We wouldn't be asking you if we didn't think it was relevant.

GWEN: Whatever. You could read my police interview, but why bother? I can recite the story by heart now.

MUÑEZ: Would you tell us about your sister's incident?

* * *

Lizzy—Elizabeth—was three years older than me, and she was aiming for the Devino Scholarship, too. Until senior year. Senior year was when everything—well, I don't know how to say it otherwise, so I'll have to be vulgar. Everything went to shit.

Her year started out normal. She was doing honor society, tutoring, basketball, journalism. Naturally, she was acing all her classes. We didn't realize how much of her schedule was a lie until Principal Mendoza contacted us, close to the end of the first semester. It's not my parents' fault they didn't know. Lizzy had been forging their signatures for months to get out of her extracurriculars. And then she went . . . somewhere. Did something. Mum and Dad tried to figure it all out. Mum picked up extra jobs to pay for counseling. But it was too late by then. Every time I saw her, she looked like she'd slept less and worried more. She stank like an open bottle of beer and she hid pills in the bottom of her underwear drawer. Rumors followed her like the smell. People said she slept with anyone who asked, that she was having an affair with a teacher, with someone's parent, that she did so much coke she put a hole in her nose . . . the wolves will spread any gossip, and the nastier the better.

The night she died, she snuck out of the house after Mum and Dad went to sleep. I was studying for math, so I had my music up and my head down. I didn't realize her car was gone until around one, when I was pulling the window shades down to get ready for bed.

I stared at the place where her battered old Hyundai Accent had been—she'd saved up for sixteen months and bought it used. But she wasn't supposed to take it out this late. Staring at the empty spot, I could feel dread filling my stomach. I told myself it was just a party, she'd go and get drunk and fall asleep on someone's couch, come home the next day and get grounded. I told myself it was her life and she could ruin it if she wanted.

The phone rang in Mum's room, this insistent chime like an old rotary phone. A few moments later I heard Mum's voice, sleep laden, irritable.

It must be Lizzy, I thought. She was calling because she was drunk or high and needed a ride. But when Mum's voice came again, it wasn't angry. "William," she said. I imagined her shaking my father's shoulder. "Wake up. Get Gwendolyn."

"What's happening?" I asked as soon as the door opened. Dad's face was drawn, haggard but awake.

"Get a coat and get in the truck. It's your sister."

"Why do I have to go get her?" I grumbled, but the dread in my stomach expanded, eating a hole in my belly until I thought my heart would drop through. I put some jeans on over my boy shorts and stuck my feet in my boots, then grabbed my coat.

The road was slick from the rainstorm, but Mum didn't care. She kept her foot on the gas, pressing down until we slid half a lane and my dad shouted, *"Bronwyn!"*

"I'm fine," she snapped back, and that was when I realized how *not* fine she truly was. Her hands shook, so she gripped the steering wheel to steady them. Her knuckles were white, bones ready to pop from the skin. I looked over to see a tear drop from her chin onto her lap.

"Who was on the phone?" I said.

"No one," Mum began, but Dad put a hand on her arm.

The moonlight shone through the windshield, turning his face pale and cragged like the landscape around us. "It was the police, Gwen."

"Why?" My voice quavered, higher than normal. Like my heartbeat. "Where are we going?"

Jefferson-Lorne is a town that you can cross in ten minutes flat, so I got my answer soon enough. We passed Anna's Run and turned onto a little side road that leads into the mountains. Mum drove until we saw the flashing blue and red lights, and she parked next to a trailhead and a little black Hyundai Accent. The Accent had been parked haphazardly across three spaces, stopped not a foot from the edge of the ravine.

"Stay in the car," Mum said as she unbuckled her seat belt.

"She deserves to know—" Dad argued.

Mum gave him a look that would stop a grizzly in its tracks. It's a look I'd never seen her give before, and I hope I never see it again. "Gwendolyn," she said, and her Welsh accent came out thick. "Stay. In. The. Car."

"Okay." I pulled my coat tight around me. Dad gave me a last worried look before he got out.

I leaned against the dash of our truck. In the blinding, dizzying red and blue, I saw the shadows of my parents meet two other shadows, ones with radios at their shoulders and guns at their hips. One of them held up an empty square bottle. Then my parents disappeared down the trailhead, following the police.

They found my sister at the bottom of that trail.

They wouldn't let me see her body.

We had a closed-casket funeral. I never got to say goodbye. The last memory I have of her is the rusting Hyundai, parked on the edge of the ravine. One rev of the engine from flying over. For a long time I wondered why she bothered to get out.

I wish I knew more. I know she was found full of whiskey and uppers. I know her bank account was emptied, presumably to pay off her dealer.

And . . . I know that Emma thought she knew more about the case than any of the detectives from Fort Collins or Denver. Lizzy was Emma's peer mentor when we were freshmen, and Emma worshipped her. She clearly couldn't accept that some girls fall. She couldn't accept that Lizzy just wasn't the girl she'd been. She couldn't let it—well, die. Emma became obsessed.

Fucking Emma.

MUÑEZ: So you and Emma didn't get along?

GWEN: Honestly, no. It wasn't just the Lizzy stuff and the Devino Scholarship. Emma was . . . How do I put this? Performative. For example, the day of the bullying seminar. She got up, did her little song and dance, got the attention of the whole school, and waltzed out. I wanted to rip her throat out. My family, we can't mourn for five minutes. Everyone's always tossing our grief out for the whole world to see.

MUÑEZ: It's understandable that Emma's actions at the seminar angered you. Did she ever tell you why she did it? Are you still angry with her?

GWEN: No. Yes. I don't know.

I wanted to confront her, but as soon as she broke the seminar, Garson and Mendoza hauled her away, and I only saw her making a pinched face as she followed them down the hall, looking so scared that for a moment, she had me convinced. But like I said: she's performative.

Anyway, I got to go through a day of *Poor Gwen* and people treating me like a broken doll. "Don't talk about Lizzy. Don't mention Lizzy." And I finally caught up to Emma as she hurried down the concrete steps that bridged the front of the school with the parking lot, right after school was over. I grabbed her by the shoulder and spun her around.

She'd been crying. Her whole face was blotchy and her short blond hair hung limp and greasy. She looked like a mouse— trembling and harmless and terrified. It made me feel bad for a second. But she'd lied to the whole school and exposed my pain. The least she could do was face me now. "*What* is your problem?" I demanded.

Emma stared at the ground. "Nothing," she whispered.

I got closer. "Bringing up my sister? Contradicting the police? Humiliating me? If you're going to make up stories, you can have some respect for the dead." I almost shoved her, but I made myself move away. I didn't want detention. I have a perfect record. "And if you think it's going to get me off my game, you're wrong about that, too," I added. Because she was always at my throat. Way more competitive than people realized.

Emma still wouldn't meet my eyes. "I know. I just—I cared about Lizzy. She was like a big sister to me, too."

My hand clenched, ready to throw a punch. How *dare* she?

How dare she act like they were sisters, like she cared more than me? Like she could solve a nonexistent mystery because she loved Lizzy more? I stood, trembling with rage, unsure of whether I should cry or scream or hit her. . . . She just turned away and hurried down the stairs, and I went to yearbook and tried to ignore all the extra sympathy I got. And that was that.

See, I know this about Emma—she loved stories. She was always working on one. Whenever I saw her, she had her notebook out and she was writing. Before class got started. After she finished a quiz. Even when the teacher was talking. She wrote like she'd never be able to get it all out of her head. So when she started going on at length about my sister? It was obviously another story. Maybe she had some compulsion to do it, I don't know. Or maybe she wanted to distract me from focusing on the Devino Scholarship, and she didn't mind using dirty tricks.

Most students can't hack the schedule we kept for the competition. Emma's in AP Physics, AP English 2, AP Comparative Government, and AP Calculus. Last year we were in AP English 1, AP United States History, and Spanish together. If there's an Advanced Placement class, she takes it. And she's never gone below a 93 percent. I lost a couple of percentage points to her on the last physics test, but I got a perfect score in APCoGo and she only managed a 97. Add to that all the extracurriculars—last year, Emma and I both had speech and debate, National Honor Society, the *Jefferson-Lorne Inquirer*, and yearbook club. We both worked as student administrators for the office. And she had cheer, while I did mathletes and community service at the Lorne Maternity Ward. This year she's only doing the paper, cheer, and Honor Society.

MUÑEZ: You seem to know a lot about Emma.

GWEN: Look, it was clear from sophomore year that we were both going for the Devino Scholarship. Maybe that doesn't seem like much to you, but here's what it meant to me: one of us would be going to college for free, and the other wouldn't be going to college at all. Do you get that?

I'm not going to let sentimentality get in the way of my future.

MUÑEZ: So you think that both Emma and Lizzy died the same way, by accident?

GWEN: I don't know. It doesn't have anything to do with me. The police are the ones who said Lizzy's death was accidental. I read the report. Didn't you?

MUÑEZ: You read the police report?

GWEN: Everyone in Lorne has read that fucking report. The redacted one, of course. The police said it was standard procedure, and that they'd cut the most gruesome details for our peace of mind. And honestly, if I ever find the person who leaked that report . . . well, maybe I shouldn't be saying that sort of thing to you. But it hurt my parents so bad.

Anyway, are we done? Because calculus started ten minutes ago, and I'm supposed to present to the class.

Sorry, it's just, in case you can't tell, I'm a very busy person. I have a lot going on. It's not easy having to be the best at everything.

<u>Diary Entry</u>

Emma Baines—September 9, 2017

Way back when, Lizzy took me for a drive to commemorate the end of our mentorship. We sat on the bridge over Anna's Run and she took a little book out of her backpack. Her diary, she said as she threw it as hard as she could into the water. Every time she ran out of pages and had to get a new one, she came out here and gave the old one a Lorne Burial. "No one deserves to know my secrets but Anna," she said.

I don't think I deserve to know her secrets. But maybe the police need to. There wasn't a diary among her effects, but what if the police didn't know to look for it? If there is some afterlife, Lizzy, and you're watching me, I hope you're not mad.

Maybe I should've visited the Sayers before now. It just seemed so—so trite to show up after Lizzy died, with flowers and an insipid card. And then I didn't know what to do instead, and then I started wondering what had really *happened to Lizzy, and all that led to me staring down their front door like it was going to open onto the mouth of hell. The paint was half white, half rust from where it had washed off in the weather, and the door hung crooked on a swollen frame.*

I crunched over brittle grass and came face-to-face with the door. The doorbell looked like it had been installed during the Gold Rush, so I knocked before I could lose my nerve.

The door opened a crack and Mrs. Sayer's brown eye appeared. "Emma! All right? Wonderful to see you." She sounded like she meant it. I heard the same warmth in her voice that she'd always saved for me when I came over to do homework, or to catch a ride with Lizzy to speech and debate. I almost burst into tears right there. I thought she would be angry with me for abandoning them. I'd always wondered if they blamed me, somehow, for the things that happened to Lizzy. "What can I do for you?"

I swallowed the lump in my throat and managed to lie without choking. "I'm in a group project with Gwen. I just need to drop off some things."

I wasn't worried that she'd suspect me. Adults never do. I have so much practice lying to Dad, and for Dad. I've aced the innocent little white-girl act.

Mrs. Sayer opened the door and let me in. "You thirsty? You want a Coke?"

"No thanks." I still don't trust Dad not to find out when I drink soft drinks. Even the Gatorade we get at cheer practice is almost too much for him.

Mrs. Sayer shut the door behind me and locked it before moving toward the kitchen, a tiny space with a sink, a dish rack, one cupboard, and about three inches of counter space. Everything was linoleum and faded but clean. "Cup of tea?" she said.

I was on a timeline. Dad expected me home from yearbook between 4:45 and 4:52, depending on traffic. All the same—"Tea would be great." I had enough time to sit with Mrs. Sayer for five minutes. Besides, she always makes this comforting tea, thick with milk and sugar.

"You know, it's lovely to see you again," Mrs. Sayer said as she turned on the kettle. "Tell me, what's up at school?"

Mr. and Mrs. Sayer are such good people it makes me want to cry. Always being so kind to me, even though I'm competing with their daughter for a life-changing scholarship. I ran my finger along the duct-taped edge of the tartan-patterned couch. "It's good. School's good. Our cheer team is really good this year. I think we're going to make it to regionals."

"I wish Gwen had joined a team this year. I was captain of the football team in my day." She still doesn't say soccer, even though she's been here for years. "But she prefers running. That girl will take on the whole world alone if she can. I hope she's good in your group project." Mrs. Sayer shook her head, smiling.

"She's good at everything." I was proud how I managed to stifle the bitterness that always rises like bile when I think of Gwen. Still, I wasn't here for a nice chat. "I'm just going to set my notes on her desk."

Mrs. Sayer nodded and pointed out the door to Gwen's room.

When she opened the fridge, I slipped into Lizzy's room instead.

I froze inside the door. The room was so . . . stifling. A mausoleum. Lizzy's bed still had the Disney coverlet on, the one her mom had sewn from flannel and she'd painted with fabric paints. She wanted to work for Disney when she got out of college. Her desk still had her AP Psych book and a battered copy of Macbeth. In one corner of the desk the dust had been disturbed, and Lizzy's senior picture leaned against the laminated chipboard edge, right next to a picture of her smiling next to a decorated horse skull attached to a sheet, some kind of Welsh tradition. Two tea lights sat in front of the photo, and a little bowl with crumbs at the bottom. She looked so happy. What happened to you, Lizzy?

I swallowed my sorrow and bent down to check under her bed. Her parents must have cleaned up, but how much would they have snooped? Would they be afraid to touch her things, or obsessed with *finding out how she had descended into . . . whatever it was? I slid underneath the bed to check between the mattress and the frame, I rummaged in her desk drawers and dresser. But I didn't find any false bottoms or hidden compartments.*

I tried to breathe evenly, but I could feel my pulse rising. If Mrs. Sayer wanted to ask me something, if Gwen came home early . . . I started to pull books off Lizzy's shelf, heedless of the way I disturbed the dust. This was such a bad idea. Maybe I should've just texted Gwen about it, asked her to see if she could find Lizzy's diary. But that would've meant talking to Gwen, and trying to explain myself, and that's never ever gone well.

Then I saw the Bible, and I knew. The top of the book bulged, like something small was caught inside. I slid it down from the top shelf and let it fall open. The tiny black notebook was the perfect size. I flipped it open, just to be sure.

Saw my lacrosse star today. He promised he'd see me later, but it looks like later is later this week. It's so frustrating, but it's only a little while. A year. I can think of a year like a group of a few months. And a few months isn't much time, right?

Secret boyfriend. Could that be the source of the boot prints?

I stuck the diary in the front pocket of my backpack and slid the Bible back into place, then rubbed at the book spines and the shelf to erase the rest of the dust. Maybe no one will notice. Then I waited until I heard Mrs. Sayer clanking a pan and slipped out of Lizzy's room.

I feel bad for deceiving them. But I'm also determined to find the truth. I need facts before I bring this up. Before I wipe that kindly smile off Mrs. Sayer's face. She lost her kid—the least I can do is give her a reason to go back to that night.

THE JOCK

CLINE: The date is Thursday, December 6, 2018, the time is twelve oh five. Interviewing James Schill. Thank you for coming in. We just have a few questions for you. You were with Claude Vanderly last night, correct?

JAMIE: Okay. This is going to sound—this is going to sound ridiculous. But I have to ask you a favor. Don't tell my mom about this? Like, I'm happy to say that you interviewed me, but I don't want Mom knowing it was about Claude. These are confidential, right?

CLINE: Absolutely.

JAMIE: Cool. Yes, Claude was with me last night. We, um, study together and stuff. We'd made plans for her to come over after lights-out so that Mom wouldn't catch on.

I don't normally sneak around. It's just—Claude. Her mom and my mom hate each other for some reason, and Mom thinks that Claude invites the devil in. And Claude, um. Likes staying over. Which Mom doesn't think is appropriate.

CLINE: What time did Miss Vanderly come over?

JAMIE: It was way late. She was supposed to come around eleven so we could do math homework. Don't tell her I know this, but she waits to do it until I can help her. So I always finish it in advance so that I can be clear on the explanations before we do it together.

She didn't show, though, and I sort of fell asleep on my homework with the window open. She climbed through at three something, I don't remember exactly. She told me she'd been held up doing something, but it was nothing important.

CLINE: Did she seem upset? Unhappy? Acting unusual?

JAMIE: She seemed fine. She seemed like Claude. Energetic, full of life, ready for anything. . . . Um, could you take that last bit off the record?

CLINE: She didn't give a hint as to where she'd been?

JAMIE: I don't remember. We were kind of busy—busy *doing math*. But it was probably a party. Claude always goes to parties. Her mom doesn't care as long as she drives safe. Anywhere else she might have been—well, it was probably a misunderstanding. That's what I'm hoping, you know? This is a big misunderstanding.

CLINE: A girl in your class is missing and presumed dead. I'm not sure what there is to misunderstand here, Mr. Schill.

9

THE PARTY GIRL

CLINE: The date is Thursday, December 6, 2018, the time is twelve fifteen p.m. Second interview with Claude Vanderly, so welcome back. We'd just like to reiterate, for the record, where you were last night.

CLAUDE: Seriously? At Jamie's. I can say it in another language, if you like. Estuve en la casa de Jamie anoche.

CLINE: You got to Mr. Schill's house *after* three in the morning. Maybe you can tell us where you were before then.

CLAUDE: Like it matters. You can't arrest me for crawling through someone's window at an undetermined time. Yeah, I have some inside knowledge to this little process. For example, I know you don't have enough evidence to charge me *just* because I was banging Jamie later than you thought I was, so you're going to sit here and hope I incriminate myself. Which won't work, because I have nothing to hide. It wasn't even my idea to keep my visits with Jamie a secret. It's only because his Stepford mom would have an aneurysm if she knew I was staying over.

Look, I was at a party, all right? Until, I don't know. Till three.

CLINE: You weren't at Jamie's at three?

CLAUDE: Two forty-five, then. Jesus fucking christ. It's a ten-minute drive through Jefferson-Lorne.

CLINE: Claude, I'd like you to calm down.

CLAUDE: *Don't* tell me to calm down.

CLINE: I'd like you to calm down, and I'd like you to start from the beginning of your day yesterday.

(silence)

CLINE: What did you do yesterday? What was your schedule?

CLAUDE: Fine. Fine. If we keep this short and sweet, maybe I can salvage some of my lunch hour.

Get ready to be shocked: On Emma's last day, I *came to school*. Obviously. I drove from home, and got here around eight, because I like to sleep and I don't move so quick in the mornings. You can confirm my time stamp with the Ham on this one. Then I went to my classes like normal. Precalc, physics, AP Lit. And then lunch, which I always leave school for, because have you *seen* the lunch they offer at the cafeteria?

My mom's not really the lunch-making type. Sometimes I make my own, sometimes I buy. I almost always leave school for it, though. It's nice to just drive.

Jefferson-Lorne . . . sometimes it feels submerged, forgotten. The curves of Highway 7 whip around the canyon above us, and every day cars trundle past on their way to Kansas or

Wyoming or Rocky Mountain National Park. They don't see us, hidden beneath the swirl of aspen and pine. And when I drive out on the highway, I can pretend that I'm leaving Lorne behind forever. No more dealing with people who ask pointedly if I shouldn't be in school. No one tells me that my dyed hair or thick eyeliner are an "interesting" look. No one whispers nasty names when they think I can't hear. On the road I'm just me. All the things I want to be, none of society's judgment.

I had my lunch with me yesterday, so I was going to drive and eat. Maybe take Janine up to a little trailhead overlooking the peaks and just sit. I headed for the car, doing my usual check to make sure the security guard wasn't going to try and stop me. And . . . Emma was there, actually.

She was talking to someone, but I can't tell you who. It looked like a girl, but it was a boy's lacrosse hoodie with the hood pulled up. Number 217. February 17 is my mom's birthday, so it caught my eye.

I don't know what they were talking about, but Emma looked troubled. Maybe pissed. And I thought it was weird to see her out here at all, because if there's one thing I know about Emma, it's that she was obsessed with becoming valedictorian. She was neck and neck with Gwen Sayer, and we all knew that whoever got to be valedictorian would take the Devino Scholarship.

They didn't notice me, and I didn't go say hi. Emma's life was none of my business. And neither is her death. And that's the last I saw of her.

I swear it.

Then, as I headed for Janine, my two least favorite people in JLH pulled into the parking lot. Heather Halifax and her Bratz doll of a friend, Holden.

Heather has a voice so shrill it could melt acid. The Geneva Convention has banned the use of her voice in war. And I don't love bitching about a girl's voice like I'm trying to fit into the Dude-Bro Nation, but just as often it's the *content* Heather spews that fills me with rage. Girls have to be perfect and virginal and part of the church choir in order to get her stamp of approval. All boys have to be is hot. Also, we had a slight altercation concerning Heather's boyfriend last year, so Heather thinks I can fuck off and die, and she's not afraid to express that sentiment. So I ended up ditching my plans and stuffing myself into a spare corner at school, turning my headphones up until it was time for AP Comparative Government.

Wait a sec. I guess I lied because I did see Emma in APCoGo. Emma's always quiet, and for the past few months, she's been even quieter than normal, pulling her shoulders around like they could act as some sort of shell. That's . . . sort of how she is. It's not hard to forget about her. I think that's what she wants. Wanted.

We were given a practice test to go over in groups. For some people, like Emma, this means putting her head down and doing the test. Heather Halifax was using it as a chance to plan her weekend. "There's supposed to be a party at Greg's place, but I don't know. I mean, he has a hot tub—but Leigh said he's being treated for chlamydia, and I just don't know if my parents would let me hang around with someone like that."

She let out a dramatic sigh. "It's so difficult keeping up with who's filthy." She pitched her voice a little louder, to make sure it carried to me. "I'll bet *Claude* knows. Claude, you know all about who's got chlamydia, don't you?"

"Can't help you," I replied. "Though I did see your mom in line at the pharmacy. Maybe the two are related." I hate *your mom* jokes. They stink of unoriginality. But where Heather is concerned, I'll say anything to piss her off. It's my fatal flaw.

The kid in front of me snorted. Heather's pencil went sailing past my head. I bit my lip to keep my smile in and leaned over my paper.

"Damn it, I forgot my pencil case." Heather sighed. "Emma. Hey, *Emma*."

I peered through my hair at Emma. Her nose was just an inch above her paper, eyes narrowed as she concentrated. If she heard Heather, she didn't react.

"*Em-ma*." Heather snapped her fingers just under Emma's ear.

Emma sprang back. Her hands clenched so tight she snapped her pencil in two. Her eyes widened and her mouth parted slightly. She looked like a mouse caught in a live trap. She looked so terrified.

"Whoa," Heather said. "Don't freak out. Can I borrow a pencil?"

Emma's shoulders came up to her ears. She grabbed a pencil from her cloth case and practically threw it at Heather. Then she turned back to her paper, without a word.

Weird, right?

***

CLINE: What was Emma writing in?

CLAUDE: A . . . notebook?

CLINE: Like a diary?

CLAUDE: Standard, five-subject, college-ruled. How the hell should I know if she was doing her diary? She'd be the type to have one. But it's not like we took diary breaks in class. And I don't even know what she'd write about. *Dear Diary, Gwennie's so mean, I'm so smart.* Emma's problems are none of my business.

And by the way, I didn't kill her.

CLINE: Why don't we fill in the gap between school and going to Jamie's place?

CLAUDE: Track meet, check in with Garson. Dinner, check in with mom. We ate at Red Runner. After dinner, I drove.

CLINE: To the party?

CLAUDE: What? Yeah, I spent a little while at the party. But I drove. I like to drive. I took Janine out and I drove on Highway 7. It's safer than the town road, it has reception most of the year, it never floods. It smells like pine and woodsmoke. I'm closer to the peaks and the Milky Way. The Universe, God, whatever you call it . . . I'm closer to her, too. I just . . . needed it, last night. To calm myself down.

Seems sketchy, doesn't it?

CLINE: We're only trying to establish a timeline.

CLAUDE: I stopped at a gas station around one in the morning. The Bradley near Allenstown. Check it. Check their surveillance, their receipts . . . seriously.

CLINE: We'll take a look if we think it's relevant.

CLAUDE: I mean it. I was there and I can prove it. I'm not a liar and I don't kill girls.

CLINE: Claude, I'd like you to calm down again—

CLAUDE: Fuck that. *Fuck* it. I'll be as angry as I want. I didn't do anything, and you're wasting my time and yours with this ridiculous questioning. So if you don't have any evidence, I'm out.

That's what I thought. Nice talking to you.

December 6, 2018
What are your friends saying?

Lyla Ionescu: Emma, you were a bright light in this world, a fun dance partner, the smartest girl at school, and so kind. I know every single person at JLH will mourn you. I will remember the long bus trips to competitions, stuffing our faces with fries and shakes at the Morning House after a hard practice at the gym, and the fry attack will always be one of my favorite memories.

A source very close to the investigation has told me that the police are considering that the video might be a hoax. Like ??? Poor Emma is relying on them to find whoever pushed her, and they can't be bothered? They're just interviewing every JLH student like we all might have something to do with it? This is such a joke, like even I know where I would start. Seriously guys, round up every tall hobo in town and figure this out!! #EvenICouldDoThat #JusticeForEmma

    Samantha Johnson: PREACH
    Ben Nakayama: RIP Emma :(
    Shay Brayden: ikr?
    Natalie Powell: wtf lyla she never came to the Morning House with us she wasnt even there for the fry attack

Shay Brayden: RIP Emma I know u are up there looking down on us, pls let the police find the sicko who did this!!! #JusticeForEmma

Samantha Johnson: WHERE WILL THIS END? We can't even value girls enough to get our asses in gear when one of them is FILMED being MURDERED?!?!?!?! We must start valuing the lives of our women and demand EQUAL JUSTICE FOR ALL #JUSTICEFOREMMA

James Schill: We will miss u Emma #RIP #JusticeForEmma

Kyle Landry: yeah but the important ? is who am I gonna crib my math homework off now? #thesearetherealquestions
Steven Bulowski: Gwen?
Kyle Landry: no way man shes fuckn scary
Ben Nakayama: #toosoon

Michael Bryson: #JusticeForEmma cmon dudes get your heads out your asses

Avery Cross: Emma, I won't cry because it's over, I'll smile because it happened. But I stand with anyone who wants #JusticeForEmma and I'm willing to help in any way I can.
Michael Bryson: so sorry babe your the best

Jefferson-Lorne Inquirer: We are currently considering op-ed submissions concerning Emma Baines's case and the decision of the police to ignore, for now, the Facebook video that went viral and alerted the town of Jefferson-Lorne to her disappearance. Please keep submissions tasteful. #Justice-ForEmma

   Lyla Ionescu: @Gwendolyn Sayer surely you'll trade an opinion for extra credit . . .

10

PRETTY VULTURES

Rumors rush.

They sweep the streets, filling up the gutters like a flash flood of gossip. They wash through the parking lot of the dead girl's high school in a susurration of whispers—*Did you know? Wasn't she—?* The river of grief runs wide, but it is the undercurrent of curiosity that will pull them all under.

It is a crisp day, the kind that comes and goes in a mountain town. Soon it will snow, promising the patronage of fake-tan businessmen and their freshly waxed skis; tomorrow it will be like summer again. Nature here is fickle, playing nice before it strikes with a storm or a drought or a wildfire.

The cheer team sits at a table next to a spindly pine tree, all in black in honor of their fallen comrade. They watch the clouds roll in and drink up the last of their lunch period. Behind them the yellow bricks of Jefferson-Lorne loom.

The whispers whorl and spin around this table, afraid to stop and dip in. The squad meets any attempt of rumormongering with glares and sniffles about respect. But beneath their somber expressions, the curiosity bites, perhaps harder than for anyone else.

Lyla places a hand over her heart as she recounts the story of her gym fight with Gwen. "I have never seen that level of disrespect for another human being," she swears. "How cold does a bitch have to be, not to get the bigger picture when somebody *dies*?"

"I wish Mr. Darrow hadn't left. He would have stepped in." Avery sits next to Lyla. She traded the morning's pink sweater for a black hoodie, and she pulls the sleeves down over her hands before propping her elbows on the table. Her boyfriend, Michael, slides closer on her other side, until their thighs touch on the bench.

"I'm glad he did. I think Gwen got herself a nice arm injury." Lyla shakes her head, still offended by Gwen's existence.

"Why is she like that?" asks Natalie around a bite of Caesar salad. Only Natalie keeps eating salad in the dead of winter. The rest warm themselves on pumpkin and butternut squash soup heated in the cafeteria microwave.

"She's a classic sociopath." Lyla pushes an imaginary pair of glasses back up her nose, a sure sign that she's about to start talking out of her ass. Her dad's a detective with a two-year degree in psychology that Lyla likes to appropriate as often as she can get away with it. "Remember, you know—Lizzy? They told Gwen to take as much time as she needed mourning. And how many days do you think she took? None. Zero. She hit all of her extracurriculars. She didn't even skip *mathletes* that week." She leans back and puffs a cold breath into the air. "Besides, she's got motive, more than anyone else. She fits as a killer."

The rest of the table leans in, drinking up Lyla's words. Avery toys with her own lunch, a can of Monster Michael smuggled in for her. "She's not a sociopath; she just needs to deal with things differently than we do. Maybe we shouldn't judge people we don't know very well."

"Aves." Lyla throws an arm around Avery's waist, ignoring the other girl's slight flinch. "You know I love you, right? And I love you because you always believe the best of people. It's, like, your superpower. You're *that* good at it. But Gwen's not good people. She's a total cutthroat and I can one hundred and fifty percent believe she murdered Emma to get rid of the competition. Girl has a dark streak. Runs in the family, I think."

For a second, there's silence, the nervous flutter of eyes around the table. Has Lyla gone too far? But she's not finished. "Do you remember seventh grade, speech and debate competition? Gwen and Kyle Landry were the finalists. *She* walked away with a hundred-dollar gift card; *he* was too embarrassed to come out of the bathroom until everyone had gone home. I've said it before, I'll say it again: laxatives in his water bottle."

Natalie and Shay giggle at the memory.

"She's ruthless," Lyla states. "Just like Lizzy. We all know what *she* did."

"Not for sure," Shay jumps in.

"I know for sure. Brittany Landry said she missed half

their AP English class with Mr. Pendler. Yet she got a perfect score on her fall final. A teacher could've adjusted her grades, no problem."

"Who do you think it was?" A stray piece of lettuce hangs from Natalie's lower lip.

"Mrs. Willingham," Lyla says, leaning in. Somebody at the table gasps. Avery's face flickers with hurt. "I'm not joking. The Ham came here five years ago, right? I heard she's bi and got kicked out of her last school for having an affair with a student. A *female* student."

"Mrs. Willingham's married to a man," Avery points out.

"So? My dad cheated on my mom like five times before she divorced him," Natalie says.

"Maybe you just think she sleeps around because she's bi," Avery mutters.

Shay leans over and takes Avery's hands. Michael presses in protectively. "Aves, we know you're not like that," she says.

"Don't be so sensitive, Aves," Lyla says, defensiveness creeping into her voice.

And good Avery acquiesces, because that's what her kind of girl does. And she knows her friends trust her—but what sort of trust will it be when the rumors swing *her* way?

"Anyway, it was either a teacher or a parent. And I think it's a teacher," Lyla says.

"I think we're talking about a dead girl." Avery's face has gone pale, her voice hard, and her feet tap uncontrollably on the brown grass. She kicks a pine cone. "Being with a teacher is super illegal. You just sound like the Lily Fransen accusers."

Lyla snorts. "This is nothing like Lily Fransen. Lily Fransen was groomed and raped. But Lizzy? She just flew off the handle. And the rumors were everywhere. No smoke without fire, right?"

"Rumors are just rumors. None of us even knew her." Avery's face twists. "Lizzy and a teacher, Gwen and Emma . . . I wouldn't want people to talk about *me* doing stuff like this without looking at the evidence first."

Michael chuckles and slides an arm around her, just under Lyla's. Avery's trapped between them. "Babe, no one's going to accuse you of murder. Do you know what it takes to get away with it?"

Avery stiffens, face going blank.

"Seriously. It's not like planning a routine," Lyla adds.

Others chime in. Determining the time, the place, catching the victim alone, getting rid of DNA evidence . . . these are things that sweet, good, well-meaning, *simple* Avery cannot possibly do. Red spreads up her face like a rash, and the bottoms of her eyes fill. She can't move, not without pushing away from Lyla and Michael, not without showing her friends how their words slide under her skin.

Natalie squeaks in panic, and the whole table falls silent. They look up to see Officer Cline strolling up. His lips stretch in anything but a smile. "Having a nice lunch?"

On Avery's face, the captain smile reappears, a bit wobbly. "Trying to remember the good times."

"You were all on the cheer team with Emma?" Cline asks.

The girls nod. Michael says, "Not all of us," which makes a couple of them giggle nervously.

The detective's attention snaps to him, and suddenly, Michael looks like he wishes he'd never spoken at all. "Lacrosse, right? I come to the odd game. Used to be on the team, too. What's your number?"

"Uh, two-seventeen," Michael mutters.

Cline's eyes glint. "Mine was three-thirty. This your girl-friend?" He gestures to Avery. Michael nods. "You don't mind if I borrow her a minute, do you, son?"

"No, of course not." The relief in Michael's voice earns him a glare from Lyla.

Cline's attention has shifted, from the lacrosse star to the cheer captain. "We have a few follow-up questions for you, Miss Cross," he says.

"Anything I can do to help." Avery brushes off the unre-sisting arms of Michael and Lyla and climbs over the bench. Around her, the expressions of the team and their assorted boyfriends flicker.

The humans of Lorne are as fickle as the weather.

"See you later?" she says.

"Yeah." Michael manages a smile.

Avery tugs on the drawstrings of the black hoodie and tucks her hands in the pockets.

And as she walks, the river changes. The whispers twist toward this new disruption in the current. Maybe Avery Cross will change the flow of the river—or maybe she's another vic-tim of it, about to get washed downstream.

THE HELPER

CLINE: How long have you been with Michael Bryson?

AVERY: Um . . . I don't really get why . . . ? Two years.

CLINE: You're comfortable with each other.

AVERY: Yes.

CLINE: You borrow his clothes?

AVERY: Um. I guess? Sometimes?

CLINE: Another student saw a girl in Mr. Bryson's lacrosse hoodie in the parking lot, with Emma Baines, yesterday afternoon. Was that you?

AVERY: Oh! Oh, I'm so sorry. I completely forgot about that. It's just because I—I haven't been thinking properly. You understand, right? I'm still reeling from all this. And, I mean, I did come to you. I have nothing to hide.

I did talk to Emma in the parking lot. It must've been . . . around lunch. Yes, it was lunch because we'd agreed to use the lunch hour for working on a routine.

While I don't like to speak ill of my friends, or of the dead, or, well, of anyone, the truth is that Emma always needed help on routines. She could execute the easy stuff, but she couldn't be the base for a basic lift and the girl was terrible with memorizing choreography. I think she had too much else on her mind, to tell you the truth. I find clearing your head is the best first step to a perfect routine.

But Emma didn't join the team for the same reasons as the rest of us. You know, because we love to dance. And also to be a spirit of positivity in the school. Emma joined because she knew it would look good on her résumé. College was the most important thing in Emma's life. But even if she didn't think of us as a big family, I did. I wanted to help her, because we help family. Since Gwen had track, Emma needed a sports activity, too.

Emma was dragging us down this year. And yes, before you say anything judgy, cheer is a real sport. We lost points at a couple of early competitions because we weren't coherent enough on the floor. She's often half a beat behind everyone else, and she doesn't put in the effort to fix that. Natalie and Shay have pushed me to kick her off the team more than once, and they don't think it's right to let her stay on for the credit when she doesn't put in the work. But I . . . really wanted Emma to succeed. I guess I felt a little bad for her, really. I would hate to be that alone.

I couldn't help feeling she needed me somehow.

Emma came in for our lunch date frustrated, but I tried to ignore it and focus on the music. Emma didn't bite. Her moves were sloppy, she missed a bar of choreography, and when I stopped to go over things slowly, she rolled her eyes at me. A bit rude, right? Not that I want to be a jerk about it. All I said was "What's going on with you?"

I didn't think I asked it like a snot or a . . . you know . . . bitch. But she couldn't take it. She stormed out, without her bag or any of her gear. I grabbed her backpack and rushed after her, spotting her as she streaked down the hallway toward the front doors.

I had her stuff and my stuff, so I was a little weighed down, but I *am* the cheer captain, and physical activity is kind of my specialty. I caught up to Emma in the parking lot. "You forgot your backpack," I puffed.

Emma turned. Tears ran down her face in a river. I dropped my bags and leaned in, wrapping my arms around her. "What's going on?" I asked again.

"I had a meeting with Mr. Garson today." She sniffed and I dug around in my pocket for a tissue. You know Mr. Garson, right? He's killer. He's our co-coach and the head coach for the lacrosse team. I twisted my knee last year and Mom said I shouldn't compete for the rest of the semester. But Mr. G helped me rehabilitate and got me back on the floor in four weeks. He's the student counselor, too—he's so easy to talk to, you sort of forget you're talking to an adult. He gets us the help we need, and Emma had been seeing him twice a week since her, um, Lizzy outburst. "He said I should think about alternative options if I didn't get the Devino Scholarship."

My heart sank for my friend. "Does he think Gwen's ahead in the game?"

"I don't know. He said he couldn't talk about other students, that this was our time to devote to me and my future. He's talking about options and after-school jobs. He asked if I had a college fund." Her face screwed up again.

Emma's home life was really private, but my dad is kinda friends with her dad, so I pick a few things up. I knew there was no college fund. I knew there was no job. Emma's dad has refused her both. The Devino Fund was basically her only chance to go to college.

I don't think her dad wanted her to leave.

I searched for something encouraging to say. "Your grades are great, and the competition's only a few weeks away. I'll help you. We'll get the team to the regional finals. That can help you too." Even as I said it, I felt a little guilty. Because Emma winning the scholarship would mean that Gwen would be the one stuck in Lorne. Gwen's not my friend like Emma is, but I don't like doing things that hurt other people. I'm not that kind of girl.

"What if it's not enough? I'm not going to be trapped in this stupid town for the rest of my life. Coming to lacrosse games because there's nothing better to do. Waiting for Main Street to flood every spring, so we literally can't get out. Dying of boredom or alcoholism or—" She choked.

I hugged her again. She trembled against me, rigid with fear. At the time I thought it was all about the Devino Scholarship, the prospect of staying in Lorne forever. But maybe it was something different.

She might have told me, if Heather Halifax hadn't strolled by with her best friend, Holden. "What's up with you two?" she asked curiously.

"We're fine," I said.

Maybe I said it a little sharply, because Heather held up her hands in defense. "All right, I'll stay out of your business." She smiled at me, but it seemed suspicious. People like to think I'm sleeping with half the cheer team because I'm bi.

"We'll get you out of this," I said to Emma when Heather and Holden were gone, and I meant it. Maybe Emma saw that I did. She smiled, and, sir, I'm an *expert* on fake smiles. This one was real.

There was a party last night, but I'm sure Emma wasn't there. Her dad didn't let her go to any parties because there might be alcohol or weed or boys. Even after cheer competitions, he'd pick her right up from wherever the meet was and drive her home. She never hung out with us when we went to the Morning House or got coffee, which meant that while all the girls were becoming better friends, she was sort of stuck on the outside.

She said once that she wished she could join us at the Morning House after practice. I offered to drive her home early, before her dad got off shift. She said he'd know anyway. She said he even kept cameras in the house to make sure she didn't sneak out after bedtime.

CLINE: Cameras?

AVERY: Oh. I shouldn't have said that. I'm so sorry. Can we, like, strike it from the record or something? He's the police chief, so I'm sure he had his reasons. Maybe that's standard police officer protocol, what would I know? I really don't want it getting back to him, and like I said, my dad and her dad are kind of buddy-buddy.

Honestly, if you find any clues at all, they'll be in her diary. I told you about her diary, right? She wrote in it all the time, and since it was by hand, it's not like anyone can spy on that. It would be the one place that Emma had freedom from everything. From everyone in her life, even herself.

And if she had something in that diary that she didn't want her dad reading, she wouldn't keep it at home. She'd stash it here. Did you check her locker?

CLINE: We are looking into all aspects of this case. Thank you for taking the time, Miss Cross.

AVERY: I know it's stupid. Of course you've checked her locker. I'm not the detective here. But she didn't just have the one locker—you know that, right? Just want to be as helpful as possible. She had her own locker for gym, for one thing. Oh, and she also had a desk at the high school paper. The diary has to be in one of those places.

Emma Baines—September 21, 2017

Diary, if I don't come to school tomorrow, I hope the police ransack my stuff and find you. And when they do, they'll flip to this page. POLICE: MY DAD DID IT. HE KILLED ME AND HE BURIED MY BODY SOMEWHERE YOU'LL NEVER FIND.

Oh, who am I kidding. Dad is *the police. Dad, if you end up reading this:*

Ugh. I don't even know what to say.

The problem is, the cheer squad doesn't get it. They're all "Everyone's parents are overprotective, Emma." Avery goes on about how her mom measures her weight each day, and okay, like, that probably does suck, but dammit, Avery Cross, I still have a freaking baby monitor and nanny cam in my room. Dad saw me get up at two in the morning and work on my APCoGo paper. And then he TOLD ME OFF for it over breakfast.

He dropped the bomb after that. He said, "I've changed my mind about the Devino Scholarship."

I almost choked on my cornflakes. "What?" Mom and Dad hardly agreed about anything, as far as I could remember, but the one thing they were united about was my studies. I should always devote myself to my studies. Of course, as soon as Mom left town with a trucker, she stopped giving a shit about my studies. She hasn't called in the last three years. So I guess it was only Dad who really cared. Well, not anymore.

"You need to stay in Lorne. I'll get you a job at the station after school. We can always use another dispatcher and assistant in the

office, *and if you do well we can send you to the academy in Fort Collins."*

"No." *I wasn't thinking. I never say no to Dad, not like that. It's always couched in soft language, like* what about *or* I've been thinking. *I realized my mistake as I saw his face turn red. But a rare anger swelled in me. Some things he can decide as my father. But not my life. Not my future.* "I don't want to be a police officer."

"Then we'll get you something else. The Christmas shop is always hiring, and in a few years we're going to have a big boom. Lorne's going to be the next ski town. Everyone's saying it, and Greg Cross is building like it's going to happen yesterday. The tourists will want their fancy coffees, and their fancy cafés, and their private security. You'll have plenty of opportunities here."

They weren't the opportunities I wanted. But I didn't know how to say it.

Dad caught the look on my face. I expected him to scream or snap. But he put his spoon back in his cereal and his voice softened. "I need you here, Emma. I need you safe. You're all I've got since your mother . . ." He stopped, swallowed, stared hard at his breakfast.

And then I realized why he didn't scream. I was supposed to feel sorry for him. Poor Chief Baines, he spends so much time caring about his daughter when his evil wife abandoned him. What happens when he's injured on the job? What happens when he's old? Emma can't abandon him, too.

Only Emma didn't ask to be abandoned by her mom. Emma didn't ask for security cameras through the whole house. Emma didn't even ask to be born. The rage came back, and worse. "Really? You want me safe? Or do you just want me here? Controlled?"

Dad's lip curled. "You're not going to college. It's a waste of time for people who think they're better than everyone else. And while you live in my house, you follow my rules."

"If I win the scholarship, you can't stop me."

"You don't talk to me that way," Dad barked.

"I'm not Mom," I shouted. All the color drained from Dad's face, like I'd sucker-punched him. My brain was stuck on a loop of shitshitshit *and my whole body wanted to run. But I stood my ground.* "I'm not going to leave and never come back. But that's what this is about, right? Mom, me, women in general?"

"Get your coat," he said. "You're going to be late for school."

The problem is, I am turning into Mom. *I hate her, too, but all the same, I want to leave this place and never come back. And if Dad wanted to prove to me that he cared? About me, about women in Lorne, about futures?*

He should've investigated Lizzy's death like a murder.

12

LIKE MOTHER, LIKE DAUGHTER

"Hi, Mom." Claude's voice is quiet, lacking the ragged-rough edge that she brings out for her classmates and teachers. She's crouched against the end of a long line of lockers at the edge of a hall, squashed between gray-brown metal and yellow brick, bag tucked between her knees. She runs her finger along the spine of a textbook inside it.

"Is something wrong?" Mom says. In the background, Claude can hear the beginnings of a heated argument.

"I can call you back if you're busy—"

"No. Don't worry about that—" Mom turns away from the phone and Claude hears, in distinct but hushed tones, "Can you fuckers be *quiet*?" Her voice softens again as she comes back. "Okay, honey. What do you need?"

"It's about Emma Baines. They've interviewed me twice and I know they don't believe me—"

"Claude, calm down." Mom's voice is even. Claude takes a deep breath. Lets it out slowly. "Have they charged you with anything?"

"No, but they clearly think I had something to do with it." Her fingers snag on the zipper, tugging it back and forth.

Mom's voice is gentle. "We're going to take this one thing at a time, okay, Claude?"

Claude sniffs. But the tears haven't dropped yet. "'Kay."

"Finish the school day. I know I don't normally say this, but don't push the status quo. Come right home and we'll figure the whole mess out. And Claude?"

"Yeah?"

"If they detain you after school, *don't say anything*. They can't question you without your lawyer present." Mom takes a deep breath. "It's going to be fine. They're letting your reputation color their opinions. You didn't do anything wrong last night."

"No, I didn't." The bell rings and she flinches. Doors scrape open for passing period. "I gotta go. Love you." Claude smiles at her mother's reply before ending the call.

Passing period is filled with whispers. All day they've incubated, and now they're coming up for air. Emma took pills. Emma cheated. Emma liked risks. Emma was on the verge of solving Lizzy Sayer's murder. No one knows truth from lie, and no one cares. There is only one truth, the universal one—the dead girl is tragic. She can't be anything else. Her story sucks at the town, pulls the vitality like endless matchstick-hot summer days without rain. It looms, larger than the mountains that surround Lorne. And everyone in the hall drinks up that story, spitting it back out with a new rumor attached.

It started snowing last period. Fat flakes fall past the windows at the top of the hall and the big glass wall at the end. Students pull sweaters from their lockers and curse Colorado's weather gods. Then, with a last quip, they head for their final class of the day.

Claude carefully touches her finger to the space under her eyes, collecting her unshed tears so they don't ruin the eyeliner she reapplied after lunch. She runs a hand through her short black hair, and when she picks up her bag, she's back to her usual *fuck you* appearance—skinny jeans, leather Docs, chipped polychrome nail polish, bored expression.

A few people eye her as they pass, perhaps eager to see if Claude Vanderly is as collected as she was before her first interview this morning. Claude leans against the lockers, staring at the gray world outside and the snow that sticks to the windows.

One boy stares a little too long, so she turns her head. She looks him up and down, assessing his sharp chin, the way his hair brushes his jaw, his large eyes under a sweep of too-long eyelashes. He blushes and walks right into a door before realizing he probably should have opened it first.

The second bell rings. The halls are empty.

Claude pushes off the wall and begins to prowl. Her boots click on the floor, echoing in a hall that is suddenly silent. She leans around the corner, and there's Emma's locker.

In its sea of dirty-dishwater compatriots, her locker bursts with color. A bouquet of garish multicolored roses has been taped to the front. Cards surround it, spilling apologies, love, and remorse with the frenzy of unsaid prayer. *Please don't blame us.*

The community that cares, now that their consciences are at stake.

A detective stands in front of Emma's locker, spinning the combination lock. On the third try he swings it open—just as Principal Mendoza calls down the hall for him.

His shoes squeak like caught mice as he leaves without closing the locker. The police of Lorne truly are fools. But their inability is Claude's good fortune. She steps out from behind the corner. As she does, two freshmen girls approach. One of them says something behind a curtain of loose blond hair. The other one giggles. They shush each other, like they're sneaking out on a date.

They don't notice the sound of Claude's Docs on the floor. "Fuck off," she hisses. They stare at her in openmouthed amazement for a moment. Then they fuck off. Their laughter erupts behind her, but she doesn't care about them. One long finger touches a cream envelope with Emma's name written neatly in blue pen. For a moment Claude lingers at the envelope's flap—then she turns her attention to the locker itself.

The inside of the locker would be neat, except for the notes that have been shoved through the slats. More *you were the greatest*s from people who've only known Emma as "that girl." People are scrambling for even the smallest excuses to say they knew her. A couple of notebooks lean against one side of the locker.

Claude's eyes narrow at the sight of the notebooks, but

they're not what she's looking for. She pulls a nail file out of her pocket. Sliding it into a crack at the bottom of the locker, she jiggles the nail file, then again. The bottom pops up with a soft sound. Reaching in, her hands curl around something. She pulls out a battered iPhone. One eyebrow arches. She drops the phone into her bag and reaches back into the secret compartment. She rummages until she hears a crinkle. Her expression twists in satisfaction.

Claude pulls out a bag of tiny white pills. It goes into the messenger bag, too. Then she slides the false bottom back into place with a *click*.

A muffled "thanks" from the conversation around the corner makes her leap back. She spins on her heel, takes a few trotting steps, and when she's out of sight, she stops and straightens her clothes.

Claude doesn't go to class. She goes straight to her car.

The Vanderly home is a little two-story box tucked on the "wrong side" of the mountain, the side that was developed during the mining days. The Vanderly women have lived there since time immemorial, which means the cabin is half Grandma's attic, half hectic-lawyer single mom. A cuckoo clock sits on the wall next to pictures of the Vanderly family from four generations back. Ms. Vanderly's law diploma is crammed among them. A high shelf running around the living room wall holds a ceramic angel collection that props up vinyl records Claude and her mom rescued from flea markets and estate sales.

Claude and Mom sit at a rickety wooden table covered in bills, newspaper pages, and junk mail, eating Red Runner takeout. Mom's eyes sag from fatigue. A pile of notebooks—math, history, psychology—sits in in front of the third chair, as though obscuring it from view.

"Lily Fransen's case got dismissed," Mom says.

Claude drops her burger in disgust. "What the *fuck*."

"Statute of limitations was past."

"Yeah, because she was younger than me when it happened." Claude rubs at her eye, then looks down at her uneaten food.

Mom puts a hand on her arm. "I thought life would be easier for you than it was for me. That the world would change faster. But all we have now is smear campaigns and interviews and . . . dead girls." She raises an eyebrow, but Claude doesn't look up. "Want to tell me what happened?"

Claude shrugs. "They asked me where I was last night. They asked me if I knew her, they asked me what I did between yesterday and today. Then they pulled me back in around lunch and asked everything all over again."

"What did you tell them?"

Claude sighs. Her burger bun sags with too much ketchup, and a pickle falls out as she lifts it again. "I don't need the third degree from you, too."

A line appears between Mom's eyes, but a moment later it's smoothed out, and she's all sympathy. "I don't want them targeting you." They both know how easy it would be. The school slut could have gotten into a fight with Emma over a boy. The school vandal could have taken a prank too far. The school delinquent could have been one step from psychotic the whole time. Claude happens to be all three of those.

Claude nods grudgingly and takes another bite of the burger, washing it down with orange juice. "I told them the truth."

"The whole truth?"

Claude puts the burger down and looks her mother right in the eye.

They wait. The silence turns cold and brittle.

The door rattles as someone hammers on the other side. Mom's face flushes. She glances at Claude; Claude shakes her head. It's eight in the evening and they're not accustomed to uninvited guests.

The Vanderly household abhors guns, but as Mom slides toward the door on the balls of her feet, she grabs a baseball bat from where it rests against the balding couch.

The pounding comes again. "Open up! Police!"

Mom's apprehension coalesces into cold anger. She unlocks the door. "There's no need to break down my door. What can I help you with, sirs?"

The cop all but punches her in the face with the paper, brandished like a talisman. But he drops it when he sees Ms. Vanderly's sharp cheeks and wide brown eyes, the curly mane of hair. He tries not to stare at the triangle of skin exposed by the unbuttoned collar of her dress shirt. His face softens a bit. Men have a tendency to go gooey around her. "Sorry, ma'am. But we have a warrant to search the premises."

"What?" But Mom has no choice. She steps aside and allows a team of three to shove past her. The last cop has a German shepherd on a leash. "How did you get that? You can't come in here and implicate my daughter, just because you don't have any real evidence—"

No one's listening, least of all Claude. The moment she sees the German shepherd, she springs from the table and leaps for the living room, where her bag is tucked against the couch. The nearest cop scoops it up, putting out a hand to keep Claude at bay. He turns the bag over and dumps its contents on the floor.

"If you're going to riffle through our lives, the least you can do is treat my child's belongings with re . . . spect. . . ." Mom's voice peters out as the cop leans down and pulls a plastic bag from the mess. The German shepherd barks.

The pills are white, small, round. Not terribly interesting. The cop hands them off and leans down again, pulling a phone from the chaos of notes and pens and open candy wrappers. "This yours?"

He looks past her to where two phones sit on the table.

With a gloved hand he activates the lock screen. The photo is of a girl, smiling. A girl with ice-blond hair cut close to her chin. A girl who's gone with the current.

The world rushes through Claude, dragging her down, stealing her breath. She hears the cop muttering the usual "You have the right to remain silent . . ." but his voice is lost in the river of noise—the bark of the dog, the shouts of the cops, the click of the handcuffs as they slide around her wrist.

And standing in the middle, silent, the rock around which the noise froths—Ms. Vanderly, staring. Shocked into a rare loss of words.

It doesn't last. She swallows, and her voice comes back, louder than the rest, cutting through the cacophony. "Don't say anything, Claude. *Anything*. We're getting a lawyer. Do you understand? *Don't say anything*."

And then Claude's mother is lost, left behind, as the current sweeps downstream.

THE LORNE EXAMINER ONLINE
Thursday, December 6, 2018, 7:00 P.M.
Missing Persons Case Officially Declared Murder

Police arrested a suspect this evening in connection with the death of Emma Baines, a high school senior at Jefferson-Lorne High School.

The Baines case, previously categorized as a missing persons case, was declared a murder investigation when a video posted to the girl's Facebook page was further examined by the police and determined to be authentic.

The video, which has been removed, depicted a girl fitting Emma's description being pushed into the water over the bridge at Anna's Run. Anna's Run is a popular teen hangout spot, but the water narrows dangerously upstream, cutting through the deep channel just under the bridge and creating a powerful undertow. The police believe that the push was deliberate, and made by someone familiar with the danger of the area.

No details regarding the suspect have been released.

STUDY BUDDIES

Gwen should be telling Heather Halifax to get back to work. It's her job as a tutor, after all. But it's too late to focus properly. She sneaks a look at her phone every few seconds as Heather finishes flicking through the *Lorne Examiner Online*. "So they let him off," she says at last. "Senator Hunterton," she clarifies when Gwen raises her eyebrows. "Maybe I can write my APCoGo final paper on abuses of power and gender imbalance."

"You'd probably get an A," Gwen says. "But imagine presenting to the class."

"But, uh, wasn't Lily Fransen really hot at the time?" Heather parodies in her patent stupid-boy voice. She tucks a strand of auburn hair behind her ear. Heather's smart enough not to need tutoring; in her own words, she's just lazy. And it's easy credit for Gwen, who was angling to be more community-oriented than Emma. Plus she likes Heather. Heather doesn't bring up Lizzy all the time, and she's pretty easygoing where everyone but Claude Vanderly is concerned.

Around them, the library is quiet. Most everyone has gone home by now. A group of girls piles on four beanbags, sleeping or doing algebra homework or arguing quietly. A couple of guys are having a heart-to-heart in the corner.

"Today's weird." Heather stretches. "Let's just cancel it and go home." But she looks like she's going out later—her hair falls in perfect ringlets and she spent the first half of tutoring reapplying her makeup while answering Gwen's pop quiz. She wears a soft burgundy V-neck sweater that dips to show her cleavage. "I'll buy you an iced coffee to put on your shoulder." She rolls her eyes, as though to reiterate how stupid she thinks Gwen is for her competition in the gym.

"No thanks." Heather's nice and everything, but being around her makes Gwen uncomfortable. Heather's always offering to buy her stuff. She has so much money she doesn't care. Instead of trading in her old iPhone for credit on the new, she gave it to Gwen so that Gwen could have a phone. It doesn't have a SIM card, but at least it has an internet connection. She used to offer to drive them to Starbucks during study hour, too. Gwen knows Heather would buy her whatever eight-dollar drink and muffin she wanted. She doesn't hate Heather for it, but she sort of resents her. Gwen's never imagined dropping eight bucks on someone else, for no reason at all.

Mr. Pendler leans on the table. "How we doing, humans?"

Heather smiles at him. "Fine." She leans forward a little, and his eyes momentarily follow the neckline of her sweater before snapping back to her face.

"Getting in good study time?"

"It's great, thanks." Gwen busies herself with flipping through notes.

"We're closing in fifteen minutes. Time to wrap up." He makes little finger guns, then heads for the pile of girls.

Heather watches him leave. "I wish he were ten years younger," she says.

"Really?" Gwen mutters.

"Yeah. I'm not going to go for, like, a thirty-five-year-old."

"Maybe we should get back to APCoGo and, you know, abuses of power," Gwen says.

Heather flaps her hand. "It's not the same. Women can have relationships with older men." She picks up her phone, frowning at something on the screen.

"For a certain value of older and a certain value of women," Gwen replies under her breath.

Heather's not listening. "Oh, *shit*," she says, mouth dropping open. "Sweet Jesus. Claude Vanderly's been arrested."

She says it loudly and gleefully enough for the rest of the library to hear. For a moment, silence reigns. Then chairs scrape back as students rush to crowd around her phone. Gwen leans in to read upside down.

"No way," Heather breathes as she scrolls.

"It's fake," says Ben Nakayama.

"I agree. What is this site?" says Samantha Johnson. She scribbles in her notebook; no doubt she's starting an op-ed for the *JLH Inquirer*. "And who the hell is Adams West?" Her question is met with general dissent from the students as they all deny knowledge or involvement.

"Okay, humans, break it up." Mr. Pendler and his finger

guns are back, herding students away from Heather's phone. "This is study time, not gossip time. Miss Halifax, do I need to confiscate that?"

"No," Heather says, but he pulls the phone from her hands. Mr. Pendler frowns as he scans the blog, and Gwen's heart drops through her stomach.

The nightmare has started, and it's only going to get worse.

Jefferson-Lorne Police Officially Can't Detective for Shit

By now you've heard: Police arrested a suspect tonight in connection with the death of Emma Baines, a senior at Jefferson-Lorne High School.

Slow. Clap.

Not only that, but their target is literally the first person you'd suspect: Claude Vanderly.

If that girl's as good at murder as she is at sarcasm and blow jobs—according to the rumors, that is—we should all be pretty fucking afraid.

No doubt the police think their work is done, but I'm not convinced. The resident delinquent makes an easy scapegoat, but it took the JLPD *this* long to confirm that the girl in the viral video was indeed Emma. Pray tell, what other missing blondes were last seen at Anna's Run in the previous twenty-four hours?

Congrats again on your incredible sleuthing, JLPD.

I don't just want to know that it was Vanderly who did it (if she did). I want to know why. The quiet ones always have secrets, so what was Emma's? The real key to this case is who is that secret going to bring down? And does anyone else know it?

If you do, I recommend picking up a change-of-address form on the way home.

Because I'm going to find that secret. And I'm going to expose the truth, the whole truth, and whatever I find along the way.

Sincerely yours,

Adams West

14

THE UNFAITHFUL

The snow falls, and gray wipes the world clean. Even when night descends, it can't seem to penetrate the low-hanging clouds that have blocked the mountains around Lorne from view. The town exists alone in space, separate from reality.

The gym doors at the back of the main building burst open, and the cheer squad comes out. They shiver and squeal together at the cold, pulling hoodies over their heads, hunching their shoulders to their ears. Breaths puff like smoke.

They move with care around each other, each conscious of the girl missing from their orbit. When they exchange hugs at the edge of the parking lot, they linger as though they're not sure they can let go.

Avery wraps her arms around Tanya. "I know it was a long practice today," she says. "But we had so much to work through." Both the routine and Emma. They'd clustered around Lyla's phone, reading and rereading. "We're going to kill it on Saturday."

Shay comes up and puts a hand on Tanya's shoulder. "My mom'll give you a ride home. You can't wait for the bus in this."

"Thanks." Tanya and Shay wave to the rest as Shay's mom pulls into the pickup area.

"Drive safe," Avery says as Natalie unlocks her new VW Bug.

"Of course." Natalie slips in and slams the door.

And then it's just Lyla and Avery, headed for Avery's car. "Starbucks?" Lyla says hopefully.

"Dad said I have to be home in fifteen minutes." Which is true but also a convenient excuse for avoiding two-thousand-calorie drinks. Avery runs a hand over her stomach.

Lyla shrugs. "All right. Feel good about the routine?"

"This one'll be hard. But we'll get through it," Avery says. They have to.

"Yeah. As long as no one keeps getting called in for interviews." Lyla unpins her dark hair, massaging her scalp as she tucks bobby pins through a belt loop. She casts a sidelong glance at Avery, but Avery's intently stepping around piles of slush, careful not to ruin her ballet flats. "I mean, they've already done you twice."

Avery rubs the back of her neck. "I offered to help, remember?"

"Of course." But Lyla sounds relieved. "Are you giving them good stuff? Stuff they can use? Stuff that can help Emma?"

"Yeah." Avery looks up, staring at the slate sky, at the snow that falls in clumps. The perfect weather for careening over the side of the ravine, or crashing into the mountain. Sliding off bridges and into rivers. She taps her foot, as if pressing on an imaginary accelerator.

"Awesome. They might be getting somewhere because of you. My dad texted me during practice to say they already had a suspect in custody."

Avery's head whips around. "So it's true? Is it—?" She doesn't say *Claude*.

"He didn't tell me. But according to Adams West . . ."

"Yeah." Avery unlocks her Prius. Yesterday, Adams West didn't exist. Now he's promising to burn the world down. "Murder's a little off the deep end, though. Even for her."

Lyla shrugs. "I don't know. Claude likes to . . . try new things."

"*Lyla*," Avery gasps.

"Calm down, Aves." Lyla laughs. When she laughs in this snow, she looks like a fairy tale, a princess among peasants. "Even West is skeptical, though I'd have to be an idiot to put all my trust in some random blogger. Even if he does probably go to this school."

"How can you be so sure?"

"Knowledge of the student body and general disdain for Lorne." Lyla tilts her chin up to catch snow on her eyelashes. "He's a Lorner, through and through."

"Or maybe he's a forty-year-old in Denver who makes fake blogs out of big news stories," Avery says.

"No, he's from here. And he's definitely our age. I'm betting he's hot." Lyla giggles and leans over the hood of the car. "It's something in the way he writes."

Avery shakes her head as they slip into the Prius. "You're too obsessed with hot guys, Lyla."

"Of course you'd think that. You've got a hot guy, and I'm still waiting on mine. The most action I get is covering for you." Lyla bites her lip. "So did your parents ever ask you about it?"

"About Adams West?" Avery's busy slipping off her wet shoes and doesn't look at Lyla.

"*No*, Aves. About where you were last night."

"Oh." She swallows again and tosses the ballet flats behind her seat. "I said I was at your place. That's still cool, right?"

"Of course. You know I have your back. We girls gotta stick together." Lyla leans over to knock Avery with her shoulder and gives her a conspiratorial smile. "My parents were asleep at eleven, so if anyone asks, you came over around twelve, and you left early this morning because you forgot something at home."

"Thanks, Lyla." Avery finally smiles, a soft and real smile. "That means a lot."

"I'm happy to help. As long as you give me details. Which you've been *really bad at* so far."

Avery starts up the Prius. "I know. I just . . . don't know how to talk about it. My parents would kill me if they thought Michael and I are—um. You know. And they really like him. They say he's such a good boy." The perfect boy to marry right out of high school and start a Jefferson-Lorne family with.

"Aves, I'm happy to keep your relationship-saving secret sex life a secret, as long as you agree to spill *some* of that secret."

"Relationship-saving?"

"Don't play innocent." Lyla arches a brow. "Michael was

convinced you and Emma were . . ." She tilts her head as she leans in to adjust the heat. "He was practically crawling up my ass, trying to get me to admit to covering for you." She puts her hand on Avery's arm. "Don't feel guilty about last night."

"I don't," Avery says, but her eyes are on Lyla's hand, not her face.

"You needed to make time for him. You almost had *me* convinced that you were cheating with Emma." She squeezes. "I'm gonna dump my stuff in the trunk—hang on."

"No! I mean, here, I've got it."

Avery grabs Lyla's bag and hops out, tiptoeing over to the trunk. She pops it open and tosses a black hoodie over a pair of too-large hiking boots, still wet and crusting with mud.

"Didn't you wear that yesterday?" Lyla says over her shoulder.

Avery spins as if seeing a ghost.

"No." The lie comes out easy, forceful, with no room for error. "That's an old lacrosse hoodie. Sorry. It's such a mess back here. I didn't want to get your stuff filthy."

Lyla stares for a moment at the misshapen bundle only partly hidden beneath the sweatshirt. The rubber toe of one boot poking out. The mud, dense and dark, like the kind that coats the banks of the river. "Pine Nation doesn't make boots in women's sizes."

"They're Dad's. I sort of, um. Borrowed them." Avery twitches the muddy hoodie over the edge of the boot.

Lyla puts one hand on the top of the trunk, fixing Avery

with her stare. "Why? What were you and Michael doing last night?"

Avery swallows. "He wanted to do it . . . somewhere different."

Lyla snorts. "Shut up. You guys did it *outside*?"

"Shh," Avery pleads, looking around the deserted parking lot.

Lyla takes her hand off the trunk. "I need details. Five minutes ago."

"Okay, okay, I'll tell you everything." Avery's face is beet red. She slams the trunk closed. "Let's just get into the car first. It's freezing out here."

As they drive away she spins a story. Of hands, and lips. Of whispered giggles and hitched sighs. Of stolen, forbidden time.

Not all of it is a lie.

<u>Diary Entry</u>
Emma Baines—October 4, 2017

Lizzy's diary is quite enlightening. That secret-boyfriend thing? Suspicions confirmed. And not just that, he's an older guy. Like, statutory-rape older. That's why she kept it secret.

The boyfriend seems to coincide with . . . the other stuff. The Jack and pills stuff. And call me crazy (everyone else does, and if my diary calls me crazy I'm definitely out of my mind), but I wonder if the two things are related. Older guy, who gets Lizzy into some bad habits—he could go to jail not only for dating an underage girl, but for getting her booze and drugs. What if she wanted to break up with him? What if he wanted to break up with her but was afraid she'd go to the cops in revenge? In her last few months she wasn't exactly thinking clearly. What if she threatened him and he panicked?

What if he was a cop, and he could cover up the evidence?

All I know is that Lizzy's boyfriend wasn't a high school student. And since the biggest exodus is right after high school, it's feasible that he's still in Lorne. If he is, and he doesn't want the truth of their relationship getting out . . . I need a name and evidence before I go to the police. And I know where I can find one. Lizzy never put his identification down on paper, but she did write this: I sent THE PHOTOS today. It's all detailed on No. 2. Still fanning myself.

I think No. 2 is a secret account. If I find that account, maybe I can find him.

I need to tread carefully, but I also need to keep going. That's what journalists do. That's what friends do.

15

THE FENCE

CLINE: The date is Thursday, December 6, 2018. Nine thirty-three p.m. Third interview with Claude Vanderly. Presiding officers Muñez and Cline.

Miss Vanderly?

. . . Miss Vanderly?

CLAUDE: I can hear you.

CLINE: What was your relationship with Emma Baines?

Miss Vanderly, did you push Emma Baines into Anna's Run?

CLAUDE: I did not.

CLINE: Miss Vanderly, did Emma have something on you? Maybe she had evidence linking you to a supplier of these?

CLAUDE: I don't know anything about those pills.

CLINE: You don't know about the pills that we dumped out of your bag?

CLAUDE: Nothing.

CLINE: You're eighteen, which means you can be legally tried as an adult. Do you realize what will happen if we bring charges against you? Charges of distributing medication without a prescription? Charges of murder?

Claude, I know you're a good girl at heart.

CLAUDE: And here's me thinking the murder charges were going to be the biggest lie you told tonight.

CLINE: Sometimes, people get caught up in things and don't know how to get out of it. Maybe you did someone a favor once, and now you're blackmailed into doing it. Is that how you started selling pills? We see this story a lot. It doesn't have to be as shameful as you think. And if you work with us, maybe we can get you leniency for cooperation.

CLAUDE: I can't help you.

CLINE: The pills came out of your bag. The phone, *Emma's* phone, came out of your bag. Where did you get them from?

Tell us, Claude. Where did they come from? While we can still make a deal with you.

CLAUDE: I . . . I got them from her locker, all right?

CLINE: Which locker?

CLAUDE: Her locker at school. The main one. With all the flowers and shit around it. That's where I got the pills and the phone.

CLINE: And why were you there? At the locker?

Come on, Claude. Help us help you. Because if you don't, you're going to go up before a judge, and he's going to know about all of it. That you've been in trouble before. That you've been on the wrong side of the law. That you have a problematic history.

Do you want that, Claude?

CLAUDE: No.

CLINE: Tell us why you took the phone.

CLAUDE: I didn't mean to! I just—I heard Emma had some things in her locker. Not real bad things. Just caffeine pills and stuff. I, uh, thought they'd be useful. And when I saw her phone . . . I don't know. Maybe I could sell it or something. I don't even know what's on it.

CLINE: Can you unlock it for me?

CLAUDE: No.

CLINE: Claude, do you need me to remind you how serious this situation is?

CLAUDE: How am I supposed to open it? It's not my phone.

CLINE: Forgive me if I'm skeptical.

CLAUDE: Fine.

Wrong password.

Wrong password.

Wrong password.

And . . . now it's locked.

Your turn. Don't you have some sort of secret police computer-hacking program that can get you into any phone? Can't you violate Emma's privacy with a special investigation law?

CLINE: Even if we had the right to open Emma's phone, we don't have the means. Best we can do is restore it to factory settings.

CLAUDE: You can't get it open?

CLINE: You sound distressed. Everything all right?

CLAUDE: Yeah. Yeah. Everything's fine. I'm just surprised.

I thought you fucking fascists could do anything.

CLINE: (sighing) Tell us about your last conversation with Emma.

CLAUDE: Already did.

CLINE: You didn't tell us about the phone call.

Your phone record shows three minutes of conversation. Emma's phone to yours. Tell us about it.

CLAUDE: Um. I was driving. I was on my way to Steve's party. You remember the party you grilled me about earlier today. So I was going, and Emma called. I don't know why—it's not like we're friends. I told her she should come.

CLINE: Did she come to the party?

CLAUDE: No.

CLINE: Did you go to the party?

CLAUDE: Yes.

CLINE: Did you know Emma wanted to buy a gun?

CLAUDE: . . . What?

CLINE: What was she afraid of, Claude? Was it you?

CLAUDE: I don't know anything about her disappearance *or* a gun. I didn't kill her.

CLINE: You *do* know something. You and Emma had something going on, and if you won't tell us, we'll have to guess. You know what I think? It sounds like you were dealing to her. Maybe you need a secret place to do it, so you pick Anna's Run. It's got a reputation, it's secluded, and if anyone did go there, the river's so loud they wouldn't hear your conversation. Right?

CLAUDE: Wrong. None of this is true.

CLINE: I think Emma called you last night. She wanted to meet, maybe to buy more. Only, something's off when you get there. Maybe she didn't bring the money. Maybe she owed you. Maybe you needed the money for something. Your car's transmission sounds like it's suffering.

CLAUDE: You broke into Janine?

CLINE: Maybe Emma threatened you. Her dad's the chief of police, after all. She could get you into big trouble, and she'd walk away without a stain on her reputation. She'd leave Lorne far behind, while you were stuck here dealing pills to the next generation, dodging citations and jail time. She held your life over your head, didn't she? She and the corrupt system she's part of. The system that rejects you, calls you names, whispers about you behind your back . . .

CLAUDE: That's not what happened.

CLINE: What did happen, Claude?

I'm sorry, this is a private conversation.

CHRISTOPHER GRANT: And I'm this young lady's counsel.

CLINE: I see. Please take a seat.

GRANT: That won't be necessary. You have no grounds to hold my client. We'll be leaving.

CLINE: We have evidence—

GRANT: The phone? The phone number's not connected to Emma Baines in any way. Which means that charges toward my client of intending to distribute a controlled substance to Miss Baines are circumstantial and nothing more. Let's go, Claude.

FROM: Will Tabor
TO: Detective Camilla Muñez
DATE: December 6, 9:24 p.m.
SUBJECT: Forensics study and preliminary examination—
smartphone—case number 27-95-1682

The forensics team found partial prints belonging to two distinct persons, possibly a partial of a third person. The last print is so far unidentifiable. The first set of prints belongs to Claude Vanderly, the second set belongs to Avery Amelia Cross. We'll keep working on the third.

The tech team here hasn't had preliminary luck with unlocking the phone. We'll be sending it back to JLPD with a squad car first thing in the morning. Maybe Avery Cross can help you.

16

THE SISTER

Snow makes the world silent. As Gwen walks, rotating her arm, lights flicker in the homes around her like a toy Christmas village owned by one of her wealthier peers. Cars still in their summer tires sag on the side of the road. A cracked plastic play set already has two inches of snow.

The front walk of the Sayer house is blanketed in a thick white layer. Gwen's father isn't home yet. Stems and thorns give a muted snap underfoot as Gwen makes her way to the front door. The click it makes as it unlocks is as loud as a shout.

The lights are all down inside, save for one lamp in their joke of a living room. The linoleum underfoot is warped and crackles as she steps on an air bubble. Gwen's mum sits against the least duct-taped side of the couch with a book beside her and her head in her hands. An untouched glass of wine is on the battered coffee table. Gwen's parents used to enjoy a glass of wine each evening. Before Lizzy enjoyed wine a little too much. The kitchen area is dark, but Gwen smells chicken and potatoes and rosemary.

Mum looks up as Gwen kicks off her boots. "Where have you been?" she asks thickly.

"School. Then speech and debate. Then tutoring, so I missed the bus." Gwen covers the shaking of her hands by hanging up her coat.

"I rang you." Mum's voice is ragged but tentative. She doesn't know how to be stern anymore. Another thing destroyed in the wake of Lizzy's death—her confidence. Her knowledge, so sure before, that she was a good parent. That she was good enough.

Gwen hates Lizzy for that. And she hates herself for hating.

"I know. I was at school, so I didn't pick up."

"You should have messaged me between classes."

"And then you'd come and get me? I told you I wanted to go to school." Shivering, Gwen starts toward the kitchen. "And it was the right call."

Before, Mum would have challenged that. She'd have stood up and put her hands on her hips, saying, "Oh, was it?" before lecturing Gwen on who the mother was in this situation. Now she says nothing, just gets to her feet and follows Gwen to the kitchen, crossing her arms as she leans against the refrigerator.

Mum used to be a fearsome woman, a woman who'd lost and found her voice. She comes from a Puritan family in Bridgend and she describes her childhood the way other people would describe being in a cult. When she was seventeen, a charming missionary from the States lodged with her family for six months. When he moved back to California, he took Bronwyn with him, and he gave her a black eye twice a week for three years. She fled all the way to Lorne to be rid of him—or maybe it was just that she met Gwen's dad there and found out that some men aren't trash. She didn't want a paper trail leading husband number one to her, so she cleans for whatever the housewives of Lorne will pay her. Dad's education finished at high school, and even though Mr. Mecklin's a generous supervisor, he can't promote Dad without the right certifications. They never used to care; Mum always said she knew from experience that there were worse things than being poor.

Mum wasn't ashamed to talk about her past life, before Lizzy. Now she's quiet, and she prays when she thinks no one's listening.

Gwen hates the idea that Mum might pray over her. That Mum might wonder if her children are punishments from God, sent for abandoning her oppressive faith, for divorcing an abusive shit and marrying a man who's never raised his hand against them.

At last the kettle clicks and Gwen pours a cup of tea for her and Mum, adds milk and sugar, and goes over to her chair. She feels like a disappointment. She's not sure what to say.

Mum follows every movement. "Some vicious speech and debate?" she says, nodding to Gwen's arm and the way she winces every time she lifts it. Mum opens the freezer and grabs a bag of frozen peas.

"I slipped on ice." Gwen picks up her phone, puts it down. She has to do something to quiet her hands, quiet her mind.

Mum slings the bag of peas over Gwen's shoulder. "You should have called me. I would have come."

"Did Dad put winter tires on the truck yet?" Trick question. They can't afford winter tires.

Mum is silent for a moment. Then she shakes her head. "You can't do this, Gwen. You can't lie to me first and justify it after. That's what—" She stops.

The silence is back, and cruel.

"I'm not her," Gwen says. She clenches her hands to keep them from shaking.

Mum stares at the table, blinking rapidly. Then she leans over and rearranges the bag, businesslike again. "No walking to school tomorrow, all right?" Mum says. As if Gwen hadn't spoken at all.

"I'll take the bus." Victory feels hollow.

Mum gets up and checks on the oven. Gwen's stomach growls as the scent of lemon, butter, and chicken wafts out. "Was school worth it?" Mum moves to the sink and starts to peel some carrots.

"Yes," Gwen replies automatically. Mum turns and regards her with a raised eyebrow. Gwen's obstinacy is talking again. "I don't know," she admits. "They didn't announce the scholarship today."

"And what does that mean?" Mum scoffs.

"It means Emma won." She tries to keep her voice neutral, but bitterness infects it.

"You've got to be patient. This town is . . . going through something." Mum falls silent. They're both thinking about

Anna's Run. About the girls who went down to see Anna and never came back. Mum's fingers come to the chain at her neck, the gold cross she put on again the first time Lizzy came home drunk. Then she shakes her head. "But what else did you do today? Did you talk to Mr. Pendler about your poem?" Gwen had a poem printed in the *Lorne Examiner* two weeks ago. Mum thinks Mr. Pendler will boost her grade, even though she already has 103 percent in his class.

"I don't want to talk to Mr. Pendler," Gwen mumbles, glaring at the table. Her phone buzzes. She frowns at it, types something quickly. She tunes back in to Mum in time to hear her say, "And your comparative government class?"

"School was just school, okay?" Like so many other things in her life, she can't quite keep her voice under control. Mum's shoulders hunch over the sink. The Mum of before would have told Gwen how she should speak to her mother. The Mum of now doesn't say anything. So it's up to Gwen to try. "Sorry. I just . . . I don't want to talk about it. You were right. Everyone at school was weird, The police are looking through Emma's things. . . . But I'm still right about going." She adjusts the ice on her shoulder so she can use her phone without it sliding off. "Anyway. We decorating for Christmas?"

The Sayer family always has a big Christmas. Grandma and Uncle Louis and Aunt Selma all live in Lorne and agree that the Sayers have the best kitchen. Uncle Monty and his kids and his wife, Sisi, and *her* kids make the trip down from South Dakota. The extended family loves coming to Lorne. They think the mountain town is romantic. They like to ogle the big lodges that business execs buy to feel like mountain men every once in a while. Uncle Monty always brings a tree he chopped down himself and strapped to the top of their Land Rover.

"We always do," Mum says, but she glances at Lizzy's door.

They used to decorate the house as a Thanksgiving tradition. Lizzy hated the holiday—American imperialism incarnate, she said. But Mum and Dad insisted that Thanksgiving was about family, and would be held in the Sayer house. So Lizzy decorated for Christmas to give them something else to celebrate instead.

Thanksgiving sucked this year.

Mum hands Gwen another carrot. "Where's Dad?" Gwen asks.

Mum has moved on to opening cans of corn. "He'll be home when he's home. We can eat without him tonight."

"Is he working late or something?" This feels like another trick question. Mr. Mecklin would never demand that Dad stay after six.

"Mmm," Mum replies. Like that's an answer.

And just like that, the silence is back.

"I should do my homework," Gwen says, but she knows she won't. She can't focus. She can't think about homework or sleep or even school, where the whispers follow her in the halls and Emma's name is like a noose. Slowly creeping closer, slipping around Gwen's neck, choking.

So instead of going into her room, she goes into Lizzy's, for the first time since her sister died.

Mum hasn't changed a thing. From the fabric-painted

Disney coverlet to the books on her desk and the faded photo of the Mari Lwyd, the skeleton mare. The charm bracelet Lizzy made in art class, mocking all the rich girls with their expensive Pandora charms. The books half read on her dresser. She'd once ranted at Gwen about how much *Macbeth* sucked because it was all blamed on Lady Macbeth and it only reinforced the Crazy Woman stereotype—Gwen sometimes wonders if she was drunk that day.

When Lizzy started high school she read Shakespeare to Gwen, saying it would give her an edge. Saying you had to perform Shakespeare to really enjoy him. They put on silly voices until their impromptu drama sessions became fits of giggles. Then Lizzy would brush Gwen's hair, braiding and unbraiding it and winding it with fake flowers she brought home from theater productions.

"I feel bad for Olivia," Gwen said one night as Lizzy brushed her hair. They'd finished *Twelfth Night* earlier that evening. Lizzy had her hair long tonight, too, via the magic of cheap extensions. She wouldn't let Gwen get her own hair cut for the world. "Olivia thought she was marrying one person and ended up with another."

"Viola was lying the whole time, too." Lizzy's fingers began to twist at the nape of Gwen's neck. "She even lied about her gender."

"A girl's gotta make some cash," Gwen said. "But Olivia genuinely loved her."

"You don't think Olivia would have been worried to discover she married a girl?"

Gwen shrugged.

The movement at her braid stilled. "You wouldn't mind marrying a girl," Lizzy said. Her voice was so careful, so neutral.

Gwen's voice cracked. "Um . . . I don't know."

She wanted to cry, like it was something terrible. Something she hadn't really put into words before. A great disappointment in herself.

"It's okay." Lizzy's arms came around in a hug. "It's okay."

And then she was crying, because she *knew* it was okay, *of course* it was okay to be gay. But there was a big difference between accepting that someone else might be gay and accepting that she might.

Gwen never cared about boys. She'd always assumed she was too busy with her studies to be interested, but then Samantha Johnson had burst out laughing at a joke during speech and debate, and Gwen's heart had stopped. And she'd buried it in the back of her mind, something to think about later when she wasn't fighting for a scholarship or the top slot at school or a trophy from any clubs—and she'd sort of hoped that by the time she got to college, she'd realize she liked boys after all.

"We don't have to talk about it," Lizzy said, smoothing Gwen's hair, undoing the braid and starting to brush again. Gwen wiped under her eyes. She felt foolish for crying. It had been the shock more than anything. "But you're my little sister. You can tell me anything, okay? And when you're ready to talk to Mum and Dad about it, I'll be right beside you."

That's a promise Lizzy can't keep.

They were supposed to take the world by storm together.

They were supposed to get full scholarships and make bank and buy Mum and Dad a house with real foundations. They were supposed to fund scholarships of their own to get more girls out of poverty. They were supposed to do it all together.

Neither of them was supposed to end up they way they are: one dead, one in way, way over her head.

Gwen moves away from *Macbeth*. Her hands find the top drawer, her fingers hesitate on the knob. The last time she opened this drawer—the last time she was in this room—was the day of Lizzy's funeral. She shoved the note in this drawer, too sick to think about it. She thought she'd eventually be ready.

She was wrong.

The note is in a shaky hand, not like Lizzy's usual neat print at all. One corner is fuzzy, like a tear fell and Lizzy tried to wipe it away. *I love you, Pilipala.* Her nickname for Gwen. It means butterfly in Welsh. *Please don't be mad. I couldn't stay today but I promise I'll be there tomorrow. I'll always be right beside you.*

Gwen found the note on her desk that night, shoved it to the side so she could work. Lizzy's promises had been hollow back then, just like Lizzy herself. And Gwen *had* been mad. Booze and parties and boys were more important to Lizzy than her own sister. So Gwen decided that her sister was less important than history essays, and practicing her French, and doing her algebra. And she'd ignored the texts that said **heeeeey** and **hey G** and **hey polypsis**, which was supposed to be *Pilipala*, but Lizzy was obviously too drunk to see the autocorrect. And she'd ignored the call, figuring her big sister could get in trouble with Mum if she wanted something.

And now Gwen will never know what Lizzy was calling about.

She can't breathe. Gwen shuts the desk, and the snap of the drawer is like emerging for air. She already walks on a blade-thin edge, and thinking of Lizzy just clouds her mind. She turns away from the desk, from the bed and the bookcase—and she sees them. Those stupid plastic extensions. Draped over Lizzy's chair in an array of colors.

And Gwen realizes: she has to sneak out of the house for the second time today.

By the time she gets to Anna's Run, mud cakes her boots and knees where she slipped. Her jeans are soaked up to midcalf. The ground ahead of her is a patchwork of black and white. Aspen and evergreen trees crowd her. But she can hear Anna, ever hungry. The scent of the forest hangs thick, pine sap and crisp new snow.

And though she knows the sound of the Run will mask the footsteps of anyone coming up behind her, she activates the flashlight on her telephone and starts to search. She moves toward the little bridge.

She should have thought this through. She's going to be valedictorian now, but she can't manage simple logistics? Even if she'd remembered this morning, before the snow began—

The snow. She stops. The area's been disturbed by footprints, going back and forth. The FBI hasn't been here for hours, and the footprints all have the same pattern and size. Gwen takes a deep breath, willing herself calm. But in addition to pine and juniper, the faint scent of woodsmoke tickles her nose.

Fire. Footprints. What if it's—

The water roars. A branch snaps wetly behind her. And though Gwen has always thought of herself as the girl in control, she can't control the scream that slips out.

Diary Entry

Emma Baines—October 29, 2017

Things I haven't found out from Lizzy's diary:

Who her secret boyfriend was, or who she might have been afraid of.

Things I have found out:

That she has a crush on Jack Black's character from the Kung Fu Panda *series. wtf???*

That she thinks her mum's roast chicken dinner is dry but she'd never tell her.

That she has this weird hair-braid-y tradition with Gwen. I guess it's something sisters do. When they talk to each other about all the things that frustrate them.

That Gwen <u>cheated on her advanced-track exam at the beginning of high school.</u>

And <u>Gwen is in the closet and I'm not supposed to know.</u>

Wtf do I do with this information?? Gwen's only in the running for the scholarship because she took the advanced-track exam and got permission to take AP courses without doing the prerequisites. If I told Principal Mendoza she cheated, she'd be pushed back into the regular track, or worse.

I'd win. I'd get out of Lorne, away from Dad.

But it feels wrong. If I expose her, I'll have to show Principal Mendoza how I found out. Not only does that make me the weirdo who snuck into a grieving house and stole a dead girl's diary—not only does it alert Lizzy's secret boyfriend to the diary's existence—it also outs Gwen to the world.

Lizzy wrote about how stressed Gwen was. About how she was afraid of failing the exam, of not being good enough. Of missing out on her college education before she had the chance to try for it. Her entire future rested on one test. And I know cheating is bad, and I do feel a tiny *bit superior for passing it without cheating. But. Maybe I understand why Gwen did it. We all deserve a chance to excel, don't we? And if she was really so unfit for the fast track, why are we neck and neck?*

Lizzy wrote about the parents, too. Gwen thought they'd freak if they realized she was gay. Lizzy worried about Gwen's mental health, her happiness, the high stress of trying to be the best and being in the closet at the same time. Her parents are nice, but you never know where people land on the gay-okay track, and her mum is an ex-fundamentalist.

Can I really out Gwen to win? I mean, cheating is totally unethical, and if she won the scholarship it would be so unfair. But this feels underhanded, too.

THE DELINQUENT

Snow flurries, frenetic, as though it finally discovered that it's falling in Lorne and now it can never escape. The little police station hasn't bothered to clear its parking lot, and only three cars sit out front. Inside it's no warmer than outside, and Ms. Vanderly still wears her coat, fine black wool that seems out of place against the cheap plastic and chipboard. Her gloved fingers tap on the desk of the unfortunate night officer.

She leaps up as Claude and Mr. Grant emerge from the bowels of the station. Mr. Grant leans over the desk to shake her hand. Then she envelops Claude in an embrace Claude doesn't return. Her face is pale, her makeup faded. She's not wearing her *fuck you* expression anymore. But she hasn't cried yet, either.

"Are you all right?" Claude's mom cups her cheek with one hand.

"I'm fine." She says it without any of her usual confidence or bravado and her words ring hollow.

Mom turns on the officer who followed Claude and Mr. Grant out. "I expect an apology. Written. In full."

The officer folds his arms. "We're just doing our jobs, ma'am."

"Your job is to find the truth, not terrorize kids."

The cop is unfazed by her righteous fury. He hands her a slip of paper. "I'll get your things from the evidence locker. You'll be able to pick up the car in a couple of days."

"I want it now," Mom says.

"It's still being examined."

Mom glances at Mr. Grant. He clears his throat and says, "If my client is no longer a suspect, then the seizure of her property is illegal. We want it now."

The cop's mouth curls, but he doesn't have a choice. He turns his sneer on Claude one last time. Then he goes to get the keys.

Claude holds it together until they're out in the snow. Then she lets the air kiss her burning face, lets the tears fall hot. She barely hears Mom say goodbye to Mr. Grant. She can't hear anything except the clink of her handcuffs. She can't see anything except the cold tabletop. She's never feared the police before now. But fifteen minutes in a cold room, and she nearly confessed.

Mom's arms come around her again. "It's going to be okay," she says. Claude nods like she believes her.

It stopped being okay a long time ago. And it's been a hell of a day—why try to lie to herself?

She feels her mom draw back. She forces her eyes open. Mom's offering up a tissue. Claude wipes her nose.

"Claude . . ." Mom takes a deep breath.

But Claude's eye is caught by the figure behind her, moving slowly, shifting from foot to foot. "Jamie?"

Mom turns. Jamie Schill coughs. He looks like a marshmallow in his puff coat. His cheeks are red with cold, but his brown eyes make her forget, for a moment, that she stands in a police parking lot surrounded by trouble. "What are you doing here?" Claude asks. Her stupid heart squeezes painfully. Probably the stress. "How did you . . . ?"

Jamie holds up his phone. "You're on a blog," he starts.

"What? Give me that." Mom snatches the phone from his hand. She reads through the post two, three times. "Well, at least this West guy is on your side. Maybe." She hands the phone back. "But it changes things." She starts toward her car.

As Claude moves to follow her, Jamie coughs. "Um, can I talk to you?" Her heart squeezes again.

Mom stops by the car. "I'll wait. Claude, you have one minute. We need to talk."

As Jamie tries to scrub the red out of his cheeks, Claude thinks. She's never heard Mom trot out *we need to talk*.

That bodes well.

"So," she says, and swallows until the roughness in her voice goes away. "How'd you sneak out? Did you stage an alien abduction in your room?" Jamie's supposed to be at his house by nine on a school night. No exceptions. But he even managed to commandeer his mom's van.

Jamie's mouth twists in an almost smile. "Maybe I pretended to be on a mission from the CIA."

"Maybe you got a clone to sleep in your bed."

His expression flashes back to serious. "I said there was an emergency with Michael, actually. I promised I'd be home

132

twenty minutes ago." Jamie ruffles his hair. With his red cheeks and brown eyes he looks innocent. Disarming. The squeeze in her chest is followed by a stab. Fuck.

He hesitates, then pushes everything out, as though it will take him less effort that way. "Look, I know you didn't . . . you know. Because I know where you were that night."

He doesn't. He really doesn't.

"I know you were at Steve's party, because Steve told me you hooked up with Kyle Landry on top of the mini fridge in the garage."

"Ew," she says before she can stop herself.

"You didn't hook up with him?"

She can hear him trying so, so hard not to be hopeful. "I don't know what to tell you, Jamie." She doesn't. She wants to punch Steve in the dick until he cries, but his lie is convenient. If everyone at JLH spreads the rumor, the police won't look too deeply into whether she was there at all.

"It's okay. Really." He swallows, and she can see him thinking, *It's okay, I'll make it okay*, and that just makes it worse. Because it's only okay if he truly thinks so. "I respect you, and you don't have to be exclusive if you don't want. But . . . be honest with me. Please?"

She can't be honest. She can't say that she's never hooked up with two guys in one night. She can't say that right now, all she wants to do is lie on the couch and make up super- hero identities for their teachers and fall asleep on Jamie's lap and *not* have sex. She can't say that it's actually sweet how he pushes his nose into her back when he's waking up after a night together. That he tries to get her to drink his protein shake. She can't say that she likes doing homework with him because he cares so much that he starts to make boring subjects actually interesting.

She likes his honest, earnest expression. She likes the length of his eyelashes and the tiny ring of green in his brown eyes. She likes his puff coat. He looks huggable and soft.

She can't afford to think like that.

Claude rearranges her expression. The secret to omitting the truth is to not look like you're choosing your words carefully to hide something. "I'm not trying to play you." Not like he means, anyway. "I can't have a boyfriend, Jamie."

"Can't, or don't want to?" he asks, and that goddamn hope is back in his eyes.

She *doesn't* want a boyfriend. She doesn't. And Jamie—she *needs* for him not to be her boyfriend. Things are only going to get worse from here, and when the shit hits the fan, Jamie shouldn't be in the blast zone. She can do that much for him. So she puts her hand on his arm, and squeezes lightly, and says, "What's the difference?"

She slides into the Volvo and stops trying not to cry. Her skin prickles in the sudden warm air, and she sticks her bare fingers up against the grate, letting heat blast them.

"Everything all right?" Mom watches Jamie turn, slowly, and go back to his van.

"It's fine. He just wants to be my knight in shining armor."

Mom forces a soft laugh. "No Vanderly ever needed that."

The van pulls away with a crunch of tires on snow. Lights flicker in the neon signs across the street proclaiming Lorne's lone gym, lone liquor store, lone Realtor, and hundredth ski shop. The magic that snow brings to Lorne obscures them momentarily, a coat of paint over the worst of the grime. For a long minute, the Vanderly women don't say anything. But silence has never been a big hit with them. "Claude, how did you get that phone?" Mom asks.

"I found it," Claude whispers.

"Claude, you know what kind of answer that is." A bullshit answer. All the same, Claude can't bring herself to look up. She picks at her nail polish.

Mom sighs. "What about the pills. Are they yours?"

"Yes."

"What the *fuck*, Claude?" Her mother's gaze is hard and angry. Claude can feel it, even though she still can't muster the courage to look up. "Did they do a drug test?"

"Yeah."

Mom takes a steeling breath. "Well, you must have passed, or they wouldn't have let you go. But honestly, pills? What are you doing with them? Where did you get them?"

"They're not for me. They're for another girl at school, Avery Cross. She—she left them in Emma's locker, and I said I'd get them out for her. The phone was in there with them."

Mom's eyes narrow. "Avery Cross, the cheer captain? You're not even friends with her. Why are you risking jail time?"

Claude can't answer. She doesn't have a convincing enough lie.

"Do you think she might have set you up?"

"Doubt it," Claude says thickly. She's cried enough for one

day, *she's cried enough for one day*, but damn it all if she didn't want one fucking person on this earth to think well of her. And that person just lost faith.

"Claude, you shouldn't have gone anywhere near that locker. That complicates things."

"I know," mutters Claude.

"No going out for a while," Mom says. "No Jamie, no hitting a party. You need to lie low until I get you out of this mess. And now that your name's all over a blog, people are going to show up for photos. They'll ask for interviews. They'll twist your words and call you names. You're not going to add fuel to the fire."

"So I'm grounded," Claude says hollowly.

"If that's how you want to put it." Mom's cold fingers wrap around Claude's. "Claude, don't fight me on this. It's my job to deal with this stuff."

"I know," Claude says, and gets out of the car. She hops into Janine and starts the engine. There's one other thing she knows.

This is going to be bigger than anything Lorne's seen in the last fifty years. How is her mom supposed to be prepared for that?

They drive slowly, down streets Lorne's snowplow hasn't hit yet. The world outside is silent, and Claude keeps the radio off. Something hollow starts to grow in the pit of her stomach. She should be exhausted from three interrogations and an arrest. Instead, her ears prick at every sound and she flinches when the windshield wipers squeak. They pass houses with flickering Christmas lights and she keeps her head rigid, facing forward. She won't give anyone in the windows the vindication of seeing Claude Vanderly ashamed. All the same, what does it matter? *They already know. They already know all they need to know about you.* And soon enough the police will be back, and it won't matter how many favors Mom can call in, because they'll know exactly what Claude did.

At home Mom cleans up the chaos that dinner became. When Claude moves to help, Mom puts a hand on her shoulder. "Just get some rest, all right, hon? You still have to go to school tomorrow."

"Seriously?" After the day she's had, she needs a full week off.

"Seriously. Trust me, the rumors will only be worse if you don't. I'm just trying to help."

"Thanks," she says, and leans in to her mother's hug. Then she goes into her room.

In here there's nothing to distract her from her stupid, pounding heart, or to keep her from seeing Jamie's face when she closes her eyes. She hates that she wishes he were here. She hates that she misses him. She hates that she's afraid. All the same, she peers through the windows above her bed. No lurking shadows, no filling-in footprints. The snow would have revealed if anyone was watching her. Still, she can't shake the feeling. She shoves up against the corner of her bed. Her fingers move over the phone and she's halfway to calling Jamie before she realizes.

If she called, he'd pick up.

If she called, he'd be so hopeful.

She dials someone else instead. No pickup. She waits, tapping the phone with a forefinger before redialing less than two minutes later. Again, then again. No one answers. "Seriously?" she mutters. Finally she risks a text.

We've got a problem with the phone. Her hands start to shake. I think I'm in deep shit. Call me.

She puts the phone down and checks out the window again. Still no one. Still nothing. Just snow, flurrying in the light of the lamp, and the dim shapes of trees and houses beyond. The mountains are obscured by the storm, but she knows they're there. And they're more like a cage than ever.

THE LORNE EXAMINER ONLINE
December 6, 2018, 11:00 P.M.
Police Release Lone Suspect in Missing Teen Case

Police have confirmed that their primary suspect in the disappearance and possible murder of Emma Baines has been released from custody. The suspect was mistakenly thought to have been in possession of evidence belonging to the victim. She has several previous citations from the police.

"We're being very thorough," said Deputy Chief Bryson. "It's always regrettable to make a misstep, but we want to make sure we cover every single possibility. This case is very close to the Jefferson-Lorne Police Department."

The missing person, Emma Baines, is the daughter of Police Chief Mason Baines.

"We can apologize after we've found the culprit," Deputy Chief Bryson asserted. "Until then, stay out of the woods and stay out of our way."

Police are also combing the woods for any hikers. Smoke has been seen from several locations. Jefferson National Park is a common campground, and police suspect that hikers or vagrants in the woods may be witnesses to the crime. They also suspect that the blogger Adams West, whose posts have targeted Jefferson-Lorne High School and the Lorne police force, may be operating near or in the woods.

"He's not our top priority," Deputy Bryson said. "He's probably a high school student who sees this as a joke. Well, listen to me, young man: this isn't funny. If you think you know something, don't post on the internet. Come down to the station and talk to the police. It may

be a matter of life and death, literally." Deputy Bryson also urged cooperation from the high school population: "If anyone knows the identity of Adams West, please come forward. You can call anonymously or come down to the station. If Adams West knows as much about this case as he claims, he could provide incalculable help. Withholding that information is immoral and criminal, especially if it might help us find Emma alive."

Emma Baines was declared missing early this morning. Police have been mobilized from all over the state to help search for her.

AVERY: I hate this. I feel like hes breathing down my neck.

AVERY: I wish you were here

AVERY: or I was with you

AVERY: or I could see you at school

AVERY: I just don't feel safe alone

STUDY BUDDY: good thing you have a boyfriend then

AVERY: come on. You wanted secrecy as much as I did

STUDY BUDDY: it's not the secrecy that bothers me.

STUDY BUDDY: why haven't you ended it yet

AVERY: u know why

AVERY: Ill take care of it

AVERY: can I call u?

THE LIAR

The bathrooms at the Cross residence are all pristine and white, from the tiles to the marble countertop to the monogrammed towels next to the sink. Avery's arms and abs ache from her morning workout. Next to her, Mrs. Cross pulls the scale out from under the sink.

It's just a checkup. A way to keep tabs. What Mommy always said before she used it, hissing at her numbers. *We've got to stay healthy, baby.*

. . . six pounds over the limit. That's normal, hon, you're tall . . . you'll make a fantastic pyramid base. That's Mrs. Halifax, two years ago, supervising cheer squad.

Aves, come on. You gonna deep-throat that banana or does a guy have to dream? Kyle Landry, making sure she never wanted to eat in public again.

And the most insidious voice, the voice that makes her want to lock herself in the shower and scrub until her skin comes off. It always comes back to her when she stands in front of a scale.

You're perfect. Look at you. Hands creep around her waist, over the ridge at her hip. *No one else understands. But I do. Look at me. I do.*

Her fingers dig into her palms. She focuses on the pain of her nails against flesh.

She will never get that voice out of her head.

"Shhhhhoot," Mrs. Cross says, remembering halfway through her curse that Avery is here. She's never sworn in front of her daughter. "I was three pounds lighter when I bought the cocktail dress." The one she has to wear to the Halifaxes' party this weekend. "Your turn."

Avery steps on the scale and watches dully as the numbers tick up. Mrs. Cross watches over her shoulder. "Hm," she says.

The numbers are okay. But she hasn't had breakfast yet.

"Cornflakes," Mrs. Cross decides for her. "And I'll pack you something for lunch—no energy drinks." She squeezes Avery's shoulder and gives her a kiss on the cheek.

As far as mother-daughter bonding goes, Avery thinks she could do better. The white bathroom leads to a white hall, down white carpeted stairs into a white-and-maple kitchen with stainless-steel appliances. Mrs. Cross goes to the counter and pours her third cup of coffee. In the oven, pancakes are keeping warm, apparently to the benefit of no one. Avery gets the cornflakes out of the pantry.

Mr. Cross sits at the maple table, getting ready for a meeting with a Boulder millionaire. They're putting the final touches on a condominium complex on the other side of the mountain—close enough to Lorne to grab a gallon of milk when you're out, far enough from Lorne that you don't actually have to see it. "No Waffle House after practice today," he says as he slides his watch over his wrist, one eye on the paper.

They always go to Waffle House together before a competition. "Mrs. Halifax and Mr. Pendler will be there," she points out.

"That doesn't change my mind," Mr. Cross says, and there's no point in arguing. The Crosses are loving parents who don't want their baby girl out amid this murder business. And they're going to make sure the whole town knows it.

"Your mom made pancakes," Mr. Cross says as Avery pours her cornflakes into a bowl.

"Mrs. Halifax said no sugar before the tournament," Avery lies. Mr. Cross rolls his eyes. But he never gets involved in the eating habits of the Mysterious Female.

"What about you, honey?" he asks Mrs. Cross.

Mrs. Cross's mouth turns down. "I'll have a protein shake later. Not hungry right now." Avery doubts she'll have trouble slipping into her dress tomorrow. But that won't stop her from hating every lump, from calculating the light angles needed to make her look suave enough to flirt with the rest of Lorne's nouveau-riche at the Halifaxes' party. They have to go so that Mr. Cross can schmooze his way into winning corporate contracts from Manuel Mendoza. Avery always thought it weird that her principal comes to school in scuffed leather shoes and fraying suits while his brother practically weeps money.

The snow stopped some time in the night, but the sky remains a dim gray outside their kitchen window. The snowplow came up their drive at five this morning, making sure the Crosses and their champagne-for-breakfast neighbors have the convenience they need. Sometimes it makes Avery feel guilty, that her little Prius drives on a dry road while Natalie and Shay get tardy slips because the plow forgot about their neighborhood or didn't have time.

Avery's dad stretches his shoulders. "You look great, hon," he says to Mrs. Cross, and he means it. Avery gets her sincerity from him. She also gets her blond hair, her sharp chin, and her love of movement. Mr. Cross was an Olympic alternate for the ski team. Now he spends his free time on fake tans and reps at the gym that go easy on his bad knee.

Mrs. Cross rubs at an invisible crow's foot at her left eye. "Yeah. Aves, are you packed for school? Any news on that scout Mr. Garson said might be coming up?"

Avery's stomach lurches. "Not yet." Mr. G encouraged them to practice and gave them extra physical therapy sessions with advice for when the scouts came around. Mr. and Mrs. Cross are convinced that Avery's going to cheer for Harvard. None of her peers think she'll go to college at all. Kyle Landry once said she had a brain for breeding.

Some people don't have a brain at all, she'd thought. But she hadn't said it.

Mr. Cross tosses the newspaper away. "This Lily Fransen bullshit's bad for business," he says. Her ugly crying face takes up most of the front page.

"Greg," Mrs. Cross admonishes.

"It's true. I've been working on getting as much of the

Colorado Senate up here as I can. They're the ones who'll make Lorne the next Aspen or Telluride—but if they're pouring money into their legal team to fight off scandal, they're not taking vacations with the wife and kids." He shakes his head. "I almost feel bad for her. She's ruining her reputation, and for what? It's obvious he didn't do it."

"Why do you think that?"

Avery's parents turn. Avery almost covers her mouth. She hadn't meant to ask.

Mr. Cross's brow furrows. "She waited sixteen years to talk about it. Half her lifetime. And just when the senator was elected, she went to the papers. Aves, if a friend tells you she got raped, ask her when. If the answer's not 'yesterday,' it didn't happen." He squeezes her shoulder. "I know you like to stand by your friends, but don't let liars take advantage of you. I think a lot of well-meaning women were duped by Fransen, and they're probably feeling extremely foolish now that the case has been nixed."

Avery swallows. "May I be excused?" she says, just above a whisper.

A knock comes at the door. Mr. and Mrs. Cross frown at each other. "Is Michael picking you up today?" Mr. Cross says.

"No." It's probably a Jehovah's Witness, or a neighbor asking to borrow an egg. She stands up to get rid of her bowl as Mr. Cross heads through a pristine hall of marble tile and maple side tables and opens the door on two uniformed officers.

"Mr. Cross?" says the woman. It's Officer Muñez from school. "Can we come in?"

Mr. Cross angles himself so that he blocks the hall with his body. "What can I help you with?"

"We'd like to speak with your daughter, please." Her voice is firm and even.

Mr. Cross's is, too. Only someone who knows him well would recognize the rising rage he quells in his first word. "Avery's getting ready for school. Now's not a good time."

"We just have a few questions," she says.

"Then you can ask me." His tone takes on a hard edge. "Or after Avery gets home tonight."

Officer Cline clears his throat. "It's just a few questions, sir. Nothing out of the ordinary. You don't even have to leave the room." He steps forward, and Mr. Cross falls back. Muñez follows with pursed lips.

Mrs. Cross smiles falsely at them. "Would you like some coffee? We were devastated to hear about Emma. You'll tell her father, won't you?"

There's a tightness in Avery's chest. Her stomach is ice and her insides churn. She closes her eyes for a moment, does a brisk count as though they're about to start a routine. She runs through the first half of "Thriller" in her head. They did that one for Halloween, and everyone but Emma went the extra mile. The whole school loved it.

"Aves, where's your backpack? I'll pack your lunch while you answer the nice gentleman's questions." Mrs. Cross puts down her coffee cup and comes over to give Avery a supportive kiss on the top of her head.

Avery folds her hands and tries to keep her leg from

bouncing. "Hi." Her voice is shy and scared when it should be fearless.

"Hi, Avery. You remember us?" Avery nods. "We need to talk to you about a couple of things, okay?"

Smart people call lawyers in these situations, right? Avery glances at Mr. Cross. He nods like it's going to be okay. Because Avery's such a good girl, she's got nothing to hide, and her parents are behind her all the way.

"Okay."

"We're sorry about Emma." Muñez does look sorry. "We're doing everything we can to find out what happened."

"So what are you doing here?" Mr. Cross folds his arms, the shining knight for his princess daughter.

"Greg," Mrs. Cross whisper-snaps from the kitchen counter.

"We've been talking to a few people on the case," Officer Muñez says.

"Claude Vanderly," Avery says. Cline and Muñez share a look. "It was on this blog," she explains, trying to tame the heat in her cheeks.

"Do you know anything about the Adams West blog?" Cline says.

"Just that it popped up. Without any warning or anything. Nobody knows who the guy is, and now he's saying that you arrested Claude and—stuff." She doesn't need to go over West's opinion on the arrest.

"Miss Vanderly was tapped as a consultant," Muñez says, and behind her Mrs. Cross slurps from her coffee, looking at

Mr. Cross in disbelief. "She was found in possession of some pharmaceutical medication." Mr. Cross snorts. "She said Emma was dealing them. She said they were for you."

The kitchen is suddenly large, and Avery is so small. She should be used to all eyes on her, but being the center of attention in a cheer routine isn't really like being the center of a police investigation. "I—" she begins.

"That's ridiculous." Mr. Cross pushes his chair back and comes around to Avery. He puts a hand on her shoulder, as if to protect her. She's pinned to her chair. Her pulse rises in leaps and bounds. Her knee hits the table. "Avery doesn't associate with people like that."

Officer Cline leans forward. "*Are* you and Claude friends?" His tone is kind enough, but Avery's gaze catches on his broad shoulders, his blond buzz cut, the scar on one hand. The gun at his hip.

"No," she whispers.

Muñez is more to the point. "Would you be willing to take a drug test?"

"No." Mrs. Cross's voice is sharp and, though the cops wouldn't know it, fearful. She puts on her angry face and comes around the table, so that she stands behind Avery's chair with her husband. To Avery, it's prison. "You said you had routine questions. How dare you accuse my daughter? She's been nothing but compliant."

"Miss Cross, would you be willing to take a drug test?" Cline says it now.

"I think you should go." Mr. Cross's hand presses down.

Avery can't breathe. A shock of cold washes over her, like she just dived into the river. "Listening to the lies of a juvenile delinquent and ignoring facts is not the way of the police of Lorne. Maybe you do things differently in the big city, but here—"

"We are *not* interviewing you," Muñez snaps. She turns her attention back to Avery. Her expression softens but her fingers clench around a cheap plastic pen. "Miss Cross?"

"I can't," Avery says. She can barely hear herself.

"That's right," her dad says.

But Muñez glances at Cline. "You can't? Or you won't?"

"This isn't necessary," Mrs. Cross says, but she sounds doubtful for the first time. "You've had your answer, and you can go."

She's suffocating. She can't breathe. "I can't."

"Why not?" says Officer Cline.

"We do hope you find Emma's killer, but you can look elsewhere." Mr. Cross moves away from her chair at last to herd the cops out.

"We'll get a warrant if we think we have to." Cline stands, pushing his shoulders back. Reminding Mr. Cross that he's not so big after all. "And that won't look nearly as good as your daughter's willing cooperation."

"I'll fail," she blurts.

The kitchen goes still. Avery gasps as her mother's fingers dig into her shoulder.

Officer Muñez clears her throat and flips open her black notebook. "What will you test positive on?"

"Valium."

Cline and Muñez look at each other again. It's what they found in the locker.

Mrs. Cross sags behind her. "That's it?" she laughs, convincingly enough that the cops believe her. "Honey, why didn't you tell me? I'd have set up an appointment with my therapist for you. I have a prescription, officers," she explains, and moves away from the table.

Muñez and Cline look at Avery. "I borrowed it from my mom's bathroom," she says, quiet as a mouse. Quiet as a good little cheerleader who's so ashamed.

Muñez and Cline look at Mrs. Cross. Mrs. Cross says, "You want me to show you my prescription bottle?"

"Yes, please," Cline says, and she heads back through the marble hallway toward the stairs.

Cline waits at the bottom of the stairs. Muñez stands and tucks the notebook back into her belt. "We trust you on this," she says. *For now*, she plainly means to add, but doesn't. "We're not here about your mom's pills, but don't self-medicate, okay? Even if you think it's not hurting you, it's hurting you."

"Yes, ma'am," Avery whispers.

Mrs. Cross trots back down the stairs and hands the bottle to Cline. "We'll get Aves a slip for it," she says. "We had no idea she was so stressed."

Cline says something to her in an undertone. Then Muñez joins him, and Mrs. Cross opens the door for them.

At the threshold, Cline stops. He turns, and against the light of the door Avery can only see his silhouette. But she knows he's looking at her. "If you need anything, or if you think of anything, you'll get in touch?" he says.

"*We'll* get in touch," Mr. Cross replies for her, and ushers them out.

As soon as the door shuts behind them, Mrs. Cross comes back in. Her face is pale, her hands shaking—and Avery doesn't think it's the effects of too much coffee. She opens the bottle and pours the pills out on the table. "Valium?" she says, so quietly Avery can't hear her breathe. She quickly counts the pills by twos. "Avery, I thought you understood. No drugs, no drinking. No trouble with the police."

Tears swim in her eyes. "I—" But she doesn't know what to say. It *is* what her parents taught her. No drugs, no drinking, no being bi, no illicit soda, no unsanctioned carbs, no fats, no snacks, no sleepovers with anyone but Lyla, who's so aggressively heterosexual she deserves a medal. No gaining more than three pounds above her target weight. She knows the noes are for her own good. But she's still suffocating.

"Were you lying? Or is it really Valium?" Mr. Cross says. His voice is thunder.

Avery just nods. She can't speak past the lump in her throat.

Her mom's already lost it. She dabs at her cheeks with a Kleenex, careful even now not to smudge her makeup. "Why?" she chokes. "We take care of you. We love you. We've always protected you, and you do *this*? And we find out from the police?"

"I'm sorry." She knows how stupid it sounds. Her face is burning and turning blotchy as she tries to maintain control. "I've been . . . stressed. . . ."

"About what?" Mrs. Cross shouts. "What makes your life so hard?"

Avery knows the question is genuine. Her parents *want* to hear why.

She also knows she can't tell them.

Mr. Cross takes her arm and steers her back to sitting. Avery lets him. There's a faint buzzing to the world, like she's hearing it through an old radio. Mrs. Cross dabs at her face with a new tissue. "We can't talk about this outside the house. Do you understand?"

Because if word gets out and Heather Halifax hears that Avery Cross sneaks Valium, she might tell Mommy and Daddy, and Mommy Halifax will kick Aves off the cheer team, and Daddy Halifax won't make the right introductions for her parents at his party. The Harvard cheer squad will say no—every college will. Avery nods.

"We've worked hard to build up this life for you, Aves. Other people would kill to be where you are now. Don't throw it away." Mr. Cross straightens his tie. "I can't be late for my meeting."

Mrs. Cross nods, a brittle, broken movement. Avery doesn't look up from the table. She *knows* she hasn't had real hardship in her life. Not like Emma or Natalie or Shay or Gwen. She doesn't choose the anxiety any more than she chooses to feel sick whenever she takes a sip of Lyla's milkshake.

For a while, all is silent. The tears come, even though Avery tries to prevent them. After a minute or two she feels a cool hand pressing a tissue to her face, too. "Come on," her mom says gently, wiping carefully around Avery's eyes. "Buck up."

Because big girls don't cry, and nothing hurts happy Avery. Their eyes briefly meet. "Is there anything else you want to tell me?"

Avery shakes her head. "Nothing."

Silence for another moment. She almost thinks her mom won't push it. Then Mrs. Cross breathes out hard through her nose. "Avery."

Avery thinks she'll say something more, but instead she stands. She goes out to the hall, grabbing Avery's backpack from where it sits at the bottom of the stairs. She comes back and upends it on the table.

"What are you doing?" The fear gives way to anger. "I said nothing."

"Which means you lied to me again." Mrs. Cross sorts through tissues, notebooks, homework assignments, spare tampons. "Where do you go when you sneak out at night?"

They know about that?

"Are you going to Michael's?"

She should say yes. All it would take is one nod.

Mrs. Cross looks down at the table, scattered with Avery's belongings. She examines them almost clinically, as though they belong to a stranger and she needs to reconstruct an entire life. "I don't see any condoms. Are you using them?"

"*Mom!*"

"That doesn't answer my question." her mom's eyes have taken on a steely glint. The shock of her baby taking drugs has given way to rage. "I need to know."

Avery doesn't answer. She doesn't know how. If she pretended she snuck out for Michael, her mom would call

Michael's mom, and then Michael would say he hadn't seen her after dark for weeks, and then it would be an endless stream of *who* and *why* and it would ruin everything.

"Repack," Mrs. Cross says. "I'm going through your gym bag, and then I'm driving you to school. Your room will get a thorough cleaning while you're gone, and you're coming home with me straight after cheer. We'll talk more when you get home." She takes a deep breath. "And you're grounded. Obviously."

"You need this." Natalie passes Avery her makeup kit at lunch.

"Thanks. Sweat it all off during gym," Avery says. *Definitely didn't cry in the bathroom.* The cafeteria's crowded, and noise bounces off the brick walls. The wolf pack is tucked against a corner, leaning against lockers and the door of a supply closet. The sky outside is slate and low-hanging, and it's too cold to go out, and so the world is constricted to this tiny space where all of Jefferson-Lorne High is crammed.

"You're going to the party tonight, right?" Shay calls over the noise.

"Of course." Lyla takes a drink from her Gatorade. "Jason's going to be there, and I've got to snag him before any of you other bitches do." Shay and Natalie giggle.

"No drinking at the party." Avery doesn't feel like being the mom of the group today, but she has to. She runs her tennis shoe back and forth on the linoleum and keeps her skirt pulled down. "Remember we've got the competition tomorrow. And you have to be fresh on Monday so we can hit the ground running for next week's away game."

"Aves." Lyla puts a hand on her knee. "Relax. We'll do fine. We can take a night off. You're coming, right?"

"I can't," Avery says, just as Michael says, "Of course."

Michael turns to her with reproachful brown eyes. Across the hall a bunch of students *oohs* as the freshman dance committee drops a glittering snowflake with a three-foot diameter instead of hanging it from the ceiling. Somebody shouts, *"Glitter bomb!"*

"Babe, you said we'd go together."

"No I didn't." Avery's tone rises defensively.

"Yeah, you did," Lyla said. "Last week. Remember? I said Kyle would definitely have beer, and maybe weed, and Claude would be there, and then you said you couldn't let Michael go alone—"

The other wolves are watching carefully. The persistent rumor that Claude once lured Michael into a supply closet rears its ugly head about once a semester. Avery swallows bile and hunger, putting her uneaten bowl of soup off to the side. "Well, I can't." She hasn't told them she's grounded.

"You're going to miss out," Lyla says.

"Yeah, we're going to make our signature cocktail," says Shay. Their signature cocktail is pink Gatorade and vodka. "Aves, you love that." Avery doesn't love it, but everyone else does, so she goes along.

"You can take a night off, Aves." Michael tries to slide an arm around her. "You don't have to practice every free minute."

She doesn't shove his arm away like she wants to. But she doesn't tuck into it, either. "I'm not going."

Her voice is louder than normal to compensate for the noise level around them. And god, she's heard Michael use this assertive tone dozens of times. But the pack stares at her like she sharpened her nails and tried to rip Lyla's heart out.

"Oh . . . kay." Lyla talks like she would to a bear. But her expression says, *Psycho much?* "Take it easy, Aves. You don't have to do it if you don't want." Like she didn't just start a pile-on. "What's got you so worked up?"

Everything. Her parents and drug tests. Anna's Run. Emma. The cafeteria cheering as the freshmen successfully put up their monster snowflake. The party Kyle didn't cancel even though a girl is dead. Michael, and being with Michael, and being with someone else and knowing how wrong it is. "I'm just not allowed to go out right now. Because of Emma." She hates herself a little for lying, but she knows her mom would want her to. The Crosses don't want to be the type of parents who have to ground their kid. "My mom thinks the police are going to arrest Adams West at whatever party I go to."

"Ohmygod, mine too." Shay frames her face with her hands. "I'm going to have to sneak out tonight. Mom thinks I'm going to get abducted and tossed in the river."

"My mom thinks West did it. Like, the murder. And she thinks he sits next to me in math. And history. And APCoGo. And everything. She's worse than the cops." Natalie takes the eye shadow kit back from Avery and slings it into her backpack. "She thinks he's out for the whole squad."

Lyla raises her eyebrows a few times. "Maybe he is."

"Noooo." Natalie scoots closer to Shay, who giggles again.

"He stalks through the halls." Lyla leans in. Pitches her voice low. "Exposing the embarrassing secrets of JLH, one by one. Feeding on young, innocent blood." Her gaze flicks to Avery. "So Aves is right out."

The squad *ooh*s. "That's not funny," Avery snaps. She brings her knees up to her face like a shield. The air thickens and the semiscandalized solid noises cut out. Lyla curls her lip. "It's a joke, Aves." Avery doesn't smile or demure or say sorry. "Jesus." Lyla picks up her prepackaged soup and takes a sip out of the container.

Avery doesn't know how to reply. She doesn't know how the police investigation has already become something to joke about. A cold sweat breaks out under her arms. The room spins and she's pretty sure she wants to throw up.

Michael puts a hand on her knee and presses his nose against her jaw. She used to find it endearing. Now it's all she can do not to yell at him to stop.

She turns her head, and he kisses the corner of her mouth. "I need to talk to you after school," she says.

Poor Michael shrugs. He has no idea what's coming. "Okay."

Lyla's talking again. "Anyway, I *do* think West is here at JLH. Who else could have this kind of information? I bet he was boinking Claude at the time and that's how he knows she's innocent." Lyla gasps. "Oh my god, do you think it's Kyle?"

Michael laughs. "Kyle's dumber than a bag of rocks. It's more likely to be Aves than Kyle."

She's *definitely* going to throw up. Avery leans over to Lyla. "Do you have a tampon?"

Lyla digs around in her backpack. "So *that's* why you're all weird."

Avery grabs the tampon and virtually launches to her feet. She doesn't even say thanks.

She doesn't head for the nearest bathroom, which'll be full of girls avoiding lunch and speculating on murders and bloggers and other things she wants to escape. She goes to the empty one at the end of the hall. There's only one girl in the stall there. Avery puts the wrapped tampon behind the sink— no need to waste it—and turns on the tap. She dabs her cheeks and presses a wet paper towel to her forehead.

She has to go back out. She has to be perfect Avery Cross. Not the Valium-using, lying little girl the police are investigating. But right now, she can't. She can't face the wolves.

The toilet flushes. Before Avery can flee, the stall unlocks and out storms Gwen Sayer, all intent and fury shoved into a girl. She sticks her hands under the tap, then looks up. Their eyes meet in the mirror—Gwen, dark and serious and angry, Avery, smudged and blotchy and dripping water from the paper towel plastered to her forehead. *Oh, shit.*

"Again," Avery says, putting her hands on her hips. The wolf pack groans, but good-naturedly. "Break for Gatorade, then back at it. Two minutes."

They make a beeline for the zero-sugar cherry Gatorade that Mr. G buys by the case. It's officially for the lacrosse team, but he lets them nab extras, especially when they're cooped up in the gym because it's too wet outside to do back handsprings. It's impossible to hear the music amid the shouts and clash of lacrosse sticks, and Avery's on the cusp of an SAT-vocabulary-worthy headache. But she can't quit. It's just half an hour more. She goes over to Mr. Pendler and Mr. G. Mr. Pendler's filling in for Mrs. Halifax, who was "unavoidably detained" today and couldn't make it to practice. As she approaches, Avery tugs the skirt of her uniform down.

"The squad's getting tired," Mr. G says. "They're making mistakes. Be careful out there."

"We'll practice till it's perfect," Avery says with her trademark chipper smile.

"You know, Aves, in theater they say a bad dress rehearsal means a good opening night," Mr. Pendler offers. "Maybe you just need to get the mistakes out of your system."

"You'll be pumped up on adrenaline tomorrow," Mr. G adds. "I think you'll do great."

The smile turns up a notch. "Thanks."

"Watch out for the jumps. They can be dangerous when you're this practiced out," Mr. G says.

Avery nods. Of course she's not going to tell the girls to avoid the jumps. She goes back to the circle of cheerleaders and grabs her own Gatorade.

"What about Mark?" Lyla's still speculating on the identity of Adams West.

Shay wrinkles her nose. "He's way too nice. He'd never start a public speculation blog." She taps the Gatorade with a long nail.

"You're right." Lyla sighs. She frowns at something on the edge of the bleachers. "What is *she* doing here?"

Avery glances over her shoulder. Gwen picks her way down from the top of the bleachers. The battered and thrice-labeled *JLH Inquirer* camera swings from her neck.

"I guess she's doing a piece on the lacrosse team," Avery says, shrugging.

"Unbelievable." Lyla shakes her head. "Emma's not even declared *dead* and the bitch is going after her extracurriculars."

"That's cold," Shay agrees.

Gwen looks down. She spots the whole cheer team, staring. Avery spins around, but she can feel the burn start in her cheeks, flushing downward. "Time's up." Her voice is a knife's edge. "Get in formation."

"Hang on, I want to see where she's going." Lyla bends around Avery to get a better look.

"*Now.*" She surprises even herself with the snap of the word.

"Jeez, jeez. All right." Lyla rolls her eyes and turns back. The rest of the team hastens to get into place. Lyla mutters something that makes the freshman next to her giggle.

The count's off from the start. A good captain would stop and make everyone start over. But Avery's not a good captain. She's a selfish one. She launches into a lift half a moment before Natalie gets a solid grip, feels her shoe slip out of the cradle. She lands ankle first, then rolls, smacking her head on the gym floor. Pain rattles her jaw and explodes in the back of her head. When her eyes flutter open, the wolves gather around her, silhouettes blocking the light.

A larger dark shape parts the waters. Mr. G says, "Avery? Can you hear me?" The girls back off. "How many fingers am I holding up?"

"My ankle," she groans. She thinks about throwing her wrist over her forehead, but that'd be too dramatic.

He slides an arm under her back to guide her up. "Come over to the bleachers and have a seat. I have to get the lacrosse team out of here, so can you ladies clean yourselves up? Great practice today—you're really going to kill it tomorrow."

"I'm so sorry, Aves," Natalie squeaks, fingers crushed against her mouth. "Are you going to be okay?"

"Yeah. It was my fault." She hops toward the bleachers, one hand on her temple. "I probably just need to ice it."

Lyla scoots in and slings her arms around Avery's shoulder. "Aves, this is awful," she says, and sounds a little miserable, like maybe she thinks she threw Avery off with her comments. "What are you going to do about tomorrow? You can't cheer on a bad ankle."

"Good thing you're my second, right?" Avery says with a weak smile.

Lyla's arm tightens. "Avery Cross, don't you dare make me do that jump. Get better."

"I will." She'll have a miracle cure by tomorrow, walking on the ankle like nothing's wrong at all. Because nothing is.

"We need space to work, girls." Mr. G makes a herding motion with his hands. "Avery will be fine. Don't worry."

They chatter as they pack up. Some of them send a few worried glances Avery's way, but they don't talk to her again.

The slam of the gym door brings silence at last, punctuated only by the occasional squeak of Mr. G's shoes as he rummages around in the supply room and trots back to the bleachers.

"Let's take a look at that." He rolls her sock down, fingers brushing against her flesh. She flinches and gasps involuntarily. "Hurts?" he says.

"Yes." She'd hate herself for the tremble in her voice, but at least she's *trying* to sound pathetic.

His hand rests on her calf just above her ankle. "I warned you it was dangerous to keep going when the whole squad was tired." His fingers tighten fractionally.

Avery nods. Her mouth is dry.

"You know I'm looking out for you." The hand moves up her calf, more toward her knee. She squeaks. "Hurts?" Mr. G asks again.

"It's fine," she whispers.

"Keep your ankle up. I'd say take some painkillers, but I guess you'll have to talk to your mom about that."

Because of course Mrs. Cross called Mr. G. She trusts him. Everyone trusts him.

Mr. G's other hand moves to her shoulder. "I'm not here to judge you. I just want to help you. I know you've been hit hard by the news, and working with the police is just an extra stress." His hand squeezes. "You know you can always talk to me, right?"

And though she still wants to throw up, Avery smiles at him. "I know, Mr. G. That's why you're my favorite."

The gym door crashes open. Avery jumps and winces again as her ankle bounces off the bleachers. Mr. G pats her leg.

Michael comes into the gym. He glances between her and Mr. G, brow furrowing. "I grabbed you some Monster. Everything all right?"

"Always nice to have a boyfriend to look after you, isn't it?" Mr. G stands up. "I'm going to get a bandage. Don't put any weight on that leg."

"Wait—" Avery fumbles as he makes for the gym doors. "I need to talk to you!"

"I thought you needed to talk to me," Michael points out.

She stares at him for a moment, openmouthed. "I can't," she says finally, too brusque and too cold.

She sees the hurt in his eyes before he shoves it down. "All right. I mean, you were the one who wanted it. Maybe I can walk you to your car?"

"My mom's picking me up," she says, cringing. "But, um, we can wait together?"

"Sure." He hands her the can of Monster. "We can talk while we wait."

The last thing she needs is to break up with her boyfriend in front of her mom. So she pops the tab on the Monster. If she takes a couple of quick sips, she can appease him and maybe get him to hold the can when Mrs. Cross shows up. She gets to her feet, leaning on his arm. "How was lacrosse?"

JLPD cares more about some blogger than they do about Emma Baines

Do you smell that in the air? The smell of snow and river water? Do your Christmas carols drown out Anna? Do the twinkling, cheery lights help you forget the dark woods beyond Lorne? Well, happy fucking holidays, nerds.

You know who I hope isn't having a good holiday season? The JLPD. They'll be working overtime on the Baines case this weekend, and whose fault is that? I told you Claude Vanderly was a dead end. I told you it was useless. Maybe you should've listened to me instead of searching high and low for my identity.

You'll never find it, so stop trying.

In other news, the JLPD suspects someone from JLH as the culprit in Emma's death. Oh, really? Are these the detecting skills for which we pay hard-earned tax dollars? Let's see. Who does that narrow the pool of suspects down to?

Oh yeah. Everyone.

I know what you're all thinking. *What about you, West? How do you know so much? How close are you to all this?* Ordinarily, I'd be flattered that you're all so obsessed with me. But we have bigger problems. You're so focused on who I am, you forget that you never even cared who Emma was. Fuck that. You don't even *know* who Emma was. You're in love with a fake dead girl. And if you want to get to know the real Emma?

You should have put in effort before she died.

Everyone puts on a false face. Now her true one is lost to

time. It's just too bad no one can find her diary. Now *that* might tell us something interesting.

Sincerely,

Adams West

Emma Baines—February 1, 2018

I still can't believe I snuck out. This is how fucking weird things are getting. I'm sneaking out, *risking death a la Dad, but I have to know what happened. Lizzy, this is for you. This is for us.*

The boot prints belonged to a slightly small foot, but after today's excursion I'm pretty sure it was a man's boot. According to Reddit the print belongs to a Pine Nation hiking boot with a rubber sole, probably a 6' waterproof deluxe. If anywhere had them, it'd be Lorne's Hunting and Sport.

Problem: the camping store's only open 9–5. If Dad realizes I snuck out, he will bury me in the backyard, I swear to god.

I thought about waiting and skipping out on cheer practice. I thought about calling the store instead of going over in person. But if Lizzy truly was killed, I couldn't do a half-assed job of finding the murderer.

Lucky for me, Dad poked his head in while I was finishing my AP Calc homework. "I'm going to work in the garage for a bit," he said. "What's for dinner?"

"Chili," I said off the top of my head, because I knew I'd be chopping onions for it and Dad hates the smell of raw onion. Lucky I'm such a good liar and can keep my face casual. I wanted to pump my fist in victory. Dad's been working on a new sliding closet door with an inlay of stained wood carved like the Rockies. It's taking him forever, and that forever is exactly what I needed.

I was not *in luck when I got to the camping goods store. First I ran into Principal Mendoza—literally. If he ever mentions this to Dad, I'm a dead girl. "Hello, Emma," he said, taking my shoulders to stabilize me. "How's cheer?"*

"Fine."

"Your spring fling dance is going to be magical." He wiggled his fingers. "Let me know if you need help with the makeup. I used to do theater."

"Yep." So not here for you, Mendoza.

My second blunder was that I forgot who manages the camping goods store. Art Miller, an old buddy of Dad's. They used to go fishing together, before Dad got married. I don't know why Dad didn't get back to it after Mom left—I mean, of course I know, he wouldn't take me along and he wouldn't let me stay home alone—but they still chat sometimes.

Art found me crouched in the shoe section, looking for the Pine Nation brand. "Can I help you?"

I looked up. I realized my mistake. Art's eyes widened in recognition and the lies started coming. "You sure can," I said in my brightest happy voice. I pretend I'm Avery sometimes. It really helps when you want to manipulate people. "I'm trying to buy my dad a surprise present. I noticed his old boots are getting a little worn out"—I brandished my phone with the bootprint photo—"and I know new ones are outside the police budget." Art smiled. Cute little girl, taking good care of Dad. I had him. "So I was recommended some Pine Nations."

Art frowned as he went through his mental stock. "We don't carry those. But we can order 'em in, if you like. What's his shoe size?"

"Um, I don't know." I tried to pass off my blush as embarrassment. "But I was actually hoping to ask if anyone else bought some. You know, so I can find out how they fit. Shoes can be so finicky."

I turned my smile up, hoping he'd launch into the Girls just love talking about shoes *mode of thinking instead of whatever was going through his mind instead.*

"They're good," *said a voice from across the store. Art and I looked around. Principal Mendoza stood by the counter, ready to check out. He saw my frown and clarified.* "Pine Nations. They're a good boot. The entire faculty got them at Greg Cross's Christmas party."

God. Damn. It. Everyone has them. Every single teacher?! This is worse than if Art had said that no one ordered them at all.

Art was oblivious to my dilemma. He rambled on, telling increasingly unlikely stories of fishing trips with Dad, asking me about the Devino Scholarship, chatting about his college days river rafting and rock climbing. Like, come on, Art, some of us are gonna get murdered if Dad finds out we left the house. I finally coughed and said, "Maybe Principal Mendoza needs to check out."

"Right, right." *Art ambled toward the front of the store.*

We went over to the counter, where Principal Mendoza had been standing for about a million years. He waved for me to go first. "It's okay," *I said.*

"They are great," *he said.* "I wear them hiking all the time. Good for a muddy path."

And what would you know about that, Principal M?

Mendoza went on, oblivious to my suspicions. "You're friends with Avery Cross, aren't you? Her dad was the one who bought them. I guess he swears by them. Gets a new pair every year."

Every year. That's a convenient excuse to get rid of murder evidence. Mr. Cross has a lot to lose if it comes out he had an affair with a student.

Mendoza finally paid up and left. "Should I put in an order for those boots?" Art said.

"How much do your guns cost?" I blurted.

A gun, Em? Seriously? But I can't help feeling like I'm going to need one. If a man's capable of killing once to protect his secret, who's to say he won't kill again?

The guns sat on a rack behind him, gleaming with fresh oil. Long-barreled Rugers and Marlins, lit from beneath.

The look Art gave me didn't say cute now. "Depends on what you're looking for. You can get a good rifle for $800, or a nine-millimeter for about half that. But if you're not on your way to a gun show or under the supervision of your father, you're not getting a gun from me until you're twenty-one, young lady."

"It's for Dad," I said again. "Surprise present, remember? I'm old enough to go hunting with him now but all he has is his issue handgun."

"I think shoes are more in your budget."

"I'll think about it. I'll be back next week. And remember, surprise present. Don't tell Dad, please?" I tried out my winning cheer smile.

Art didn't smile back.

I'm doing a lot more than risking Dad's ire. The more people see me snooping around town, the more likely it is that the killer will find out. And I won't even be able to buy a gun to protect myself.

LYLA: hey can we talk?

MICHAEL: sure. Missing some math homework?

LYLA: Its abt Aves actually

MICHAEL: uh sure? What abt Aves?

LYLA: shes been acting weird ever since yall did . . . whatever.

MICHAEL: uh excuse me???

LYLA: come on, she told me all abt your unholy adventure wednesday night

MICHAEL: wtf we haven't been together for a week

MICHAEL: u mean the night emma died???

MICHAEL: she told me she was with u

19

THE SNEAK

Snow piles against the windows at the top of the yellow brick walls. The halls are quiet, cold; and the sounds outside are muffled by the storm. The cars are all gone, the birds asleep. The last bus left half an hour ago, and around now Mum is going to realize that Gwen wasn't on it. Again.

Gwen hardly dares to breathe. She looks each way down the hall for observers, then takes the keys she swiped from Mr. G's coat pocket at the gym and tries them with shaking fingers until she finds one that fits his office lock. She takes a deep breath, checks the hall again, then slips inside.

Mr. G's office has a deep brown faux-leather couch that looks like it came off Craigslist a million years ago. The coffee table has overlapping brown rings around the edges and the gray rug beneath is dotted with stains. The bookshelf against the office wall carries books on sports, psychology and physiology, and binders of student files. Gwen's fingers itch to touch the *S* binder. But that's not why she's here. *Focus.* She tastes something metallic in her mouth and she realizes she's biting

172

her cheek. Instead of the binders, she goes to the other side of the room, where Mr. G's desk is. Where his computer will hold, among other things, notes from his counseling sessions.

She types in her office administration key. A few clicks get her to his client folders.

Emma and Lizzy are both there. Her hand stills on the mouse, cursor hovering over Emma's file. If Emma told anyone about the test scores . . .

Maybe she should just walk away from this. Maybe she's risking too much. If she keeps her head down and her grades up—

Footfalls sound in the hall, far too close. Gwen leaps up from Mr. G's desk just as the man himself comes in.

"Gwendolyn?" He frowns.

Heat rushes to Gwen's face. "I'm sorry. Your door was open and I wanted to talk to you."

Mr. G pats his vest pockets. His eyes land on his keys, just a hair too close to Gwen's hand. She starts talking again, faster. "The police said we should report anything suspicious, right? I saw . . . somebody in the parking lot. A strange man."

"Take a seat," says Mr. G, gesturing to his couch.

Gwen sits. The couch smells like old sweat and disinfectant. Mr. G goes over to his desk—*oh shit oh shit oh shit*—but instead of looking at his computer, he opens the bottom drawer and pulls out a bandage roll. Then he comes over and sits across from Gwen in a battered office chair. "Tell me about this person you saw. Could it have been someone who works at the school?"

She talks without thinking. "He didn't look like a teacher or a parent. To be honest, he looked kind of . . . scruffy. He had on a big black coat, and combat boots, and a hat. Like a knit hat. And he looked like he hadn't shaved for like three days."

The furrow between his eyebrows deepens. "Can you tell me more about this man? What about his build and ethnicity?"

"He was white," Gwen says quickly. "And, ah, tall. Taller than you, maybe?" Mr. G's five ten. "And he was pretty skinny, I think. It was hard to tell because of the coat. It was one of those puffy coats. He kind of looked like a drunk. You know, red nose and eyes and stuff. And he had a scar, right over his lip." She draws a line between her nose and mouth to demonstrate. "Do you think it's West?"

Mr. G taps the bandage roll against his thumb. "I don't like to jump to conclusions. But I'm glad you brought this up. I'll ask Principal Mendoza about it and make sure security is checking everyone on school property." He looks pale under his gray-flecked goatee. "In the meantime, I have to get back to the gym." His hand tightens around the bandage roll. "Do you need a ride home? When I'm done at the gym I'll be able to drive you."

"No thanks." She leaves with Mr. G and tries not to think about what she didn't accomplish in his office.

Her phone buzzes as she leaves the school. Snowflakes dance in the yellow light of a streetlamp, and she fumbles with her gloves to answer the phone. "Mum?"

Mum sounds pissed. "Gwendolyn, tell me where you are *right now*."

"I'm coming home from school. I missed the bus."

"Gwen, you said you would come straight after school. You said you'd help decorate."

"I had yearbook." Like every freaking Friday this year.

"You are on thin ice. You said you'd be careful and you said you'd take the bus. If you don't want to be grounded, you need to follow our rules. I need to know where you are."

"Geez, Mum. Do you worry about where Dad is? At least you know what I'm doing." The same thing she does every week.

Mum is quiet for a terrible moment. Then she says, "You do not talk about your father that way."

Gwen should back down. Instead she says, "That's why he can do whatever he wants, right? If you policed him half as much as you police me, maybe you'd know where he goes every day after work."

More silence. Then the call disconnects.

It's been a while since Gwen pissed her mother off that much.

She used to have a rule: She could be an asshole at school, but never at home. Never to her parents, who worked so hard to keep her going, to give her a chance for the scholarship. Never to her sister, who always took time out of her studies to listen to Gwen's problems. Gwen forgot her rule when Lizzy died. How much has Mum been going through? How much of her sadness has she buried so Gwen's life can stay together? So that Gwen can get out of here? Gwen's thumb hovers over Mum's name. She should call back and apologize. She should promise to be there as soon as she can.

She feels eyes on her back. Slowly, she turns. The parking lot is empty, save for Mrs. Cross's van in the pickup area. Snow coats the asphalt. Gwen can hear nothing, not even the wind. The world is so still, so silent, that she's afraid to even breathe. There *can't* be anyone else here.

A shadow detaches from the wall.

She can't see its face, but she knows. She *knows* its eyes are fixed on her.

It steps forward, and Gwen turns. She's not the fastest in track and field, but that doesn't matter. She only has to be faster than whoever's following her.

She runs.

<u>Diary Entry</u>

Emma Baines—August 25, 2018

Someone wants to shut me up. It was just a feeling before, but now I know.

Yesterday was a shitshow. I'd decided to announce Lizzy's murder at the assembly for two reasons: first, because the seminar was bullshit, and overdosing wasn't how Lizzy died. And second—the case is too big. I can't handle it alone. I thought maybe calling it out might get the police involved. I should've seen that big fat nope *coming.*

Yesterday I was put in counseling to "consider my actions" and think about how no one appreciated my "little outburst."

But today, well. Things are about to get worse.

And in the meantime, I have daily extra sessions with Mr. G. The first one was yesterday and I'm already wondering. Did I really make this all up? Are my theories just elaborate schemes to bring sense to this senseless world?

I am right. I am right about Lizzy. *Every time I review the facts I'm convinced again. She was murdered.*

And I just revealed what I know, and no one fucking believes me. I am so sick and tired of not being believed. I'm sick of getting counseling when I should be getting protection. And now . . .

My dad didn't want extra sessions interfering with my classes, so I have to meet Mr. G after school instead. Which runs directly into my time at the Jefferson-Lorne Inquirer, *but apparently no one cares about independent journalism anymore. I still had forty-five minutes after counseling today, so I hurried for the little closet that is the* Inquirer's *newsroom. Even though most people had abandoned* the halls by this time, I still kept my head down, focusing on my sneakers. I just . . . didn't want to deal. With the looks. Some pitying (Poor Emma, she's lost her mind), *some angry* (Can't she just leave it alone?), *some sensationalist* (The freak's coming. Quick, get a good look!). *If I don't see them, I can pretend they're not happening.*

But there were two people I did have to deal with. Samantha Johnson, our editor in chief, would not *let me miss a deadline. And Mr. Pendler was our adviser.*

"You're late," *Samantha said as I came in. She's one of those people who think that being a hard-ass will somehow inspire us.*

I didn't bother to answer. She knew where I was, everyone did. Instead I went over to my side of the desk.

The old Dell computer was already on. And my notes—they weren't in the place I'd left them yesterday.

The alarm bells in my head started, softly. I ignored them. I couldn't afford to panic. "Have you been working on my article?" *I asked. Samantha does that sometimes—takes over when she thinks something's too far behind schedule. It's a bitch, but then, so is she. And I knew it when I signed up this year.*

"No." *Samantha looked at me like I'd asked if she'd kicked my puppy.*

I took a calming breath, pitched my voice even. I thought, Don't freak out, Emma. *Everyone would just think I was losing it again.* "Were you looking for something in my desk?"

"Believe it or not, I don't riffle through other people's stuff. A journalist's desk is sacred."

Mr. Pendler butted in. "No one's been near your desk, Emma." *He fixed me with a stern look.*

The alarm bells rang louder. Deeeeep *breaths. I opened the top drawer.*

My interview list was gone.

I had Lizzy's friends, exes, family, suspects, all on that list. Who would take it? And under that, my Lizzy Sayer notebook? Also missing. Every scrap of info I had on the case, every casual comment that sounded like someone might know more. The receipts that prove she was at a gas station half an hour earlier, and sober—and the note. That note would have blown her case wide open. It's all gone.

I stood, shaking in front of the computer. Sam and Mr. Pendler eyed me warily. They didn't condone the Lizzy investigation in the first place—Sam said she'd never publish it, for the good of the student body. I knew before I logged on to the computer, my files on the Lizzy case would be gone.

Anyone with an admin login could have deleted the files. Lots of people have a key to Mr. Pendler's room. Practically anyone could be responsible for the murder and cover-up. And I've just told the whole school that I know.

I can't go anywhere alone now. They must be watching me, and I'm so fucking scared, and nobody believes me.

Nobody.

CLAAAAAAUDE

Working late. Takeout menus on the fridge so get what u want but DELIVERY ONLY!! Still grounded. Love u xx

Claude can't remember the last time she was stuck inside on a Friday night. She flops on the couch. She's been watching crappy Christmas romances on Netflix for the last four hours. She should be working on her APCoGo essay, but she blew it off. And Jamie texted her: are u ok?

No, she replied, sometime in the middle of a *Miracle on 34th Street* rewatch.

U need to talk abt it?

She ignored that. If she replies he'll do something like rank the *Star Wars* tie-ins from best to worst, or have her guess whether the names he sends her belong to nail polish colors or preteen pop songs. He'd even talk her through the APCoGo essay if she asked. Anything but *the* talk he wants to have. But it'll still be lurking in the subtext. The *Is this what boyfriends/ girlfriends do?* question. And honestly? Claude doesn't fucking know. She's never had a boyfriend and she's never wanted one before. Boyfriends make pretty promises and knock you up and tell you you can't get an abortion and then three years down the line they leave you and your daughter high and dry. That's what she's heard in this house, anyway. Sex is nice and uncomplicated. Well, it *was*.

She should stop talking to him. It'd be better for everyone in the long run. He'll be sad but then he'll get a proper girl-friend and he'll stop talking to Claude and all of a sudden her best friend will have disappeared on her.

But she doesn't want to stop talking to him. His *Star Wars* ranking arguments are really compelling.

The phone buzzes again. Claude rolls her eyes and re-adjusts the plaid-pattern pillow behind her head before taking a look. But it's not Jamie. It's Margot. You coming to the party tonight? XO

Claude met Margot protesting a petition to reopen the coal mines around Lorne. Margot arranged it; Claude was the sole attendee. Margot's nice, an ex-college student from Gree-ley who works in Lorne's weed dispensary, which popped up soon after the first McMansions did. It's mostly famous for being where underage JLH students get busted trying to buy.

Margot also steals her dad's pharmaceutical pads and runs a nice little business on the side.

Claude looks at her mom's last text. What does *working late* actually mean?

Which party u thinking of?

I hear kyle landry has a pretty sick hot tub.

Claude can confirm, though she hasn't been at Kyle's place since he dumped her friend Monica. Claude firmly believes in friends before fucks—but Monica graduated last year and moved out of Lorne. That makes Kyle's house fair game.

She's still grounded. But if Mom's working a case late . . .

She sends a quick text. Im bored. When do you think youll be home?

It'll be late honey, Mom replies. Im sorry but were in deep shit over here.

And then, because Claude's mom is no fool, she texts, remember u r GROUNDED!!!

Vanderly girls. So bad at respecting authority. She switches back to her text conversation with Margot. on my way.

Kyle Landry's house is fifty years away from being the decrepit lair of a supervillain. For now, the dirt road up to his palace is strung with white twinkle lights, and a gate of curling black iron and red brick separates the house from the driveway. Kyle's house rises three stories and juts back into the mountain. Lights are tastefully draped to illuminate the faux-Greek columns, the widow's walk, the pine fence that circles the yard. Immaculately trimmed cypress trees surround the property like soldiers, and there's a manger scene out front. Someone's stuck a red plastic cup upside down on Mary's head. Ariana Grande croons from a portable speaker, a base for the party's laughter, chatter, and the occasional *"Whoop!"* Claude checks her phone before getting out of the car. She's got maybe an hour. Guilt chewed a hole in her stomach as she drove over. She wants to unwind, but she also wants Mom not to hate her.

The front door's unlocked. Ben Nakayama sits happy

drunk in the hall. "Claaaaaaude," he says, like she's what he's been waiting for all his life. This is Claude's party name. *Claaaaaaude.* "How was jail?"

Claude ignores him.

Kyle's house is a showcase of another life. The floors are dark stone tile, the walls a pristine white. A moody modern painting hangs in the foyer, with a vase of willow branches on a shelf underneath. Shoes pile in an untidy mountain below them. Through a door to the right Claude can see stuffed white brocade chairs and couches, the corner of a dark wood table. At least one heap of people is inside. To her left there's an open room with some books and board games and an out-of-her-depth freshman looking at her phone in a corner. Farther down the hall, the TV room is stuffed with people playing *Mario Kart.* They hold glasses of Coke and beer and some kind of punch that's probably a mix of everything in the Landry liquor cabinet plus orange juice.

She recognizes people in the kitchen. They lean against marble countertops that probably cost more than the entire Vanderly residence. A keg sits on the island in the middle. Shay fills a cup from a bowl with an atrocious pink cocktail in it, while Natalie pulls her brown hair into a ponytail behind.

"Hey, Claude," Shay says when she looks up. She's the lone wolf who doesn't consider Claude the absolute devil. "Beer?"

"Claaaaaaude," the rest of the kitchen choruses. Heads crane from the TV room.

Fuck, she wants a beer. But she thinks of Lizzy Sayer's Hyundai, parked haphazardly at the top of Anna's Run. "Driving tonight."

She waits for them all to ask. *How was it? Did they take your fingerprints? Did they strip search you, ha ha? Did they find the murder weapon? Did you do it?*

"Your mom let you go to a party?" Shay says instead. "You must have, like, the coolest parent of all time."

"Well, you know. No walls can hold me for long." Claude tries to sound breezy. Maybe it will help her forget her growing impulse to throw up.

"The irrepressible Claude," says Sam Galley from the corner.

"Claudini," Violet Pendler chimes from where she's tucked into his arm.

"Claude the unstoppable!" Jason Lennox calls. His cheeks are flushed, his eyes glassy. The hand that raises his cup is a little too enthusiastic, and beer sloshes over the side. "Claaaaaaude!" he bellows.

"Claaaaaaude!" they all reply.

Claude always plays a role, but the role she has for parties slips around her like a well-worn coat. Here she doesn't prowl the halls like a defiant outsider. Here she's queen. At parties her sarcasm is cutting and funny, not disruptive. Her short black hair is edgy. Her low-cut tank top and short shorts are sexy. Claude's still Claude, more or less—but instead of giving someone the middle finger, she puts a hand on their arm. She laughs at a joke even if it's a tiny bit sexist. She doesn't have to be the first and last bastion of feminist watch.

She pops the tab on a can of Coke and joins their cheer. Then she leans back and spreads her arms expansively. "What's new in the world?"

"I can't believe Mrs. Willingham cried in class." Jason smirks.

Shay and Natalie shoot him identical looks, full of daggers. "She was handing back essays and Emma's was at the bottom of the pile," Shay says in an undertone.

"I didn't realize the Ham liked Emma so much," Claude says, carefully keeping her face neutral.

"Everyone liked Emma," Natalie replies. Her expression is brittle, like it's ready to break into something more feral if Claude only gives it the chance. Ah, yes. The cheer squad that scrambles so diligently to be the ones who loved Emma best.

So Claude does the only thing she can do. She raises her can of Coke and says, "To Emma!"

"Emmmmaaaaaaaaaa," everyone in the kitchen yells.

Shay wipes away a sincere-looking tear as she brings her glass down. Natalie's eyes remain on Claude. She's been wary ever since Claude got halfway down Michael Bryson's pants at homecoming.

"Anyway, I've got a laundry list of party goals, so I'll love you and leave you." The kitchen's too one-note anyway; she can hear them toasting *Shaaaaaaaaaaaaay* as she walks out the sliding glass door that leads to the backyard. A few heads glance her way, but she doesn't feel like wasting precious minutes on any of them.

The lights of the house bounce off the clouds, making the world a strange kind of gray-bright. The air raises goose bumps in a sweep across Claude's neck and shoulders. She should put on a coat. Kyle Landry's infamous hot tub is too stuffed with sentient bikinis, so she heads toward the first knot of people she sees.

"Claude!" A hand lands on her arm and Margot pulls her into a brief hug. Margot is the kind of girl who never got a locker check in her life. She's an ex-cheerleader with a round, friendly face and blond hair that she still pulls back in a high ponytail. She's the only person Claude knows who had the option to leave Lorne forever and didn't take it. She smells of lavender incense and, under that, a little bit of weed.

"What's up? I got extras in my car—do you need?" She raises her eyebrows. *Extras* means extra prescription pills.

Claude wonders if Margot knows where she was last night. Mom's furious, heartbroken voice echoes in the back of her mind. *What the fuck, Claude?* "I can't. I gotta lie low for a while." Maybe forever. Maybe she can find some other way to make cash in this godforsaken town.

Margot's eyebrows rise for real this time. "I always thought you made too much to quit." Claude shrugs one shoulder. "All right. But if I find another dealer for JLH in the meantime, I can't just give you your job back."

"That's fine. Hey." Another idea nags at Claude. "Do you know anything about hacking phones?"

Margot takes a long, slow sip of beer. "Depends on what you need." It'll cost, too.

Claude speaks with careful casualness. "Let's say . . . someone has a locked phone, and it *may* have incriminating stuff on it. Is there a way to get in without knowing the pass code?"

"Mmmm." Margot swallows. "Do you want to wipe the phone, or just get in?"

"Just get in."

Margot shakes her head. "You're going to risk a total factory reset, which would delete everything. Maybe you can find out the password to your blackmailer's cloud?"

Claude didn't say anything about blackmail, but she's not going to tell Margot the truth.

"Hope you make it work." Margot looks sympathetic. "Let me know when you want to get going again." She pats the pocket of her vest. It crinkles.

Someone hands Claude a beer, which she holds on to as she circulates. People shout when they see her. She gets hugs, she gets cheers, she gets snacks off other people's plates. In the clear, crisp mountain air, in the alternating shadow and golden light of the house, the thing that is Claude seems to stretch and take on new shape.

"Claaaaaaude," says a boy she doesn't know. "How was jail?" His friend smacks him, but he's more than a little drunk and he pays it no mind. The people around them lean in, ready to share in her delinquency.

Claude runs her free hand through her hair, letting them follow the line of her slim arm. "It was bullshit," she says. Her smile is jagged and dangerous as river stones. "No torture, no police brutality—they barely asked me any questions." She grabs another pretzel off the plate next to her. "Seven out of ten. The last arrest was better."

They crow around her. The thing that is Claude swells off their adoration.

"Did you set the fire in the woods?" asks a freshman girl, sounding hopeful.

An odd expression flickers over Claude's face. A moment later it's back to her easygoing party self. "Course not."

The music changes out on the lawn. The few dancers stop, bewildered. But Claude just laughs. *Meat Loaf?* She puts her beer down on the lawn and beckons. "Come on. Let's show these fools how it's done." She parades to the flat stretch of green that answers for a dance floor here.

Claude's not a member of a dance squad or cheer team. She's not even graceful. But nobody laughs at her lack of style. The way she punches the air makes blood sing. Figures follow her out, and soon the grass is full of people hopping awkwardly, losing their self-consciousness as the music slides under their skin.

As Meat Loaf is replaced by another power ballad, Claude slows to adjust to the new music. A hand slips over her hip. She turns. "Man of the hour," she says.

"Yeah?" Kyle takes that as an invitation, putting his other hand on her lower back. His pale brown hair is messed up from dancing, and he smells like a combination of body spray and beer. His eyes are hazel and his arms have a nice muscular slope to them. Claude starts to relax. She's got thirty minutes before it's time to panic about Mom. "I dunno," Kyle says. "You're the one everyone's talking about. And you can get anyone to dance to . . ." He wrinkles his nose. "Whatever this is. Mark has the worst taste in music."

Claude laughs. "Meat Loaf is my mom's favorite." *Don't think about Mom.* To soothe her own guilt, she presses in. She's interested in seeing how he reacts. Whether he leaps back like the virginal *I'm going to save you from yourself* boys or whether he grabs the excuse to grind up against her.

He lets his arm slip lower down, resting just above the line of her shorts. The feeling in her belly is less sickness, more hunger.

"Ridiculous," Kyle says. "It's Top 40 or nothing."

"You're missing out," Claude says.

He smiles wider, bright Golden Boy teeth shining in the dark. "Not right now, I'm not."

Kyle Landry isn't JLH's smartest, or kindest, or most tactful boy. But his attention is all on her, and that's how Claude likes it. His fingers trace little patterns on her back and arm, leaving a trail of goose bumps in his wake.

"You're not cold, are you?" he says after a few minutes.

"I wouldn't mind going somewhere warmer." *Somewhere more private.*

He cocks an eyebrow. "Like where?"

She slides her thigh against his and is rewarded when his grip tightens on her skin. "Dunno. How about your parents' secret bunker?" she jokes.

"Huh?" Kyle looks nonplussed.

Jamie would've gone with it. Suggested a base on the moon or a cabin belonging to an outlaw from the Gold Rush days. Would've made a joke about lumberjacks.

Kyle's not Jamie. That's the point. "Never mind," Claude says. "Let's go."

His smile turns smug. He detaches from her and takes her hand, weaving toward the house. Heads turn to look as they approach, and unease tickles her spine. Kyle swaggers. One guy fist-bumps him as they pass.

It's not that Claude cares if people know what she's doing. But it's none of their business, either. She doesn't need to wave the proverbial banner high.

He leads her through the house—she ignores the chorus of *oooohs* from the kitchen—and up the stairs. They pass a couple making out in the hallway and head to the door at the end. Kyle opens it onto an expansive king-sized bed in royal blue, a pristine white carpet, and bay windows that overlook the party. A tidy bookshelf is filled with things like the *Gray's Anatomy* textbook and *The Psychology of Love*. "This . . . isn't your room," Claude guesses.

"Of course not." Kyle flips the lock. "It's my parents'."

"Seriously?" Kyle wants to have sex in his parents' bed? "I think we should do this somewhere else." Even on top of a mini fridge would be preferable.

"Nah, we'll be fine." Without preamble he grabs her wrists, pushing her back toward the bed. When she makes a tiny gasp, he leans in.

The kiss isn't gentle, like most guys are at first. Kyle mashes his mouth on her, pushing her own lips against her teeth. His tongue swipes across her firmly closed lips and smears half her chin in his saliva. She jerks back. Jamie never pulls shit like this. He's always gentle, waiting for her to say yes or to make the first move. His first preoccupation is always what's making her happy. He doesn't try to jam his tongue down her throat without even asking first.

And he always tells her how beautiful she is, right before he kisses her. Like it's so important to him that he has to remind her.

Kyle doesn't tell her she's beautiful. He doesn't say anything at all. He tries to pry her lips open like she's a walnut. Other memories rustle at the back of her mind, memories from a time she tries to keep locked up tight. Of a hand up her shirt, of threats issued in a silky voice. Of her own brain, screaming *no, no, NO*—

She twists her hands out of Kyle's grip, but it's too late. Her knees hit the back of the bed and Kyle nudges her until she sits. He fumbles with his belt. He's practically panting.

He hasn't looked at her since she said *Let's go.* His eyes are on her chest, her legs, her ass. He doesn't want her, he wants a sack of meat that will gently moan once in a while.

He wants to satisfy himself, and he doesn't care what she thinks about it.

"Hang on a sec, sport," she tries. Her voice is shaking. She has to get it under control.

Kyle doesn't notice. "Why?" His jeans fall free. She can see the tent in his black boxer shorts. "I'm ready."

"I'm not," she says.

She sees the flash of his Golden Boy grin again, and his eyes dip up to meet hers. "Let me help you with that."

She takes a deep breath. This isn't the same incident. He isn't forcing anything. She's safe, even though the door's locked and no one would help her if she screamed. It's just Kyle.

He leans down and rips open her shorts.

Her knees come up like a shot, hitting him in the side of the head. Kyle reels back. "What the hell?"

"What the hell yourself," Claude snarls. She rolls away and stands. She can't stay pinned to the bed. "I said I wasn't ready."

"Come on, you're always ready for it." His smile flickers, like he knows he maybe said something wrong. *Maybe.* "I mean, tell me what you want." And he shrugs, like her pleasure is an inconvenient roadblock, worth it only so they can get on to the truly important matter of getting *him* off.

"Actually, my mom's going to freak if she realizes I snuck out. I should probably go. Next time, Landry." She moves toward the door.

"Wait, hang on." Kyle steps in front of her. The smile has disappeared. "Please. Please, please, please. I'll do whatever you want, okay?"

Her stomach is back to churning. "You sound like I'm threatening to kill you." Her stupid voice won't stop trembling. She clenches her fist until she can get it under control. "Just—I'm not into it anymore. Next time." *Next time being absolutely never.*

"This was next time. I waited for you the whole night at Steve's party and you never showed. And, I mean, come on." His smile is a little more sheepish. "Everyone already thinks we did it. We might as well."

Claude thinks of Jamie in his puff coat, determinedly earnest. "Why does everyone already think we did it, Kyle?" Her voice is soft and serious. Dangerous.

He takes a step back, as if he senses her anger, and scratches his head. "I mean, we'd have done it if you'd actually showed up to the party." Like she didn't have a choice. Like she couldn't have resisted him.

"Who exactly claimed we had sex on a mini fridge?"

"Um . . ."

"Kyle, did you start the rumor?" She's past the shaking voice now. Never has she sounded so calm in all her life.

He leans against the door, eyes darting nervously to the side. The air between them is hot, the silence brittle. "I mean—" He coughs. "It's not the worst rumor that's ever been spread about you."

Claude forces herself to speak. "Sorry, Kyle," she says through gritted teeth. "Desperate and disgusting aren't really turn-ons. See you on Monday."

She leans past him and undoes the lock. "Oh, come on," he whines, flipping it back. "You pity-fuck Jamie Schill on the daily. I'm not more desperate than him."

She brings her knee up, slamming his erection with as much force as she can. His mouth opens in a silent wheeze. She hopes she kicked him hard enough that his parents find him here when they come home. "Go fuck yourself, Kyle Landry." She unlocks the door and storms down the hall. "Nobody's going to do it for you."

She does up the button of her shorts as she thunders down the stairs. She opens the front door before she remembers her keys. They're in her coat, and her coat is in the front room. As she storms in, two girls look up from the couch but turn away from her when they determine she's no one interesting.

"My mom won't let me hang out there," the brunette says. "She's already caught wind that it's where everyone goes to smoke."

"Huh. What about the woods?" says the blonde.

The brunette laughs. "Right now? Ever since the police said someone might be in there, she's been flipping her lid. She checks every major newspaper and the Adams West blog before she takes me to school in the morning. If she catches me in the woods, I'll be *way* more grounded than if she catches me smoking." She shrugs. "Best place to do it is here, frankly."

"So Kyle Landry can clean up the mess?" The pale girl raises her eyebrows.

"He'd deserve it," Claude mutters, finally picking up her coat.

She walks quickly down the front drive, but now that her head is beginning to clear, she realizes: there's something else to do before she goes home. She still has twenty minutes before she enters the danger zone, and that should be just enough time. She hops into Janine and pulls away from the Landry house with a screech that will hopefully wake the neighbors.

The Breakfast Club sits right off main street, right next to the Eternal Christmas store, whose animatronic Santa hasn't stopped waving from the front window since 1965. Claude flips off the machine as she goes by—Santa waves—and heads inside.

The restaurant has its usual late-night clientele: a couple of homeless guys perched over a cup of coffee, Lorne's taxi driver waiting for his next call, a few students between parties. One of them shouts, *"Claaaaaaude."*

She ignores him. She's not in party mode now.

The diner's decor is cheap plastic everything, from the linoleum on the floor to the stools at the bar that still, miraculously, have stuffing to leak. Rumors circulate every year that it's going to be shut down, replaced by a chain diner or a fancy coffee shop, but Claude doubts anyone will reuse the place. The walls are stained yellow from the days when you could smoke inside. Pictures splattered with old ketchup are framed by cracked gray wood. The faux-tile floor is so faded no one knows what the original colors were. They just have gray and darker gray now.

Still, nothing in Lorne beats the Breakfast Club for a late-night meal.

She goes up to the bar and takes a seat, scratching at a dried mustard stain on the counter. The unimpressed waitress takes her time refilling a guy's coffee, then comes over. "Two breakfast burritos, please," Claude says. "To go."

The woman heads over to the register. "Anything else?"

"Don't you want extra guac on yours?"

Claude turns. Seriously? Why does Jamie need to be here, now? Why does she need to suddenly remember that he has a dimple on either side of his mouth when he smiles? Why does he have to be smiling at all, and not in a judgy or cruel or even suggestive way?

Stupid boy, looking happy to see her.

The waitress taps her long nails on the register, looking bored. "Extra guac on both, please," Claude says.

Jamie slides onto the stool next to her. She expects a subtle jab about *two* burritos, and she readies the defenses. Instead, he just says, "You think Mr. Yamotov will let you make up your calc quiz?"

The quiz today. She'd skipped calc but forgotten about the quiz. "Probably. He loves to say that anyone can do math, so he'll be all eager to prove it."

"I don't know if anyone told you, but we have a paper due in APCoGo on Monday."

Claude tries not to smile. "You told me, Jamie."

"I did?" His eyes widen a tad too much. "The aliens have erased my memory again! See, this is why JLH should make tinfoil hats part of their dress code."

Claude gives in and smiles. For a moment they're quiet. Then she says, "I bet if there were aliens, half the staff at JLH would be one."

"Like who?"

Claude twists her mouth. "Mrs. Willingham. That's why she confiscates our phones every morning. Can't have a phone signal disabling her human projection."

"Yes. Yes. Also, Mr. Pendler. Like he always says, 'Okay, humans!' like he heard gender neutral is the new way to go but he doesn't know how to do it?"

"Yes. And Principal Mendoza, because every principal is an alien." Fact of life.

"And Mr. Darrow. No human on earth is that ready and

196

chipper in the mornings." Jamie's grinning. He has a bit of cilantro stuck between his teeth. He has dimples and a carefree smile and no smirks, no judgments, no pleading—

She wants to kiss him. And then put her head on his shoulder and listen to him ramble instead of thinking about jail and her mom and the party and stupid Kyle Landry, who would have sexually assaulted her if she hadn't kicked him. She wants to put Jamie on the couch with a blanket and make him watch *Miracle on 34th Street.* She wants to stop jumping through his window at night and walk up to his front door like a normal person.

She can't. She's made a colossal fuck-up of her life and she can't ask Jamie to be a part of that, even though he'd say yes.

Maybe. She did say no to him already, and he hasn't brought it up again tonight. *And isn't it nice that someone can respect your boundaries?* whispers the voice in the back of her head.

The waitress slaps down two foil-wrapped burritos. Claude jumps and fumbles for her wallet. She's not at the Breakfast Club to flirt with Jamie. She's not even here for herself.

"I'll see you on Monday," she says without looking up.

"Awesome," Jamie replies, as though he really does think it's awesome. Then, to the waitress: "Could I get some fries, please?"

Something alarming twinges in her chest. Something like regret.

No police cars tonight at Anna's Run, though the area's still marked off by tape. Claude slides plastic bags over her Docs, tying them at the ankle, then ducks under the tape.

The wood is pitch black. Trees and shadow are indistinguishable from each other, and Claude has to find the flashlight on her phone to keep from straying into bushes and tripping on roots. The river's rush drowns out other sounds—the sounds of passing cars, the sounds of night birds. Claude's mind floods with stories of hikers who were followed by mountain lions, and more than once she whips around, but it seems that mountain lions are more sensible than humans when it comes to Anna's Run.

She breathes in deep, picking up the scent of juniper and cold water and woodsmoke. She must be going the right direction. She goes deeper into the woods, walking as they become impossibly dark, until her flashlight is an insignificant token against the night. She comes to the muddled crime scene of the bridge.

Water sprays in cold droplets. Winter cannot freeze and tame Anna's Run. Claude steps out onto the creaking wood, leaning away from the broken railing on her left. Her breath can't reach to the bottom of her lungs until she's on safe ground again. The river roars—in approval? In anger? Desperation for another sacrifice?

She clears the police tape on the other side and keeps going.

The smell of smoke becomes stronger. The air seems a little grayer, the woods a little lighter around her. And then she starts to see the first slivers of red and orange, reflections of a campfire.

The fire blazes high. A tent is set up next to it, large enough for two. Claude steps into the circle of light. She *so* shouldn't be doing this.

"Hello?" she says.

A shadow falls across her path. She gasps and spins, holding the burrito like a weapon.

But when she sees who it is, she sighs, half laughing in relief. "Thank god it's you." She offers the burrito. "Hungry?"

OFFICIAL POLICE RADIO TRANSCRIPT ORDER CODE 31225

    JLPD TEAMS ON DUTY 1, 3

DISPATCH: Car Oscar Golf 311, are you receiving?

OG311: Car Oscar Golf 311 reading loud and clear.

DISPATCH: We've got a billing address for that phone.

OG311: Go ahead.

DISPATCH: Wenby Court, number 133, residence registered to William and Bronwyn Sayer.

OG311: Jesus. We're on our way. You unlocked the phone yet?

DISPATCH: Negative. We'll keep you updated.

OG311: Roger, Dispatch. Headed there now.

FROM: g.mendoza@fcpsjlh.com
TO: gwen.sayer@gmail.com
DATE: December 7, 2018 9:31 P.M.
SUBJECT: Devino Scholarship

Dear Miss Gwendolyn Sayer,

It is my pleasure to inform you that you have been selected to receive the prestigious Devino Scholarship. The decision was based on your academic record, your eloquence in writing and speech, your moral integrity, and your commitment to extra-curricular activities that enrich the community around you. Congratulations.

Representatives of the Devino Fund will be in touch shortly after the new year to confirm your financial status. If you choose for any reason to reject the scholarship, please let me know before the beginning of winter break so that the scholarship can go to another deserving participant. The scholarship cannot be deferred—if you decide not to attend college in the fall 2019 semester, you will forfeit the scholarship entirely.

I am very proud that we had not one but two incredible students at Jefferson-Lorne in competition for this prestigious scholar-ship, and that despite incredibly difficult personal issues, you've shown your mettle and gone after your dream. However, as much as I know it's an achievement you deserve to boast to the world, the school board and I have agreed at this time that it would be

201

best to postpone the formal announcement, out of respect for Emma Baines and the ongoing case.

Have a good weekend.

Regards,
Gabriel Mendoza
Principal, Jefferson-Lorne High School

21

THE DESPERATE ONE

The Sayers arrive late for dinner, and Mum gives Gwen surreptitious glares through the rearview mirror the whole way. Gwen keeps her arms folded and her mouth shut. She meant to apologize the minute she came through the door, but before she had the chance, Mum had practically pushed her back out into the cold again, with Dad on her heels. "Adelaide's waiting for us, and I promised I'd help with the baby."

She'd forgotten about dinner with Dad's niece Adelaide.

The Sayer family grew up in Lorne, but Adelaide moved into her husband's mobile home when she got married, which means she lives a whole twenty minutes outside the city limits. The Sayers pull into Juniper Park just past seven and park in front of Cousin Addy's single-wide. A lopsided snowman sits outside the neighbor's house. Little twinkle lights line the top of the mobile home, but they're not turned on.

Mum's scowl evaporates as Addy opens the door. "All right, Adelaide? Lovely to see you."

"Thanks, Bronwyn." Cousin Addy and Mum hug. The smell of chicken and onions and garlic wafts from behind her.

Her apron is stained with baby food and dinner. She hugs Gwen's dad, then Gwen. "How goes, Gwen?"

"Great," Gwen lies. "Where's Eric?"

"Eric has a new job." Addy's tired smile takes on new life. "Night security for First Bank in Fort Collins."

Both Addy and Eric attended JLH, like Gwen. Unlike Gwen, neither of them won a scholarship to get out of town. Eric took night classes while Addy worked two jobs and had three children. Addy and Eric do what they can to keep their mobile home looking nice, but the linoleum peels away from the corners of the rooms, and they didn't get permission to paint over the orange fleur-de-lis wallpaper put up by a previous tenant. They've hung a big poster of the northern lights over it. It clashes horribly.

Laundry is piled up on the couch; Addy's sister-in-law, Catarina, sits next to it, folding. She uses her pregnant belly as a shelf, and waves at the Sayers as they come in. They make the rounds, hugging and kissing and exclaiming over Catarina's swollen feet. "It's a boy," Mum says.

"I don't know about that," Catarina replies. Her brown skin is sallow with fatigue. "I been drinking water like I'm living in the desert. Girls are thirsty."

"It's in the way you carry. It's a boy." Mum smiles.

Next they have to dote on baby Toby, screaming with joy from his high chair. Gwen loves the kid, but god, he's giving her a headache. Addy and Eric started soon out of high school.

But that's Lorne. There's nothing to do here but work and

have sex. And what little work you do get might not be enough to pay half your rent in the trailer park.

Mum goes into the kitchen to take care of the food. Gwen squats next to Toby and Dad goes outside to where Addy's other two kids, Margaret and Lionel, are making an army of tiny snowmen.

"You heard back yet from NYU, Gwen?" Catarina calls from the couch.

Gwen pauses in the middle of feeding Toby a sliver of green cabbage. "Uh, no. Another week and I'll start to worry." She applied early decision and she's second-guessing herself. Now Dad has started disappearing from their lives, and Emma has disappeared from *everywhere*, and everything seems to be coming down at once.

She'll get through this. She *will*. And she'll get her scholarship and buy her parents their big house and maybe she'll get Addy a cottage with foundations, one that won't wash downstream in the next flash flood.

"How about the scholarship? I'm so proud of you," Addy says.

"It's not official yet," Gwen objects.

Addy waves her hand. "Everyone knows you deserve it."

Gwen can't really muster the right kind of smile. "Thanks."

They crowd around the folding table to eat. Margaret and Lionel stomp in from the snow with loud exclamations. Margaret tackles Gwen.

"You're freezing," Gwen shrieks as Margaret's hands slip under her shirt and latch onto her back.

"Me and Li made a snowball army," Margaret says, sticking out her tongue.

"What's a snowball army?" Gwen asks.

"It's a bunch of little snowmen that quickly become snow-*balls*," says Dad. He's smiling like he doesn't have to think about anything tonight. Gwen sort of hates that it's so carefree. He could show some of that at home, if he ever actually came home.

They wrangle the kids into their chairs. Addy serves a warm soup. As she sits down, Gwen can see how her body sags. Gray hair streaks either side of her temple. She tells Margaret off for splashing her spoon in her soup and admonishes Li for slurping.

If Gwen stays in Lorne, this will be what twenty-five looks like for her. She can't. She promised Lizzy she'd get a prestigious job and move her parents into a house where the pipes never freeze and they can afford to change the fuse box. She loves Addy, but she doesn't want to spend her days making coffee that she can't afford for Heather Halifax or Claude Vanderly or any of the other soon-to-be alumni of JLH. She doesn't want two or three jobs just so that she can live alone. She doesn't want to get married, and *especially* not to a boy, and she doesn't want to be out in a town like Lorne.

She helps wash dishes listlessly. She got the scholarship. All she has to do is make it to graduation. As she stacks the plastic plates into a neat pile, she prays silently—to God, who may or may not exist, to the Mari Lwyd, who might be a version of Mary or might be harmless fun, like Mum always says. *Six more months. Six months of peace.*

Gwen's not big into gods, so she's not surprised when her prayer protects her for all of half an hour. She's reading a children's book of fairy tales for Margaret and Li when the wail of sirens can be heard from outside. Mum's brow wrinkles.

"Don't worry," Addy says from where she sits, nursing Toby. "They come through twice a night. There's some meth heads who keep trying to cook something up in the middle of the park."

The sirens draw closer. Something in Gwen's chest constricts. They stop outside Addy's home and switch off.

Catarina and Addy exchange looks. Nobody speaks.

The knock comes hard and unforgiving, and everyone jumps.

"It's fine," Mum says, though she's paler than normal. Addy opens the door.

Gwen recognizes the policewoman—Muñez from school. Well, shit.

"Miss Gwen Sayer?" Muñez looks right at her. "Could we trouble you to come with us?"

"Why?"

"We have some follow-up questions in the Emma Baines case," says Officer Cline.

Gwen stands. Catarina leans forward and grabs her wrist. "You don't have to say anything without a lawyer, Gwen. You don't have to go unless they've got a warrant." She glares at Muñez.

Gwen shakes her off with a humorless smile. Catarina

should've become a comedian. As though they had money for a lawyer. "I'm happy to help," she says tonelessly.

"I'm coming," Mum says, standing too. "Don't you dare put cuffs on her."

"We have to follow procedure, ma'am." Muñez puts her hand on Gwen's shoulder and turns her toward the door. "If you want to come down to the station, you'll have to drive yourself."

"Don't," Gwen mumbles. It's not worth it. They don't have winter tires on the truck.

It's the last thing she says before she's marched out, past the Christmas lights, with her family and their neighbors gawking from the windows. She knows what they're thinking. Looks like that Gwen Sayer is as much trouble as her sister.

22

THE CHEATER

CLINE: The date is December 7, 2018, the time is 8:47 p.m. Interviewing Gwendolyn Sayer. Present are Officer Cline, Officer Muñez, and Miss Sayer.

Miss Sayer, are you comfortable? Do you need anything?

GWEN: Why am I here?

CLINE: We just need to follow up on a few things. We've had some developments in the case. For example, do you recognize this?

GWEN: It's a phone?

CLINE: Your phone?

GWEN: No.

MUÑEZ: It's connected to your address.

GWEN: My phone's in my backpack. You can check. And it doesn't have a SIM card in it, because Mum and Dad pay per minute and can only afford one number. They bought Lizzy a phone, but seeing how she used it—

Wait. That's her phone.

Why do you have it? I thought you gave us back her personal effects.

209

MUÑEZ: Do you have any idea why Claude Vanderly would be in possession of this phone?

GWEN: No. Can I have it back?

MUÑEZ: I'm afraid we have to hold on to it for now.

CLINE: Miss Sayer, may we also ask what you were doing at the Cross residence yesterday evening?

GWEN: I, ah, I don't know why you think that.

CLINE: Neighbors saw a girl matching your description knock on the Crosses' door. You spoke with Avery Cross for a few minutes, then left. Less than half an hour later, Avery Cross left her house as well.

GWEN: I don't know why Avery left home. I'm not in charge of her. Not her keeper, as my mum would say.

MUÑEZ: But could you tell us why *you* were there, Gwen?

GWEN: I . . . I wanted to give her my condolences. For Emma.

CLINE: In your previous interviews, you didn't claim to be close to Emma.

GWEN: I wasn't. But I knew Avery was. And I wanted to return a favor. A favor that Avery did me three years ago.

The smell of death is flowers. Flowers are expensive unless you pick them from the side of the road, so we rarely had them in the house. But in the days after Lizzy's funeral, flowers were everywhere. White roses and lilies and baby's breath sat on every surface, overpowering the comforting smells of food and home with a scent that choked me. I couldn't leave the house, so I held my breath, retreating to my room when I could and keeping the window open. Cards sat wherever the flowers didn't. Line after line of *We're so sorry* and *Deepest condolences*. Most of it was generic bullshit from people who didn't know Lizzy at all. A lot of cards had butterflies, which only made it harder. *Pilipala* was our thing.

I was trying to get rid of some of the flowers when the doorbell rang. Dad was at work; Mum hadn't come out of her room that day. So I answered the door. I was expecting our neighbor Mrs. Flores. She kept us in soup and lasagna for weeks after Lizzy died. I stared uncomprehending at the pink skirt, the long pale legs, the spun-gold ponytail that stuck out from behind another bouquet.

"Um. Hi," Avery Cross said.

Everything was fuzzy. I couldn't muster myself enough to be polite. "What're you doing here?"

"I got you—I mean, your family—" She thrust the bouquet in my direction. "I'm sorry about Lizzy."

I should've said *thanks*. But honestly? Avery didn't know Lizzy at all. Hell, she didn't even know me. We passed each other in the halls and had PE together. "Why?"

Avery gaped. Then she swallowed. "I guess . . . I think she didn't deserve to die. I'm sorry you have to go through it." She bit a pale pink lip. "Can I put these in some water?"

"Come in." I turned and went into the kitchen, trusting her to follow. I grabbed a dying batch of callas and upended them in the sink, refilling the vase with fresh water. When I turned back around, she stood just inside the door, wide-eyed. I imagined the house through her eyes: walls stained with the strains of living, paper crafts hanging around because we can't afford fancy art. A picture of the Mumbles, Mum's favorite place in Wales, propped up on a chest of drawers, with two plastic tea candles at the bottom corners. The tartan couch, more duct tape than fabric and sagging in the wrong places.

"Not the Buckingham Palace you're used to," I said. I didn't care whether I sounded bitter or angry or just resigned. "Probably not even the garage you're used to."

"I like it," Avery objected.

I rolled my eyes.

"It's homey. In my house, we have couches Mom won't even let me touch because they have to be perfect."

I stalked over and grabbed the flowers from her hands. "Poor little rich girl, has to live with more than one couch," I said.

Avery blushed and looked down. I felt a little bad as I dumped the flowers into the vase. "Want anything? We have a million lasagnas."

"No thanks," Avery said.

Right. Cheerleaders don't eat. She blushed again, as though she'd read my mind.

"I ate earlier."

I filled a glass from the tap and held it out to her. For part of me, it was a test. Could Little Miss Money bear to drink the water of the poor?

She took it without speaking and drank the whole thing. She asked a couple of small-talk questions, I answered. I didn't feel like chatting and she seemed to understand.

A few days after, I texted her a thank-you. We sent them

out to everyone. She said it was nothing, but it didn't mean nothing to me. No one else from school had come by. Not Lizzy's old friends, not the boys she made out with at parties, not the assholes who gave her underage self all the liquor. Avery was genuine. She was the kind of person who said sorry because she *was* sorry.

After that, we said hi occasionally as we passed in the halls. Sometimes I texted her homework assignments if she missed school. And yesterday . . . I felt like it was a debt I could repay.

CLINE: So you went over just to say sorry.

GWEN: Believe it or not, I am capable of empathy.

CLINE: Did you tell Avery Cross that you won the Devino Scholarship?

GWEN: Of course not. I didn't even know . . . How do *you* know about it?

CLINE: Congratulations.

GWEN: I . . . thought you had follow-up questions about Emma.

CLINE: You must be excited. You're going to college on a free ticket. It's pretty amazing. Even I'm proud for you. You've been working toward this moment for four years.

GWEN: Longer.

CLINE: Of course, of course. But you weren't the only one working hard. Emma was working hard, too. Harder even. She was doing better. She was ahead. She was going to win, until she disappeared. Do you know why she was doing better, Gwen?

GWEN: She wasn't doing better.

CLINE: You know why Emma was doing better.

GWEN: I don't know anything, *okay?*

MUÑEZ: You're very defensive for someone who doesn't know anything, Gwen.

CLINE: Emma knew your secret, didn't she? She knew just like we know. Were you desperate to keep her from talking?

GWEN: I . . .

MUÑEZ: It might have put your entire future in jeopardy.

GWEN: Of course I was desperate!

I'm sorry. I hate myself for cheating. I should never have done it, but I didn't kill anyone over it! It was three and a half years ago and I've busted ass *every day* to make up for it. To prove that I can. Just . . . please. I *need* to get out of here. I need to leave Lorne and the endless shitty shift jobs and the having babies at eighteen and the knowledge that I'll never ever make something of myself. Please believe me.

CLINE: I, ah . . .

MUÑEZ: That wasn't the secret we were talking about.

GWEN: Fucking . . . Well, I don't know what else you might have been talking about.

MUÑEZ: Now's not the time to be coy. Thank you for being honest about the exam, at least. We're not here to be the final arbiters of whether you deserve the scholarship or not. We're here about Emma.

CLINE: And we . . . might be able to strike a deal with you on that point.

MUÑEZ: We need help with this case. We need someone trustworthy to be our eyes and ears.

GWEN: Seriously? What is this, *CSI: Smalltown*?

MUÑEZ: Are we really in a position to joke, young lady?

Thank you. Like we said, we need your help. And if you give it to us, we're willing to overlook what you just said.

CLINE: We don't care about one little exam. You have a bright future ahead of you, and you deserve to take it. Cooperate, and you get what you want.

GWEN: Can I think about it?

No. Never mind. I'll do it.

MUÑEZ: We'll get you set up in the front office. Wear the wire at all times. And don't leave Lorne.

Diary Entry

Emma Baines—August 27, 2018

BREAKTHROUGH.

I wish I felt elated. But right now, all I feel is sick. I know who ransacked my desk at the Inquirer.

It had to be Gwen.

She has two reasons to do it. Well, three, I guess. But honestly? Only one matters.

1. Gwen's pissed at me about the Lizzy shitstorm. (Gwen's words, not mine.) And she wants to put me behind in the running for the Devino Scholarship.

2. Gwen knows I know she cheated, and she wants to put me behind in the running for the Devino Scholarship.

3. Gwen knows I know she's gay, and she wants to put me behind in the running for the Devino Scholarship.

Well, bring it on, Sayer. I can do so much worse than you. How does academic probation sound? How do you feel about getting disqualified from the scholarship? I can expose everything you are, you little liar.

Don't fuck with me. Don't fuck with this. It's so much more important than you.

I'll ruin you for her, if I have to.

DISPATCH: 911, what is your emergency?

MAN: I've got—shit. I've found someone. A, ah, body.

DISPATCH: Sir, what is your location?

MAN: I'm just off Highway 143, Maleta Drive. I'm down by the water where it slows and turns east.

DISPATCH: Please stay on the line. We're sending a car to your location now. Do you know CPR?

MAN: Uh, no. It's not gonna work. He's long gone.

DISPATCH: Okay, please stay on the line. Tell me how you came upon the body.

MAN: I was hiking, but I took a detour, you know, because the police crime scene cuts through the trail. I came down to the water so my dog could splash around where it's safe, and—well, I thought he was sleeping, till I got close.

DISPATCH: Could you describe him for me, please? Police are on their way.

MAN: Yeah, uh. He's got one of those puffy black coats. He's maybe kinda tall? And not too big around. He's probably white. He's got a beard, he's got one combat boot. He, uh—he smells.

DISPATCH: Please stay on the line. A car is almost there.

23

THE HEARTBREAKER

When the knock comes, at nine p.m., Avery knows it's the police. They don't believe she takes Valium. They've untangled her lies. They're taking her in. And she's tired enough to go with them.

Her black Adidas gym bag lies on her pink-clad bed, half full and freshly ransacked thanks to Mrs. Cross's drug check. It's a stark contrast to the princess decor of her room, the desk strewn with sparkling pens and Pandora jewelry and a pink wide-ruled notebook. She so loved being a princess when she was little. She doesn't know whether she loves it still. She just knows she's supposed to. And expectations like that sour all things.

She puts down the extra skirt she folded for the weekend game and leaves her room, skipping over the squeaky floorboard that connects her to the pristine white hall. Her parents will want her to go quietly, like good girls do when they've got nothing to be afraid of. Also, they can tell the neighbors she's "just helping."

She feels sick. But that's a good thing, she decides dully

as she heads for the stairs. Feeling sick keeps her from feeling hungry. Both she and her mom pushed most of their dinner around on their plates.

Mrs. Cross opens the front door. "Thank you for coming," she says, and gives Michael a hug.

Avery stops midway down the stairs. It's snowing again.

Michael steps in and brushes the snow off his coat, pulling his boots off as Mrs. Cross fusses over him. Avery clears her throat and they both look up, guilt flashing across their faces like spinning snow.

"Hon, I thought it would be nice if Michael came by for dessert. I need a test subject for my gingerbread cookies." Mrs. Cross makes gingerbread cookies for the Winter Fair every year, but she never wins the baking prize for them. She's been saying *This is my year* for the last six months.

Avery doesn't know why Mrs. Cross *really* asked Michael to come. Maybe she thinks he'll convince Avery to confess everything. Maybe she thinks he'll solve Avery's pill problem. She must believe they're not having sex after all. But that's the problem—the Crosses are so obsessed with appearance, even Avery doesn't know what they really want.

"I'll leave you two in the living room. No closed doors, no lying down. Half an hour." She gives Avery a hug, squeezing until Avery grunts from the pressure, then gives her a *behave yourself* glare at an angle that Michael can't see. Then she walks briskly down the hall.

"How's your ankle?" Michael says. Right. Avery "hurt her ankle."

She lets him help her into the living room, a sparse space with white carpet, white overstuffed furniture, white vases in white bookshelves that have barely any books in them. Michael settles her on a white-on-white embroidered couch and lifts her ankle up for her. "I'll get something for that."

Sweet, sweet Michael. Avery never gets the feeling that he dates her to make himself look good. He's always looking out for her. He goes into the kitchen and she hears his voice rumbling like a far-off storm. Avery plays with the cuff of her flannel pajamas. She's not ready for this. She can't see him.

But far too soon he's back. He sits, pulling her leg onto his lap, and pulls up the cuff of her pajamas. She wrinkles her nose as the ice pack touches skin, but she smiles—more of a grimace, really.

"What're you going to do about the competition tomorrow?" he asks, touching her ankle.

"Mr. G said it should be no problem. I just have to rest up tonight."

"It doesn't look swollen." He presses on it and Avery gasps. "Sorry!"

"It's okay." She chews on her lower lip. The lie feels awful and her stomach twists like the river gorged on snowmelt. "Bet you didn't come all the way over here to ice my leg." Does it sound too flirtatious? She swallows.

"Not for cookies, either. Your mom asked me to come. She said you're . . . going through stuff. Anxious."

"Always," Avery laughs.

Michael's brow furrows. He doesn't believe it. Why would he? Avery always keeps the pleasant facade.

And maybe Michael's part of the reason she's anxious.

His fingertip traces a pattern on her calf. "She said you maybe needed a friend."

"I've been taking Valium," Avery says.

"Why?" Michael's frown is deeper. Something darkens behind his eyes. *Who is this new Avery?* he's thinking. "What are you so stressed about?"

His words echoes her parents', and it cuts. "The competition tomorrow. College applications. Grades. Emma." Oh, Emma. She's been causing Avery stress longer than anyone knows.

"The competition's just a competition. It'll be fine." Michael shrugs. Avery balls her hands into fists. It's just cheerleading. It's not big and important like the lacrosse games, or the basketball games, or the football games. Everyone wants to see the pretty girls dance. Everyone agrees it's worth less.

"And I didn't think you cared about college," Michael continues, oblivious.

"Of course I care about college." She surprises herself with her bitterness. She wants to go to college. Not an Ivy League like her parents want, just somewhere she can have fun and be free of Lorne. Maybe a technical school. She wants to leave, and she doesn't want to do it as a trophy girlfriend.

"And Aves . . . I'm sorry." He keeps his eyes on her knees, like he's afraid to look at her. "I need to ask you something."

That does nothing for the flipping in her belly. "Okay?"

"Aves, can I trust you to be honest?"

No. "Ye-eess," Avery says.

Michael takes a deep breath. "Where were you that night?"

"What night?" She already knows.

"Wednesday. *That* night." He laughs softly. "Was it really just Wednesday?" Then the smile washes away. "I've been texting Lyla."

The fluttering in her stomach turns to an iron ball. "Why?" Her voice is colder than it should be, considering. She's such a hypocrite.

"'Cause we worry about you, Aves." He shakes his head, like he can't get distracted. "She asked what we did on Wednesday. You told her you were with me, you told me you were with her, and now . . ."

And now a girl is dead.

She feels hot and cold all at once. She wants to twine her fingers through Michael's, pull him down for a kiss. Make him forget about the question. More than anything, she wants to feel the heat of his mouth the same way she used to, as though it burns but she'll never get enough, as though it pushes into her and fits some empty piece she never realized she had in the puzzle of her.

But she also doesn't want that. Because she already has it. Just not with him.

"I'm . . ." Her mouth is dry. How do people form entire sentences? "I'm sorry."

It feels like a coward's way out, but her throat closes before she can say anything more. Tears start at the corners of her eyes.

Michael takes a deep breath. His hands clench around her ankle. Then he lets go, because Michael never liked to think he might hurt her.

"I was with someone else," she chokes.

He goes so still. Like her words turned him to ice, and the next thing she says might shatter him. "I didn't mean—I didn't want it to happen the way it did." *Stop talking. You're only making it worse.*

"Then why did it?" he mumbles.

"It happened too fast." Tears slip out from between her lashes. "I didn't think it through."

"That's bullshit," Michael says thickly. He presses one palm against his eye, and pain shoots through Avery's chest. She's so selfish, how does she explain? She thought it was a one-time indiscretion, like Michael's incident with Claude. Then it was a fling. Then, suddenly, it was a secret. And she never had an excuse to break up with Michael, World's Best Boyfriend.

"You always have a choice to cheat, Aves. If you didn't want me, you should've dumped me."

Avery balls her hands. "I don't want to hurt you—"

"Too fucking late." He leans against the couch but doesn't shove her leg off him. Even now he's thinking about her. But her legs prickle against him and she draws them in until her knees hit her chest. She wraps her arms around them, as though she can ball herself up and escape from the world.

"Just tell me who you're going to be holding hands with in the halls on Monday. Don't make me find out the hard way."

"I . . ." She presses her face into her knees, letting her pajamas grow wet.

"You can do that much for me." Michael's voice wobbles, pleading.

"I promised," she whispers.

"Promised to go behind my back?"

"I promised not to tell."

Michael stands up and pushes his hands through his hair until they meet at the back of his skull. "Jesus, Aves. We're past that. I'm officially dumped, okay? I just want two days to come to terms with whoever your new boyfriend is."

"I promised them I wouldn't tell," she says again, lips against her knees.

There's an ugly pause. Avery risks looking up. Michael's face is contorted, and she knows he's picking over her sentence, trying to come to a different conclusion. But Avery Cross knows how to use her words, and when to emphasize the right ones.

"*Them,*" he says at last.

"Please." Her words twist and cut inside her, vying to get out. She doesn't know if she's begging for him to understand, or listen, or even not to tell.

"Whatever. I'll see you Monday." He turns and hurries out of the living room, head down.

She doesn't go after him. She sits on the couch and keeps her forehead pressed against her knees until she hears the front door latch. Then she dumps the ice pack on the floor and runs upstairs before Mrs. Cross can come in and demand to know what's going on or say one more word about her stupid cookies.

She flops on the bed. Tears scatter across the quilt. It's a strange feeling, this hurt. She aches, but not with longing or frustration or anger. She burns mostly with shame. She should've broken up with Michael a long time ago.

But then there was the Emma problem, and the relationship that *had* to stay secret, and Michael's complete inability to be a jerk worth dumping—

She wipes her eyes. Need to talk to u, she texts, then taps the side of her phone as she waits for a reply.

Through her window she sees Michael's headlights flicker on, and an angry laugh escapes her. She can't even wait till he's gone. He pulls slowly out of her driveway, snow crunching beneath his tires. His silver-blue car disappears in the gloom.

Forget it. Im coming over. She shimmies out of her pajamas and pulls on a pair of thick spandex leggings. She hears Mrs. Cross's tread on the stairs as she pulls on a sports bra.

The door opens, a sliver of yellow light blocked by shadow. "Aves? Are you okay?" Mrs. Cross asks tentatively, because she knows the answer.

"Michael broke up with me." Avery's voice quivers. She grabs a T-shirt. "I'm going for a run."

Mrs. Cross pauses, trying to sort through all the things she wants to say. She settles on "You're still grounded, hon." She sounds sorry, but she doesn't say it. Maybe she expected Michael to walk out the moment Avery told him about the Valium. Maybe she thinks it's what Avery deserves. Well, Avery does deserve it. "And anyway, you shouldn't be out at this time of night right now." Because what would people think of the Crosses if they let their daughter run around with a murderer on the loose?

"It's going to put me off my game tomorrow." She adds a little wheedle to her voice. She knows her parents don't want anyone asking, *What's wrong with Avery? Why wasn't she doing her best?* "A run will clear my head. I'll stick to the well-lit streets. It'll help me focus and keep me from eating my feelings." She puts a hand on her belly, even though she's afraid she'll throw up if she has even a spoonful of post-breakup ice cream.

"What about your ankle?" Mrs. Cross says.

"I'll go easy on it. Mr. G said I could still do physical activity. Mom, I need this."

Mrs. Cross looks at Avery suspiciously. "If you say you're just going for a run, then okay. But if I find out you went anywhere else, you are grounded until you get married."

"It's just a run." Avery doesn't even blink. She can lie when she needs to.

Her mom stares for a long moment. Avery meets her gaze. "You have twenty minutes," Mrs. Cross says at last.

"Thanks." Avery gives her a hard hug, then jogs down the stairs. She pulls on her running shoes, slips her phone into the pocket of her leggings, and lets herself out.

She inhales a freezing lungful of air and coughs out a cloud. She shouldn't go out without a sweater or scarf or hat, but she doesn't care. She'll be fine. She's got her phone. And she doesn't have a lot of time.

She bounces on the balls of her feet a couple of times, then takes off. She doesn't go easy on her ankle. Her pace is cautious, at first, as she scopes out the snowpack and ice with her running shoes. But soon she starts to speed up. She runs like she's racing for a one-way ticket out of Lorne. She runs like her life is unraveling.

She runs like she ran in the woods, two nights ago.

Her heart drums in her ears. The soft sounds around her transform to footfalls, to the snap of twigs, to shouts behind. She doesn't look back. She just runs, and prays, and runs, and listens for Anna's growl as though she can hear it even here.

She races past the shining new fortresses of wealth her father helped build, past apartments ready for the ski industry. As she goes the buildings turn from brand-new to almost new to still nice to dilapidated. Far above, the mountains stand as silent, uncaring watchmen.

An engine rumbles. Too late she sees the black nose of a car, pulling into the driveway to her right. Instead of trying to stop, she leaps and skids on the ice. The car brakes heavily. The door opens.

Avery forces herself to slow and jog back around. She knows where she is. She's just gone by Emma's house. And Chief Baines is coming home late.

"Avery?" he calls. "That you?"

Her pulse spikes. He's the last—no, second-to-last person she wants to talk to right now. But if she keeps running, he might wonder why, might follow her, might start to unravel the long string that led her here.

"Hello, Mr. Baines. I know I'm out past curfew, but—"

Baines waves a hand. He has a scraggly three-day beard and his graying hair shines like moonlight. "So what? Come here."

She goes over and lets him pull her into a hug. His police jacket is freezing. Snow and mud and pine needles stick to the arms. Mud is splattered all down his front, and up on the hood of his car. His eyes blaze with triumph and hate and tears, even though the rest of him looks like it's about to fall apart right there on the drive as he lets her go. "You were so good to my girl." He puts a hand on her shoulder. It feels like a shackle.

"It's nothing, Mr. Baines." She wonders if he's drunk. She wonders if she could outrun him.

"No. It's not nothing. And you deserve to be the first to know."

Her heart speeds up, pushing against her ribs. It's hard to breathe.

"We found the bastard."

"Um, who?"

"West. Adams West. We're gonna release a statement tomorrow, but I had to tell you now. He's never going after you girls again."

He's grinning, dazed, squeezing her shoulder hard enough to twist the bone. And Avery's heart isn't beating so fast anymore. In fact, she's pretty sure it's stopped beating altogether.

She looks at his face, and she knows.

He hasn't found West.

"That's great," she says, maybe overdoing it with the chipper Avery voice. "That's really great. I'll look for it in the paper tomorrow and I'll tell the whole team."

"Yeah." He nods. "Yeah."

"Mr. Baines, I sort of have to get going. . . ." She smiles apologetically.

He lets go of her shoulder with a deep breath. His face still flickers between sorrow and rage and the fierce joy that comes from the hunt.

Avery takes a few steps back and flees.

She runs until she thinks she's outrun her breath. She runs until her legs are numb. She runs until the fences go from chain link to rotting posts to nothing at all, until the broken windows are nailed over with wooden boards wrapped in plastic. She runs past men who are out late cleaning the streets because the snowplow doesn't come here, past houses with drooping gutters like eyelids. She runs until she comes to a small, dark one with just one lone light on in the kitchen.

Avery ducks through the neighbor's part of the yard. In a few hours the snow will obscure her footprints, and she'll have been nothing but a ghost. That's what she needs to be: something no one sees and no one cares about.

She raps on the window she wants. Waits until it slides up a fraction. Heat flushes her face. Still, she needs to focus. "We have a huge problem."

Emma Baines—September 1, 2018

I have leads. I'm scared shitless, but I've got leads.

Foolish Mr. Pendler left his computer logged in while he and Samantha went off-campus for an interview. So I snooped and got the names of everyone who went to the Christmas party and got a pair of boots. A list of suspects.

Next up: cross-reference with alibis. From the list, there are a few who stand out. People who would have signed notes to get Lizzy out of class. People it would have been natural for her to see.

I'm not writing down names until my evidence is watertight. But I have some office sleuthing to do. Because if Lizzy had photos, a secret account, anything—*I have to connect them to someone. And then I can make this case public.*

It's gonna burn Lorne down.

A joint statement from the Jefferson-Lorne and Fort Collins Police Departments

In the late hours of Friday evening a body was discovered by hikers at the bend of the Lorne River, half a mile downstream from Anna's Run. It is presumed to have been deceased since early Thursday morning.

The body has been identified as one Randy Silverman, an on-again, off-again member of the homeless community and an ex-convict with two counts of premeditated manslaughter on his record. Wounds indicate that Mr. Silverman was fatally injured by a gunshot to the head, and officers are currently looking for the weapon. Silverman may have been responsible for pseudonymous blog posts written by "Adams West" regarding the disappearance of Emma Baines, though the police state that this is "pure conjecture" at this time.

Silverman has no recorded next of kin in Lorne. Anyone with information on Randy Silverman, or who has seen a man of approximately six feet in height, 140 pounds in weight, with a black down coat, glasses, and a scar over his upper lip, should contact the police immediately.

24

THE SECRETIVE

Claude wakes up and convulses, curling and tugging her quilt over her head. She checks her eyelashes for frost. The temperature must have dropped fifteen degrees last night.

For a moment she pretends that it doesn't matter, it's a normal Saturday, she can sleep another three hours and lounge on the couch with Mom, eating doughnuts and arguing about which reality TV show they should hate-watch today.

But as cold as it is here, it's colder in the woods.

They're running out of time.

Mom's on the phone in the living room, and through cardboard-cheap walls Claude hears, "Fine. I think ten is fine. We don't have anywhere to be today. Thanks, Steve. See you."

Claude forces herself to sit up. Her little room has posters tacked to the walls: *My Little Pony* from Jamie, a *Bat out of Hell* from Mom, a Slipknot poster from when she drove all the way down to Red Rocks to see them with Margot. One bookshelf holds her school supplies and some hand-me-down paperbacks that range from romance to hard science fiction. This, right here, is home. Claude doesn't love Lorne, but she can't imagine leaving her mom and the house and everything she has.

But there are no prisons in Lorne. So if she gets caught up in her own web, she won't have much choice in where she lives.

Mom raises her eyebrows when Claude emerges from her room. "I thought you'd be enjoying your Saturday."

"I fully intend to." She flops on the couch hard enough to bounce.

"Watch the spring," Mom says. The spring's been broken for five years.

Claude flips up the lid on the doughnut box. Not too far from Lorne is the best doughnut shop on the eastern slope. One day, when the skiiers start to winter here and the contractors are making big bucks, Starbucks will come in and buy them out and replace the doughnuts with shitty prepackaged sugar. But for now, they're the best thing about Saturday mornings. Mom always gets up early to grab some.

Claude selects a buttermilk glazed and sits back, closing her eyes. "The only thing that would make this more perfect is a cup of coffee."

"You got long legs. Go get it." Mom sits beside her, checking her phone with a frown. "You hear they found Adams West?"

Claude vaults up again. "No way."

"That's what they say." She reads the article aloud, then *hmm*s. "I doubt they'll ever find that gun. Anna's Run probably sank it."

"Are they really just going to assume it's the first improbable hobo who turns up dead?" Claude says.

Mom lifts one shoulder. "As much as I'd like to agree with you about the ineptitude of the police, for *her* sake I do hope there's evidence they're not revealing in the press release."

"Yeah." Claude gets up from the couch and grabs a cup, filling it with steaming coffee. She glances over to make sure Mom hasn't turned toward her, then pours more into a thermos. She shoves it into a corner, then turns and leans against the counter, bringing her mug up to her lips. "Um."

Her innocent tone immediately rouses suspicion. Mom turns and arches an eyebrow at her daughter.

"When Steve's done plowing the driveway, do you think I could go out for a little while?"

"It's been a day and a half since you got arrested," Mom says. "You need to lie low."

Claude takes a long sip of coffee. "It's not a school day. We're not running the rumor mill."

"Everyone in town is going to wonder what you're doing, Claude." Mom sighs. "Why now?"

"I need to see Jamie."

She meant to say a different lie, but as the words hang between them, she realizes she means it. Something in her twists like an invisible knife. There are things Jamie deserves to know. Just like there are things he *can't* know.

It's the same with Mom, really. Except the things she deserves to know and the things she can't know are all muddled up together and Claude can't figure out how to distinguish them.

"It's not like you to get worked up about a boy," Mom says.

It would be trite to say *Jamie's different*, so Claude just says, "Yeah." She stares into her cup, and the flush in her cheeks deepens as the silence grows.

At last Mom gets up from the couch. Claude's the tallest one in the house now, but as Mom wraps her arms around her, the girl folds in, pressing her forehead against her mother's shoulder.

"Claude, you know I'm here for you," Mom says. "And Jamie's nice, and he'd be a great boyfriend. But he can wait to be your boyfriend for another week."

"It's not that," Claude says.

Mom pulls back and puts a hand on Claude's shoulder. "Then what is it?"

Her brown eyes are serious, piercing. Claude looks down first. "Nothing, I guess," she says, but a bitterness seeps through her words.

Mom's hand tightens on Claude's shoulder, and Claude tenses. "I know you don't like boundaries. And I know I've encouraged you to live your own life and make your own mistakes. But maybe . . . that was the wrong call."

"No, Mom," Claude says reflexively.

"You were arrested," Mom points out. "You've been selling pills."

"It's not . . ." Claude runs a hand through her hair. Blond is starting to peek out at the root. "It's not because of you, Mom." Heat flushes over her body.

Mom's waiting for her to say something more. But Mom can't know. Not yet.

For a long moment they stand, waiting for the other one to say something. Claude can't meet her mother's gaze. The silence is only broken by the sound of Mom's phone.

She goes over to it. "Jesus Christ," she mutters, then answers. "Seriously? On a Saturday?"

Claude can't distinguish the tinny chatter on the other end, but she recognizes its urgent tone. Mom listens, then sighs. "Fine. We're snowed in until ten, but after that . . . fine. I'm getting overtime pay, right? Yeah, well, same to you." She hangs up and tosses the phone on the couch.

"I have to go back in," she says. "Claude, I'm sorry, but you have to stay home today, please. Do I have to take your keys?"

Claude swallows. "No."

Mom glares at her a moment. Then she nods. "Good. Come have a doughnut with me."

As soon as she's sure Mom's gone, Claude hops into Janine and heads out of the neighborhood at a pulse-raising fifteen miles per hour. The snow has only thickened, turning the world gray upon gray until it's hard to see which parts are road. Her windshield wipers pulse furiously, her fingers tap on the wheel.

The cheer team probably should've stayed home, but nothing makes parents fanatical like school sports and competitions. A top-heavy bus is somewhere out there, careening along mountain roads as the snow falls quicker, eliminating the world around them, blurring the distinction between mountain and air. Claude imagines it skidding around hairpin turns with a horde of shrieking cheerleaders and lacrosse play-ers inside. Then she takes a deep breath, and focuses on the road, and tries not to imagine anything.

She pulls right up to Jamie's house instead of stopping at the park like normal. Wind whistles down from the mountain and hammers against her car, making her fight to get out. She lets go of the car door and it slams shut. Snow sticks to her jacket as she hurries up the drive.

She pushes the bell before she can chicken out. Then she only has a few moments to worry about who'll open the door before it cracks.

It's him. "Claude?" Jamie cranes his neck, checking for his mom behind him. "Come in, but be quiet," he hisses.

"I can't come in." There's a hot thermos of coffee in her car, and someone in the woods who needs it. "I just . . ." And then Claude Vanderly's floundering on a boy's doorstep, try-ing to muster her courage. She never thought she'd be here.

His hair sticks up like he's just washed it. Claude catches the faint trace of his shampoo, an orange-scented monstrosity she used to tease him about. Now the smell stirs memories of early mornings in the crook of an arm and stifled giggles in the shower as his mom knocks on the door. The electric feel-ing of sneaking up to his house after midnight, the look on his face when he's thinking about kissing her.

He's got that look on his face now. That mixed with con-fusion. And Claude shouldn't do it, but an invisible hook pulls her forward and she presses her lips to his. Jamie tastes like hot cocoa and milk. He tastes like lazy mornings and the last days of school vacation. "You're beautiful," she says softly against him.

He pushes her gently away. Then he steps out and shuts the door. His eyes are a little glazed. He brings a hand to the corner of his mouth. "Are you okay?" he says.

She almost laughs. But it's a fair question. "No." Claude takes a deep breath. "If I were, maybe—" She lets the words hang, unsure of how to finish.

Jamie doesn't think about *maybe*. He puts his hands on her arms, rubbing up and down as if to warm her. "What's wrong?" She shakes her head. "You can tell me," he persists.

Her eyes grow hot. "I can't," she says, and surprises them both with the anger in her voice. Jamie freezes. "It's not—" Why is this so hard? She shakes him off to run a hand through her hair, dislodging snow. Jamie withdraws his arms. His hazel eyes are open and honest in their hurt. It was one of the things that drew Claude to him. It's one of the things that make things worse now. And she knows she owes him *some* kind of explanation, even if she can't tell him the whole truth.

"When all this blows over, maybe we could give it a shot." Jamie looks at her blankly. "I mean, being together." Those hazel eyes widen. "I just can't right now, okay? There's too much—" *Happening. At stake. About to hit the fan.* Something hot lands on her cheek, traces down to her chin.

"Claude, what's going on?" Jamie looks like he doesn't believe her. "What has to blow over? Is this about Emma?"

She can't tell him. She's too afraid that he wouldn't believe the whole truth. She's too generous with her body, isn't she?

She can hear the hissing in the halls. *Asking for it. Never said no before. Serves her right.*

"Claude." He puts a hand on her shoulder and she can't help leaning into it. "Do you know something? Should we go to the police?"

She shakes her head again. Tears spin from her eyelashes.

"Then . . . what do we do?"

"*You* don't do anything. That's the point. Just—steer clear of me, all right? And when it's all over, maybe I'll come find you."

"No." His hand tightens on her shoulder. "You said you didn't want to be together, and if you don't want it, I don't want it. But now my friend's unhappy, and I need to help." He swallows. Claude dares to look up. There's a crease between his brows, and his forehead is red from the effort of keeping tears of his own in. His hand slides down her shoulder to her bare hand, cold and half numb from the wind. She almost gasps at the warmth of him, and he squeezes her fingers. "I *want* to help you, Claude. Just tell me how."

Claude swallows. She brushes away her tears with her free hand. "You don't get it. You can't help me."

His jaw sets. "No, *you* don't get it. I'm not going to let it go until you tell me what I can do."

Claude makes a noise that's half hiccup, half sob. Of all the not-so-shining knights she's laid, this is the one who stuck around. "Okay. You want to help?"

He nods.

"Do you trust me?"

Another nod.

Claude takes a deep breath. "Lend me your shovel. And *don't follow me*."

By the time she reaches Anna's tree, snow has leaked through the bags around her Doc Martens and her feet are soaked. She slicks along the bank, cursing under her breath. The river waits, hungry, just to the other side.

Claude nudges snow aside until she hits frozen dirt, then uses the tip of the shovel like a pick to break it. *Bad idea. Bad idea.* As she leans on the shovel and starts to sweat, the words build up to a mantra. The snow muffles all sounds, but nothing can truly silence Anna. Wind blows snow down the back of her coat and into her eyes, weaves through the forks and knives and shoes and bras, all the sacrifices tied to Anna's tree. They knock together like they're laughing. Claude mutters her favorite swear words and steps on the shovel. Part of her waits for shouts and the sound of boots on snow. But everyone else is smart enough to stay inside, and all she hears is the low voice of the wind and the click and clack of the detritus above her.

She cuts the dirt away in slivers until the skin on her palms is raw. She cuts until her breath comes in ragged gasps and she can't swear anymore. She hacks until finally, finally, she hears the *chink* of metal on metal. She tosses the shovel aside and kneels, brushing at the dirt with shaking fingers until she finally wraps them around the barrel of a gun.

<u>Diary Entry</u>

Emma Baines—September 7, 2018

I wish I was dead.

I wish he'd just killed me. It would have been preferable. Preferable to living in this body and remembering every goddamn second of it.

I trusted you. I trusted all of you, and where did that get me? Praying that I'll get hit by a bus in the morning. Because what's the point, when this is what living gets you? I tried to be good, and honest, and full of integrity. And then this.

I wish I was dead.

I wish I was dead.

I wish I was dead I wish I was dead I wish I was dead I wish I was dead I wish I was dead I wish I was dead I wish I was dead I wish I was dead I wish I was dead I wish I was dead I wish I was dead I wish I was dead I wish I was dead I wish I was dead I wish I was dead I wish I was dead I wish I was dead I wish I was dead

25

THE CORNERED

Concentrating too much on her phone gives her a headache and makes her queasy, but Avery can't help it. Every time the phone buzzes, she gets a tingle in her belly that has nothing to do with car sickness, or nerves about the competition. The bus lurches but she looks at her message again.

I'm sick of keeping up appearances. After this weekend I'm ready. Consequences be damned.

If ur sure, she writes back. My parents are gonna freak but we can talk them down. Just so u know.

Lyla pops up over her shoulder and she flips the phone down into her lap. "What's up?" Lyla says. "You missed the last three cheers."

"Sorry." Avery taps the phone as it buzzes again. "I'm just, um . . ."

"Preoccupied?" Lyla hangs over the seat. "Anything going on? Anything I can help with, as, you know, your *friend*?"

Avery puts on her Happy Avery smile and shakes her head. "I'm fine."

"'Cause Michael looks really pissed. At you."

Avery risks a peek around her seat. Michael sits at the back of the bus with the lacrosse team, who are playing a game against the Greeley Steelers on Sunday. His arms are folded and he stares out the window at the blanket of white that flurries around them. As if he can feel her, he turns. Their eyes meet for a fraction of a second before she jerks back.

He could've driven himself up tomorrow. She doesn't know why he came on the bus. Except because he said he would, and he likes to keep up appearances. He's almost as concerned with them as the Cross family.

"Wow, Aves. Weird much?" Lyla says. When a freshman looks over she lowers her voice. "What happened?"

Avery swallows. "I'll tell you later." When Lyla's accompanying scream of rage won't alert the entire bus. "I'll be in the right headspace when we get there. Promise." She holds up a pinkie.

Lyla gives her an *I know this is bullshit* look but hooks her pinkie and they shake.

"Lyla, seat belt." Mr. G leans over them with a sharp expression to match his voice. Lyla flops into her seat and buckles. "Avery?" Mr. Garson says. "Everything all right?

"I'm fine." She turns her smile a little wobbly. "Just a little carsick."

His mouth turns up. "Should I confiscate your phone? It might help if you stop looking at it."

"No," Avery snaps.

Half the bus turns to look at her. It's all she can do to keep from clapping a hand over her mouth. Mr. G's smile flattens. "There's no need for that tone. Put your phone away." He turns and goes up to the front of the bus as Avery's stomach lurches.

"Jeez. Someone forgot his happy pill this morning," Lyla mutters through the gap in the seats.

Avery watches Mr. G until he sits down again at the front of the bus, in his designated chaperone seat, and gets out his own phone while talking to Mrs. Halifax and Mr. Pendler. A moment later, Avery's phone buzzes again. She checks to make sure no one's looking before she flips the screen around.

It's going to be such a relief. Don't worry about your parents. Soon you'll be 18 and they can't boss you around anymore 😑

Yeah right 😑, Avery writes back. See you tonight?

Even in a world-class blizzard, Greeley smells like cow. The stench permeates everything—the snow, the wind, the bus as they get closer, and the Stadion Hotel that will serve as their base for the competition.

Shay and Lyla scream as the bus doors open and the first blast of cold wind streams inside. Mr. G claps for them to settle down. "Thank you, girls, for breaking my eardrums," he says. Everyone giggles. "Grab your bags and get into the lobby."

They start to file out. Avery can't leave fast enough. She needs the fresh air, even if it smells like sewage. She needs the cold. She needs freedom. She thought getting out of Lorne would do it.

She was wrong.

The bus driver and Shay's mom are working together to haul gym bags from the bus's innards. Avery grabs hers and heads for the lobby, skipping around Michael and keeping her eyes on the ground.

"Hey, can we—" he says, but she doesn't look up and she doesn't stop. Let the other girls whisper about it. Let them wonder.

"Your ankle looks good," he yells after her.

Her ankle. Crap. She feels the eyes of Michael and half the cheer team on her as she goes.

"We're late."

"Relax," Lyla says as she tries their keycard for the third time. "Everything's going to be fine. Not like the competition can start on time in this weather." The lock finally beeps, and she opens the door to their room.

"You want the bed near the window or the door?" Lyla says as they enter. The beds are equally dismal singles that sag in the middle.

Avery dumps her bag on the nearest white comforter. "I don't care. Let's just get changed and get back downstairs."

"Aves, calm down." Lyla's ponytail swings as she cocks her head, suspicion written across her features. "It's going to be fine."

Avery shucks her shirt and shimmies out of her jeans. "It's not going to be fine. I'm captain. I have to be on time and ready." She pulls on her shorts and shirt. Then she looks over to where Lyla peers into the mirror. "What are you doing?"

"Do I have a zit on my chin?" Lyla beckons, jutting out her chin.

"We don't have time for this." Fear makes Avery's voice sharp. "No one's going to see it anyway, so just get your uniform on."

"So I *do* have one."

"*Lyla*," Avery explodes.

Lyla steps back. Avery realizes too late that she's breathing hard and she can't focus. "What the hell, girl?" Lyla says. "What's gotten into you?" Her eyes flicker down to Avery's ankle.

Avery focuses on the lie, bouncing on her toes. "I said we had to get ready. If we don't show, we forfeit and lose our place in the competition."

Lyla doesn't buy it. "Is this about Michael? You said you'd have your A game ready to go by the time we got here. Don't get pissy on me 'cause you guys have broken up or whatever."

"That's not what I'm pissy about," Avery half shouts.

"Then *what*?" Lyla snaps.

The knock makes them both jump. "Girls?" Mr. G says through the door. "Past time to go."

Avery gives Lyla her best *I told you so* glare. Lyla rolls her eyes. In less than twenty seconds, she's dressed.

Avery opens the door just as Mr. G's about to knock again. "It's fine—we're here," she says a little breathlessly. Mr. G raises an eyebrow at her.

"Let's go kick some ass—uh, sorry, Mr. G," Lyla says as she closes the door behind them.

"After you, ladies," Mr. G says. "I just need to run back for something."

Avery doesn't realize she left her phone in the room until they've reached the gym.

The first team in the competition heads to the floor, and the bass makes the lockers around Avery shake. Ford River High School has a newly lacquered floor, new bleachers for their parents to sit on, and a new sound system to deafen them. The smell of fresh paint and sweat is almost enough to knock Avery out. She takes a long drink of Gatorade and ushers the team in close. "This wasn't an easy semester," she says. "And maybe this is as far as we get this year. But we're going to give it all we've got, for Emma. And because we want to be the best cheer squad in northern Colorado. "

"For Emma," the others murmur.

Are you ready to go? Lyla mouths. Avery nods. She wants to throw up.

The door to the locker room opens and the previous team files in. "Good luck," says their cheer captain with a clear lack of sincerity.

"The Jefferson-Lorne Wolf Pack!" calls an announcer, and out they go. Avery takes her place as the captain, front and center. Mr. Pendler's eyes seem to pin her in place.

So Avery Cross does what she does best. She lifts her chin, looks right at him, and smiles her perfect smile. They launch into action.

Her team is good. Natalie's a little too cautious with the

lift, but they make up their quarter-beat delay and get into the rebound with perfect synchronization. Everyone's smile is real, adrenaline fueled. Even Avery's by now. They move in sharp, precise lines. And the reality is they're better than they ever were when Emma was with them.

You only ever held us back, Avery thinks, and her smile flickers a little as they take their final pose. The crowd roars for them like a river, hungry for more. For a sacrifice of young girls who will dance and pose and parade for them.

They place second. Their execution was near perfect, but their choreography lacks originality, says a judge who looks like she eats trolls for breakfast. The rest of the squad screams. Shay jumps up and down. Natalie might be crying. Mrs. Halifax gives Avery a surprising bear hug, and Mr. Pendler and Mr. G both pat her on the shoulder. "Good job." Mr. G squeezes as he hands her the second-place trophy and they all pose.

"Ohmygod," Shay says. "I've never won anything so *cool!*" She does a back handspring and nearly kicks Mr. Pendler in the face.

And then Michael is there, behind Avery. He's got flowers. Of course. "Congrats," he says, and holds them out. Avery can feel the air crystallize around them, just as she can feel the stare of her team. All they need is a bucket of popcorn to pass around, she thinks bitterly.

"Thanks," she says, taking the flowers without touching his hand.

He looks at her for a moment, then nods to himself. Then he turns away.

Mr. G claps three times. "All right, everyone. Hop on the bus. Dinner's on JLH!"

Everyone except Avery cheers.

They jog to the bus, whooping and screeching along the way. Avery welcomes the blast of warm air as she clambers in. She leans up against the window and spreads her hoodie over her lap.

The seat shifts next to her as someone sits down. Avery turns. "I don't really—"

"Did you cheat on him?" Lyla asks.

Avery stares at her, mouth open.

"It's colder between you two than it is outside. And I know you weren't with him on Wednesday night."

"Shh," Avery implores her. She looks toward the front of the bus, where their chaperones stand ticking names off a clipboard. Mr. G nods to the driver and the bus pulls out of the parking lot. "Can we talk about this later?" Avery asks.

"Will you tell me the truth?" Lyla retorts.

Avery pushes her forehead against the cold glass. "I didn't realize you liked Michael so much," she says, and her voice has a stony edge.

"You idiot," Lyla sighs, and she pulls her knees up. "I'm your best friend. I'm your best friend and you've been lying to me. I'm mad, but it's because I want to be there for you."

You can't, Avery doesn't say.

"Anyway. Party in our room, right?" Lyla doesn't wait for her to answer. "Shay *says* she snuck in some of her dad's, you know, special stuff. But last time it was watered down and super gross. I brought orange juice to help with the taste."

Avery looks out the window. She feels his eyes on her the whole way back to the hotel.

They round up in the hotel lobby. Mr. G claps for attention again. "Girls, you did a great job," he says. "I've just called Principal Mendoza, and he's really proud of you. A lot of these other schools have better funding and a bigger student population to choose from, but you're more hardworking, talented, and dedicated than any of those guys. Good work, Avery." The team claps. Shay and Natalie wolf whistle. Lyla gives her a half hug. "You made a great team and a great routine—no matter what that bitch of a judge says. Oops!" He covers his mouth in mock guilt as the team shrieks with laughter. Mrs. Halifax glares at him. "Forgot I wasn't supposed to say stuff like that. But really. Relax for twenty minutes, dinner's a five o'clock buffet. Show up on time if you don't want me to eat all the cake."

"I'm going to take a shower," Lyla says as they disperse. She shoots Avery a *come upstairs and dish* look.

When they get back to the room, Avery grabs her swimsuit and towel instead. "I'm going for a swim." She fishes through her bag. "Have you seen my phone?" There's nothing in here but an empty jolly rancher wrapper and a folded note—god, it's probably from Michael.

"Seriously?" Lyla moves to block the door. "Aves, talk to me."

She can't. She'll throw up. If she keeps lying to Lyla, she'll hate herself. But Lyla wouldn't buy the truth. "After dinner." She pushes past Lyla and flees down the hall.

Her skin feels tight and itchy. She wants to scrub it until

Avery peels away and someone new can step out. Someone brasher, louder, angrier. Avery wants to be all of these things, but she's too scared. The fear pushes into her brain, taking up space until she can't think of anything else. Of what to say to Lyla, or Michael, or the rest of the team, or the police back in Lorne.

The postage stamp of a pool already has someone swimming in it. Avery goes to the sauna, where she can be alone. The heat hits like a wall, burning her lungs. For a blissful moment, she forgets everything.

She takes a seat on the oak bench. There's something green growing on the underside but she doesn't care. A basin of water sits in the corner, next to the box of oven-hot stones. Avery closes her eyes. *Soon.* Soon it will all be over. But then what? College? She wants to go to college so that she can live with her friends and make chocolate cupcakes at four in the morning and cram for tests together in big libraries with leather-bound books. She doesn't know what she'd major in, and she won't be granted a cheer scholarship for getting a second-place trophy at a regional competition. When she said she wanted to teach dance to kids, Dad replied with "Everyone needs a hobby." He'd never pay for her to get a teaching education. She's supposed to go to Harvard, like she'd ever get in. Maybe she can trick him into sending her to Massachusetts and just never come back.

Because once this *is* over, she won't want to set foot in Lorne ever again. She doesn't want to think about it. She doesn't want to remember.

The door opens with a gust of cold air. "Lyla," Avery groans. "We'll talk about it later."

It's not Lyla.

The lights flick out, and all Avery can see is a silhouette, dressed not for the sauna but for the cold outside, from his windbreaker jacket to his Pine Nation hiking boots.

The door closes. His body blocks the door. "Do you know what surprises me the most?" he says in a dark, low voice.

She scoots back on the bench. Maybe if she can trick him into stepping away from the door, she can squeeze out around him. "Uh," she says to mask her panic. "You're not supposed to be in here. Girls' sauna."

The hiking boots shift. "What surprises me most is that it took me this long to figure out that *you* were in on it. I thought Avery Cross couldn't trick rocks. But you got me, sweetheart." His voice turns hard, the way it did when she said no in his office. "You let me believe we shared something. But you were trying to blackmail me, weren't you?"

The hair all down her arms stands on end. "No." It sounds like a plea. She hates it, and the memories it brings. *You won't tell your parents, will you? No need to go to the nurse, is there? No one else will understand you like me, will they?* No, no, no. Always no.

The figure says, "You know how I knew? The ankle. Yesterday you limped around like you thought it was broken. Today you danced perfectly. And I mean *perfectly*." Avery shivers, pulling her towel up over her bikini. "I started wondering, *why* would Avery Cross fake an ankle injury?"

Every hair on her arm prickles. "I didn't," she says, trying to bait him, pull him away from the door. But he doesn't move. Why doesn't he move?

"You wanted all of us to be distracted. Because you wanted

to give your friend the opportunity to snoop around. If you hadn't stopped pretending, I might never have realized. Bad luck, Aves."

The air swims before her. "Why are you telling me this?"

"Because I want to know who's in on it with you. Your soppy, stupid boyfriend? Your piece on the side?" He shifts, a rustle of clothing. Sweat slides down Avery's spine. "It's funny, really. Prudish Avery is in the running for school whore." His voice twists, ugly. Angry at what she wouldn't give him willingly, wouldn't let him take.

He reaches into his pocket. Avery flinches, but he brings out a phone. The screen unlocks, and Avery realizes whose it is.

"Careless girl. All I had to do was exercise my chaperone privileges. You know cheerleaders and their wild parties. I heard your roomie wanted to take a shower. Maybe when I'm finished with you, I'll go upstairs and join her."

Avery's stomach heaves. She clamps her mouth shut. At least if he's down here, it means he's not up there. Lyla's safe.

"Who else was at Anna's Run that night? You couldn't have done this alone." Her phone lights up, illuminating the plane of his cheek. "Is it *Study Buddy*?"

Cold washes over her. She surges to her feet, nearly falling off the bench. "Leave her alone," she says. She reaches for anger, but it flickers weak within her, confused and mixed with fear.

A broad hand connects with her sternum. Her skin crawls. He pushes her back onto the bench and every muscle seizes. "I'll take that as a yes."

For a moment he lingers, hand on her bikini strap, too close to the line of her breast. She can't move, can't even think anything except *This is it*. Then he steps away and moves the thermostat with a fingernail. The heat surges. "I'm not happy about this. You've always been a good girl, and you deserved better. But I can't have you jeopardizing my whole life."

What about my life? Avery thinks. But she still can't speak, and besides, she never met a man who cared about her life.

"My records show how upset you were about Emma. Crying in class, spending lunch in my office, unable to eat. You'll be just another teen suicide for poor Jefferson-Lorne." He picks up the pot of water and upends it over the stones. They hiss and roar. Steam billows out in a thick white mass. Avery coughs, gasps, coughs again. She's drowning.

By the time she stumbles to the door, he's already on the other side.

The lock turns with a click. A cruel smile plays over his face, and he taps out something on her phone with quick fingers. He turns it to the glass.

I'm scared.

Meet me at Glenmere Park. Near Stadion.

Please hurry.

Avery hammers on the glass. But a girl her size couldn't hope to break it. Not if she were clearheaded and strong and breathing dry Colorado air.

She watches as he disappears around a corner. She tries to shout but can only muster a whimper. Her mouth is dry, and her skin burns where she touches the floor, the glass, herself.

The others are settling in to dinner. Nobody else knows she's here.

And the temperature keeps climbing.

<u>Diary Entry</u>

Emma Baines—November 12, 2018

Fuck. Fuck fuck fuck. I fucked up and I fucked up BAD.

I've known for a while. It had to be him. After everything, after he utterly destroyed me . . . but I still didn't have evidence. Not until I found the phone.

I knew it was hers as soon as I saw the cracked case. I recognized the butterfly sticker on the back, and the police never found the phone. . . . After she died, a lifetime and an innocence ago, I asked Dad about it. He said it had probably ended up in the river—there was no point in looking for it. But it wasn't in the river at all.

I should have turned it over to him. Or tipped Deputy Bryson on where to find it. Now the fingerprints will get muddled, and I can't put it back in case he's realized it's gone. I don't even know why he kept it, except a lot of sickos keep mementos of their conquests. Maybe I should've taken the pom-pom, too, the hair tie with the silver heart. But I wasn't thinking clearly.

He's going to know it's me.

I have to move quickly, but who do I tell? No one will help me. Dad won't help me—he hasn't helped for months. If I speak out, they'll pluck the words and twist them from my lips, until my truth becomes marred and ugly, unrecognizable. Why didn't you come forward before? Are you sure you aren't lying? You've always been too close to poor Lizzy, Em. It only makes sense that it'd make you unhinged.

I have to get into the phone. That's my last chance. The noose draws tight.

26

THE BURGLAR

Janine inches over the road, grumbling. "Come on," Claude breathes, tapping the steering wheel. Her phone buzzes again. This is a mess. Stay safe and INSIDE. Love u xxx. "Too late, Mom."

She pulls into a neighborhood that has yet to be plowed. Kids in snowsuits hide behind packed walls of snow, hurling snowballs. Janine becomes their target as she rumbles between them. Normally Claude would curse or roll down her window and shout. Now she just wonders if *he* watches the girls in their happy, jeering youth. If he sits on his front porch in summertime as they go by in their bathing suits with their ice cream.

The neighborhood is so . . . white middle class. So normal. When she finds the right house, she's almost disappointed to see a literal picket fence around the yard. The little square block of brick has clean windows and a picture-perfect white door adorned with a wreath. A concrete porch runs around the side of the house. So domestic.

Claude checks the address one more time, then parks

around the corner. For a moment she sits, closing her eyes against the storm. But nothing can stop the storm within.

"Get in, drop off, get out," she mutters. "Get in, drop off, get out."

She goes to her trunk and grabs the gun with gloved fingers. Her teeth worry at her lip as she tucks it in her coat pocket. Then she picks up the shovel.

She goes up to the front door first and rings the bell, listening to the tinny screech echo inside. She waits a beat, then two. But there are no footsteps, and no one comes to the door, even when she rings a second time to be sure. Her body sags and her forehead hits the screen door. She sucks in air. Her mouth floods. Claude forces herself to swallow, then traipses around the porch. The window there is small, but it's harder to see from the road, and there are no windows in the house opposite for nosy neighbors to watch her.

She yanks the strings of her hoodie and pulls her scarf up until only her eyes are visible. Then she hoists the shovel and heaves it at the glass.

The first blow sends a crack spidering out, the sound of it like a thunderclap. She crouches, trying to calm her rolling stomach, trying to control the waves of heat that wash over her. She harnesses her rage, at him and at the whole world for letting there *be* people like him. And then she thinks of the lonely girls, who needed help so desperately, who needed advice or support or freedom from their peers or parents. And he was all they got.

The world carries the silence of snowfall with it. The kids

have gone inside for hot cocoa and warm blankets and a few more years of innocence. Claude gets up again.

The second punch shatters the glass.

She picks shards out of the frame, dropping them on the porch. The window screen tore in the break, and she pulls on it until she's ripped a Claude-sized hole. Then she pushes herself up, grunting, and wiggles inside.

She slides off the linoleum counter and down to the tile floor. Everything is dark. She brushes crumbs off her coat as she stands, then pats her pocket. The gun is a reassuring lump.

Dishes stack on the side of the sink. The kitchen smells like old food and standing water. The fridge has half a pizza and three cans of Coors, and a sprouting potato in the vegetable drawer. Claude grabs a beer, wanting to take something from him—then thinks better of it, puts it back. She slams the fridge door and moves away. Her boots trail snowmelt and mud into the living room.

She stops at the front of the living room, wary of the windows and anyone who might be able to see her silhouette behind them. But the house is dark and the shades are drawn. A leather couch sits across from a TV. The glass coffee table holds magazines: *GQ*, *Runner's World*, *The Atlantic*. The bookcases are stuffed with back issues and trophies from cheerleading and lacrosse competitions. Glory years gone by. He took the lacrosse team all the way to national championships when he was captain. In between the trophies sit framed certificates. *Jefferson Lorne Educator of the Year, 2016*. That one looks official. But the *Best Cheerleading Chaperone EVER* is clearly student made, and signed. Bile rises in Claude's throat. She wonders if any of those girls let his hand creep up her thigh. If they thought it was something they should want. If they thought they only had to get through it, and then things would be better. A few console games round out the bookshelf.

It's all so . . . normal. The garbage in his wastebasket. The flannel sheets on his bed. The James Patterson book on his nightstand. The toothbrush and shaver and Head & Shoulders shampoo in his bathroom. "Get in, drop off, get out," Claude whispers, but she can't help peering under the sink, opening the drawers of his dresser. There must be something here that exposes him. How can he fool the whole world into thinking he's *normal*?

Or maybe he is normal, and that's the worst possibility of all. After all, Lily Fransen was molested by a normal everyday man, and nobody cares about her now. This is Claude's reality. The school disaster can't go up against JLH's favorite member of staff. Not unless the evidence is incontrovertible. She buzzes with electric rage. She wants to take the shovel and smash everything in the goddamn house. More than anything, she wants to smash *him*, until his face is a bloody lump. Until his outside resembles what she feels on the inside.

She pulls in a breath. *Get in, drop off, get out.* Her hands are hot in her gloves. She makes a fist and moves out of the bedroom.

The study seems like a likely place. There's a small corner desk with a lopsided office chair. More shelves hold folders labeled *Taxes* or *Receipts*. One folder has *Letters from Mom*, and

Claude's stomach flips at the idea that any woman might actually love him.

She pulls the gun from her pocket and sets it on the desk. *Get out.* But her teeth catch her lower lip again. The computer monitor blinks.

They couldn't get what they needed off the phone. Maybe they can get it here. She leans over and pushes the power button. *Get out, get out,* her blood sings, but she can't. They need every piece of the puzzle.

Now she just has to figure out his password.

The lock screen pulls up. Claude tries a couple of things off the top of her head, and she's not surprised when they fail.

She starts opening the drawers of his desk. Maybe he keeps a password list. Her gloved fingers fumble over papers and receipts. She grabs a notebook and flips through it, tearing the paper in her haste.

There. A list of random characters. They're unlabeled and they may not have anything to do with passwords at all, but it's worth a shot. She lays the notebook down, next to the gun.

The front door crashes open.

Feet thunder. Everyone's shouting. Claude's heart stampedes in her chest and her blood roars like a river. She doesn't even have time to straighten. "Got him!" shouts a voice right behind her. A minute later her chin's in the keyboard as a cop holds her head down. He pulls her arms behind her and cuffs her in quick, brutal motions.

He turns her around and rips the scarf off her face. Then his eyes widen. "We got a *she*," he yells.

More cops pile into the room. Their bulletproof vests are on, and their guns are out. Deputy Chief Bryson snorts when he sees her. "Small-time dealing not enough for you these days?"

"Who ratted me out?" Claude asks. *Please not Jamie. Please not him.*

"Home security system. Technology's a wonder, ain't it?" Bryson moves in, knowing that she wants to lean back but can't, using his size and his smell and her fear to make her tremble. "Think your mom can get you out of this one?" He smiles, all teeth and shadow in the snowy gloom.

His eyes move behind her, and his smile widens as he sees the gun.

TO: Will Tabor

FROM: Detective Diego Loya

DATE: December 8, 2018, 7:12 PM.

SUBJECT: Forensics study and preliminary examination—handgun—case number 27-95-1682

We're sending over a Smith & Wesson M & P Shield 9mm, serial number SKU207248 that we suspect belonged to Randy Silverman, found in the possession of another suspect. Please run prints and ballistics ASAP, this case is of highest priority.

Thank you.

THE RUNNER

The wire itches under Gwen's shirt. She pinned it so carefully that Mum wouldn't even see its shadow as they sat down to breakfast. She's been every inch the perfect girl today. The damn microphone was enough to remind her what was at stake. But then she started wondering if the wire had a transmitting limit, and then Avery texted her he's here on the bus, and she's not sure exactly how she got to the point where she was liberating Dad's truck, but she's almost in Greeley now and her phone pinged with messages every time she got Wi-Fi and she's been praying for the last forty miles, *Don't take me now, Mary. I'll really owe you one. Except I won't turn straight for you or go to church.*

She taps the brakes and the truck slides through a stop sign. She drifts and catches traction on the other side of the empty intersection, and Gwen lets herself exhale.

Her phone rings again, and she risks a glance. Mum. Like the last sixteen times. She doesn't need to pick up; she knows she's grounded for the rest of her life—assuming she makes it home again. She left them a note, and she thought about writing why. About saying, *This is for Lizzy and for us*. In the end, she just wrote, *I'll be okay, don't worry. Please don't be mad at me. I love you.*

Of course they're mad. Just like she was mad at Lizzy's note. Unlike Lizzy, she'll be able to explain when she gets home. If she gets home.

But things are happening too fast. She recalls the pale moon of Avery's face outside her window last night, wide-eyed with fear. Avery gasping: "They found him."

No one really made a contingency plan for what happened if Randy Silverman washed up in a bend of the river. Gwen supposes it was stupid now, to hope that he might be considered an unconnected death. So she let Avery in, and she made a plan, and she kissed Aves and said it would be fine. She had the feeling, even then, that she was lying.

She's been trying not to think about him for three days. About the way he crumpled, the sound his body made as it hit the earth like a loose bag of cement.

She pulls into the parking lot of the Stadion Greeley and lets the truck roll inexorably up against a curb. Then she grabs her phone.

Where are you? Her finger hovers over the call button, but if she calls the police might overhear. They'd wonder what she was doing in Greeley when she wasn't supposed to leave Lorne. Avery's last text was about Glenmere Park. Why would she want to meet in Glenmere Park?

The phone lights up, making her jump. But it's Mum.

Again. "Hell on wheels, isn't it?" Gwen mutters in her mother's voice. It's easier than acknowledging the stab in her heart. Mum's going to think that she's just like Lizzy. She doesn't realize that Gwen's trying to save Lizzy, the only way she can now.

I'm here, she texts after a few minutes, and gets out of the car.

The parking lot of the Stadion is dead except for the bus that drove the cheer team. As Gwen enters the lobby, she spots Natalie at the desk. She ducks behind a pillar. The heat of a properly warmed building burns her cheeks. She glances around for any sign of him, but the rest of the lobby is empty. Natalie waits at the desk for a while, tapping one foot, then says a cheerful "Thank you" to the receptionist before bouncing back toward the dining area. Through blurred glass Gwen can see shapes and colors, shifting and swirling. Is Avery among them?

No. If she's scared, she'd pretend to have a headache and stay in her room. So with a final glance toward the dining room, Gwen forges into the open and approaches reception.

She feels as though she's in a sniper's sight. If he catches her—if anyone notices her and tells him she's here—then it won't just be her ass on the line. She should've told Avery to just lie low. To not give him an excuse to suspect her. What could he do on a school trip? She should be back in Lorne, dealing with the gun. Making sure Avery's safe when she returns.

She's at the desk. The receptionist purses his lips at her. "Yes?"

"I'm here to see my sister," she says. "She forgot something for the competition."

"You can go into the dining hall, but if you want to eat you'll have to pay for it," he says.

"I was thinking I could just drop it off in her room? Avery Cross." She stands on tiptoes, as though he might have a convenient list of cheerleaders and their rooms right behind the desk.

He sighs. She resists the urge to look at the door to the dining room as he taps at something. "Sure. Room 202."

She turns and walks toward the stairs, trying not to break into a run. "You're welcome," he calls after her.

She takes the stairs two at a time until she makes it to the second floor. Her knock on room 202 is too prim, but she can't risk calling out. She listens for movement on the other side of the door, and her heart leaps as she hears a light footfall.

The door opens. It's not Avery.

Lyla gapes. Gwen's mouth falls open.

Lyla gathers herself first. "What are *you* doing here?" she says, loud enough for the entire hall to hear.

Gwen's heart jolts. "Can I come in?"

"Uh, no—" Lyla says, but Gwen shoulders her aside and slips into the room.

Avery's open gym bag sits on her neatly made bed. "Where's Avery?"

"She's avoiding me. She doesn't want to . . . Wait . . ." Lyla's eyes widen. Her hands fly up to her mouth.

Gwen ignores Lyla and goes over to the bag. Maybe

Avery's just out. Maybe she left her phone in here. Gwen's fingers have started to shake. She turns over tiny bottles of shampoo, shaving foam, bath gel.

"Oh my god," Lyla says through her fingers. "*Ohmygod. Avery's been cheating on Michael with you?*"

"*Lyla.*" Gwen grits her teeth. "Please. Where's Avery?" She turns back to the gym bag. If the phone's just here—

Her fingers close around a scrap of paper.

"Oh my god, no wonder she didn't tell me anything. Don't you realize Aves can do so much better than you?"

Gwen whirls on her, crumpling the note in her fist. Lyla steps back. "Where. Is. Avery. Right. Now." She can't get her breath back. She can't shake the anger. She wants to hit something. Not Lyla. *Not Lyla.*

"Like I said, she's been avoiding me. She didn't show for dinner."

Gwen can't breathe. There's a pain in her chest, so sharp and shooting she almost doubles over. She can't do this again. She bolts for the door.

"We're going to have a little chat, you and I. If I don't just tell her to dump you," Lyla calls as the door slams. Gwen doesn't care. She only hopes Avery's still around to be affected by girlfriend drama. Her fingers squeeze, tighter and tighter around the note, written in spiky all caps:

Good girls deserve favors. Bad girls deserve the water.

Glenmere Park is black on white, trees on snow. The world ends in a cloud and flurries, but as Gwen runs past playgrounds and over the asphalt path, it resolves into a lake, spiderweb cracks shooting through thin ice. The world is silent but for her boots, crunching on snow, and her breath, ragged and clouding the night. The lake glows. She looks for a dark hole in its surface, looks for telltale footprints headed out to the ice, but she finds nothing.

No one's here.

Gwen scans the trees as she goes, slipping in her worn-down boots. She opens her mouth to call out. But she can't bring herself to do it. If Avery *is* still here—if Avery's still alive—he might be here, too. Waiting for both of them to reveal themselves.

Her lungs burn but she keeps running. She trips over a root, she slides on the path and has to catch herself with one hand. She keeps running. She circles the park twice. No one. She can't stop now. Giving up means failing, and she promised herself she wouldn't do that.

She promised Lizzy she wouldn't do that. She'd been too late in Lizzy's life; she'd sworn not to make the same mistake in death.

Her feet slip and she hits the ground with a thud.

She can't get up. There's no one to get up for.

She fails everyone in her life. Her parents, who deserve a good daughter who does what she's told. Avery, who dumped her perfectly decent boyfriend for this. Lizzy, who needed help and not judgment. Who needed someone to believe her, and to believe in her. Who died angry and afraid and alone, tumbling down a ravine. Who called but never got an answer.

Gwen tucks her knees up to her chin. Snow sears a face hot with tears and desperation. Gwen's life story: just a little too behind. If only she'd driven faster to get here. If only she'd called. If only she'd picked up the phone.

If only she'd been a better sister.

Gwen hugs her knees. Then her hand goes to her pocket, to Lizzy's note folded like a talisman. *I love you, Pilipala. Please don't be mad.*

"I love you, too," she whispers.

And the sobs come, thick and angry and hopeless, swallowed up by the storm. Gwen squeezes her eyes shut as though she can push out everything that hurts.

She doesn't see the figure at the edge of the trees. She doesn't hear him step out of the shadows.

28

THE LIVING GIRL

The world burns.

Avery passed the *I'm going to throw up* point some endless minutes ago. Everything tilts around her. Her throat is fire, her skin is melting. She'd close her eyes, but even blinking hurts. She slouches against the door and tries one last time to hit the glass, but she knows it's useless. Even stupid Avery can tell when it's time to give up. Her heart feels slow, each beat a stab in her chest. Everything fuzzes at the edges—the oak benches, the curve of her hand. The *ping* of the sauna seems far away.

There are worse ways to die. Hurtling over the edge of a slope, or crashing through icy water, at the mercy of a cruel current.

She hears a click. And then Avery knows she's in trouble, because she's falling and the air around her has turned cold, and isn't that what happens when you get heat stroke?

"What the hell?" Two arms reach under her body and pull. *No, no, no,* she thinks. He's back. And instead of leaving her to die, he's going to do something worse.

"What the hell were you doing in there, Aves?" Something presses against her hand. A water bottle. She fumbles at the cap and more competent fingers take over. She squints at them. *Focus.* Then she dares to look up.

Michael holds the bottle up to her mouth. She grips it and tips. Goose bumps rise all along her arms as she drinks, and water sluices over her chin. Her body racks with a shiver. Is water supposed to be this cold? It hurts to drink.

"Avery, what's going on. Are you . . . ?" Michael bends down until she can't help but look him in the eye. "Were you trying to . . . ?"

He thinks she was trying to kill herself. Avery forces a rusty laugh. "The door was locked from the outside," she points out. She pushes to her feet, but vertigo sends her right back down.

"Don't." Michael puts a hand on her shoulder. "What do you need?"

She needs to go. "More water."

He goes over to the tap. "I didn't see you at dinner. I thought maybe you'd stopped eating again. I thought maybe it was because I'm here. Then Lyla said you went for a swim, and . . . who locked you in?"

Would he believe her if she told him?

"Was it one of the girls?" A shadow crosses his face.

She takes the bottle and drinks again. Then she grabs her towel and uniform from the cubbyhole next to the sauna. She leans against the wall as she pulls her shorts over her still-wet bathing suit. "I have to go." Gwen's in danger. "Can I borrow your phone?"

"Hang on. You can't go anywhere. You have to sit down. You have to drink water." Michael brandishes the empty bottle. "We have to call the police."

Avery's life has been full of men telling her what to do. She's sort of done with it now. She draws herself up. "I *need* your phone," she says. She doesn't shout, and she doesn't cry. Her voice doesn't even tremble.

Michael stares for a moment. Then he fumbles in his pocket.

"Thank you."

She leans forward then and wraps her arms around him. His arms stiffen, and even when he returns the hug, he doesn't completely relax. Poor, confused Michael. "I'm sorry about everything," she says. Now her voice *does* tremble, but she might not get the chance to say this ever again. "You deserved better."

It's time to go.

She jams her feet into her shoes and heads up the back stairwell. A uniformed officer leans against the lobby desk, and the receptionist looks grave.

He's here for her. She doesn't have much time.

She ducks through the restaurant and leaves out the side door onto the patio. Slipping between closed umbrellas and stacked plastic chairs, she hops the thigh-high fence and hurries into the parking lot. The outside air is pure relief.

Glenmere Park. She checks the map on Michael's phone and sets off. The world is so quiet out here that she can hear her own heartbeat beginning to speed up.

She writes to Gwen. Its aves. DONT CALL. He has my phone. I dont know where he is. Text where u are.

The snow has lessened since their drive up, and now it falls in tiny flakes that rest on the hairs of her arm. She pads across the road, trying not to shiver, and onto the running path that circles Glenmere Park.

She checks Michael's phone. Nothing. Maybe Gwen isn't getting WiFi. Maybe she can't check her phone. Maybe she's planning what to write, or maybe she didn't even fall for his trick. Maybe she's not in Greeley at all.

If Avery called, she'd hear Gwen's voice and know she was all right.

She didn't realize how much she needed that until now.

The night is so silent. Her breath rasps like some beast. As the cold and wet sting her, it becomes harder to remember she's no longer in Lorne. It's that night. She is running for her life. Hearing the cock of a gun, the roar of the river. Screams.

Something breaks through her fear. A shuffling, broken sound. It reaches into her heart and squeezes in new, painful ways. Her feet turn toward it, and as she runs she sees a dark smudge on the ground. It takes on shape until she recognizes the fall of Gwen's hair, the faded black of her fraying coat.

She's lying on the ground. *Why is she lying on the ground?*

Avery runs. She runs faster than she knew she could. She doesn't notice the figure that has detached itself from the trees, who now steps hastily back.

"Gwen," she gasps, skidding and falling to her knees next to Gwen's body.

Gwen opens red eyes. Her face glistens in the dim light. "You're here?" she whispers.

Avery eases her up. "I'm here." She leans Gwen forward until they touch, head to shoulder, arms sliding around each other slowly like that first, uncertain time. "Did he—did anything—?"

Gwen shakes her head. "What about you?"

"He tried," Avery says, so fiercely that a laugh escapes Gwen, high and hysterical and accompanied by a fresh wave of tears.

She pulls back. "I'm sorry," she chokes.

Avery pulls up the edge of Gwen's scarf and starts to dab at her cheeks, pressing gently. "It's okay," she whispers. "Don't be sorry. It's okay." Even though it's so, so far from okay.

"But I wasn't there for you." Tears drip onto Avery's hand.

She turns her hand to cup Gwen's cheek. Those brown eyes, always so guarded, are finally vulnerable, and the hurt in them makes her want to crumble. More than that, it makes her want to be strong. To stand in the way of anything that might come at Gwen, and to turn it aside. She presses her forehead to Gwen's, then her nose, then her mouth. Gwen shudders against her. Her lips taste like salt and need. Her fingers contract around Avery's arms, and she presses forward, easing Avery's mouth open with her tongue, kissing like it's the last chance she'll ever get.

But when they pull apart at last, the despair hasn't left her eyes.

"It's not your fault," Avery says. "It's never your fault."

Like it wasn't her fault, or Claude's fault, or Lizzy's fault, or Emma's fault.

"Tell me it's going to be okay again," Gwen murmurs, and Avery knows she doesn't believe her.

"It's going to be okay. It's going to be okay." She leans forward and kisses Gwen. "It's going to be okay." One kiss for every time she says it.

They both hear it—footfalls on snow. Gwen freezes. "He's here," she whispers.

Avery wants to freeze, too. But she can't. She has someone to protect. She turns, thinking of what she can use as a weapon, knowing her fists won't be good enough.

"Put your hands in the air! Now!"

It's the police.

"Up. UP!"

Avery and Gwen jerk their arms up. Avery squints in the sudden glare of half a dozen flashlights, all pointed at her.

Two hands pull her away from Gwen. "Avery Cross?" says a gruff voice she doesn't recognize.

"Yes," she says. *It's going to be okay.*

"You're under arrest, on suspicion of murder." The cop all but pulls her to her feet. "We found the gun." He rattles off her juvenile Miranda rights. "Maybe if you come quietly, you can get a good plea deal."

It's going to be okay. It's going to be okay. They're safe now, from the worst of the monsters. From the monsters that lurk in the trees of Glenmere Park, watching the parade of officers and teens march to the Stadion Hotel parking lot, where red and blue flash in concert. The monster whose face contorts with rage as his quarry escapes again. The monster who slips into the hotel lobby while the rest of the cheer team stands, staring.

THE LORNE EXAMINER ONLINE
December 8, 2018, 7:45 P.M.
Three Teens Arrested for Murder of Fourth

On December 5, Emma Baines disappeared. Tonight, the Jefferson-Lorne Police department made three arrests.

The girls had all been questioned before. One has been skirting a juvenile detention record. One had a fierce academic competition with Emma and comes from a broken home. One took prescription drugs and may have lured Emma into a homosexual relationship.

"The girls all had holes in their stories, but there were too many variables, too many alibis to give us a clear path toward one," said Deputy Chief Bryson, the spokesperson on this case. "Once we started looking at it as a possible team effort, a lot of things fell into place."

Emma was well liked at her high school, Jefferson-Lorne, though her busy schedule meant she had few true friends. She was slated to be the recipient of the prestigious Devino Scholarship; following her disappearance, the scholarship was given to one of the young women now in custody. Emma was quiet and hardworking and had been granted early admittance to CU Boulder.

It is currently unclear as to whether a video, taken the night of Emma's disappearance and ostensibly showing her death, was to be used by the culprits as part of a blackmail pact or something more sinister. "We're still looking through all the options," said Bryson. The video shows a large figure, presumed to be dead hit man Randy Silverman, pushing Emma over the bridge at Anna's Run. Silverman's body was found in the river two days after Emma's disappearance,

277

and his gun was recovered Saturday evening. Fingerprints on the gun belong to the three suspects—and Emma Baines herself.

A candlelight vigil will be held for Emma at Jefferson-Lorne High School on Tuesday.

29

THE VICTIMS

BRYSON: It's Saturday, December 8, 2018. The time is 11:43 p.m. Deputy Chief Bryson and Chief Baines interviewing Miss Gwendolyn Sayer.

GWEN: Can I ask you something? Do my parents know I'm here? Could you tell them?

CLINE: It's Saturday, December 8, 2018. The time is 11:43 p.m. Officer Cline interviewing Miss Claude Vanderly. Miss Vanderly, would you like to tell us what you were doing with that gun?

CLAUDE: I was planting it.

What? You thought I'd come up with some excuse?

MUÑEZ: It's Saturday, December 8, 2018. The time is 11:43 p.m. Officer Muñez interviewing Miss Avery Cross. Miss Cross, congratulations.

AVERY: I— Excuse me?

MUÑEZ: Your cheer competition. I hear you placed second. Congratulations.

AVERY: Uh, thanks.

BRYSON: Gwen, can you tell us why you were in Greeley tonight?

GWEN: I was in Greeley because of him. Because of Lizzy.

BAINES: This is shit—

BRYSON: You were in Greeley because of your dead sister? Not because of Avery Cross?

GWEN: Yes, I was there for Aves. But it's more complicated than that.

BAINES: Seems simple to me. You killed my daughter. You've been scrambling to cover it up. If Bryson weren't here, I'd be turning off the security camera and this line of questioning would be taking a different direction.

BRYSON: Chief, I got this.

Gwen, go ahead. Tell us why you were in Greeley.

GWEN: Okay.

I'm ready.

It starts a while back. When Lizzy was still alive.

CLAUDE: So I've always been easy, right? I mean, that's what you'd say. I prefer the term *sexually uninhibited by bullshit gender norms*, but the world we live in puts a lot of pressure on how *other* people see me. For example, I wanted to get a job as soon as I could drive. But no one in Lorne wanted to leave me alone with the male staff, like I'd turn into Sexual Fantasy Barbie the minute the boss's back was turned. And because no one would give me a job, I started dealing pills.

CLINE: Did Emma buy pills from you?

CLAUDE: You bet she did. Adderall.

CLINE: It was Valium that was found in the locker.

CLAUDE: Well, maybe those pills weren't from me. Or for her.

CLINE: Did she ever owe you money?

CLAUDE: Nah, she was a good client. But that's not the point. She wasn't my only client. I had a lot of them. And Lizzy Sayer was one of the first.

GWEN: I was starting high school and I was going to be just like Lizzy. Top of her class, a finalist for the Devino Scholarship, well liked. She had as perfect a life you can get if you grew up eating government-provided cheese. She was supposed to be my mentor in all things.

But when we entered the official JLH mentorship program, I got paired with Brittany Landry, and Lizzy got Emma Baines. Siblings don't mentor siblings, but it bothered me that Lizzy's attention was divided. Emma was needy. Emma was ambitious. Emma wanted my scholarship. And Emma and Lizzy talked about things that Lizzy wouldn't talk about with me.

It was like she'd upgraded baby sisters.

It was Emma who told me that Lizzy had a boyfriend. "Any idea who it is?" she said, fake casually. She was always such a liar.

"None of your business," I replied, because it isn't, and also why did Emma know Lizzy had a boyfriend when I didn't?

I thought it was because—you know.

BRYSON: Because you're gay?

GWEN: Yes. It felt like she didn't think I'd understand her attraction to boys. It hurt. She said she'd always be there for me, but she wasn't letting me be there for her.

I asked her about it. She blew me off. She started staying late after school and coming home right before bed. At first, it didn't bother Mum and Dad so much. She'd always been a good kid, so they trusted her. They trusted the adults of JLH to look after her.

CLINE: Lizzy Sayer's car was found full of prescription drugs and cocaine. Was that you?

CLAUDE: The prescriptions, yes. The coke, no. Kyle Landry's the dealer for the hard stuff around here.

Hm. Probably should've kept that to myself.

Lizzy first came to me for Adderall. The preppies always do. I was starting to see her at parties, and I figured she wanted both the grades and the fun. And unlike *some people*, I don't judge. A lot of kids actually need something, for stress or for energy or for depression, but their parents won't take them to get help.

Thing is, she disappeared from the party scene. But she still showed up at my car before first period, looking like she slept in a parking lot and drank Jack for breakfast. And then she didn't want Adderall. She wanted Xanax. She wanted codeine. I said no. She wanted whatever she could buy with a crumpled twenty. And yeah, I sold it to her. I figured as long as she was coming to me, I could control what she took. I didn't *want* her doing coke.

CLINE: And it didn't bother you that Lizzy overdosed and died?

CLAUDE: Hey, fuck you. Of course it bothered me. I quit selling for ages after she died. Especially when I didn't know it was coke they found in her system.

But then I found out it wasn't really the booze and pills that killed her. It wasn't a some*thing*, it was a some*one*.

CLINE: Was it Randy Silverman? Is that why you shot him?

CLAUDE: I didn't shoot him.

CLINE: Your fingerprints were found on the gun.

CLAUDE: We struggled for it. He was trying to kill my friend. But I wasn't anywhere near it when it went off.

AVERY: I've . . . always been worried around him.

MUÑEZ: Around who?

AVERY: Mr. G. Mr. Garson.

I met him when I tried out for varsity cheer, freshman year. He and Mrs. Anderson were the judges for the varsity squad.

He seemed nice, right? Harsh but fair. He said I had potential, could maybe even get a cheer scholarship for college.

The first time I came out in my cheer uniform, I *knew* he was looking at where my hem hit my thighs. I didn't want to bend down, or squat, or high-jump.

MUÑEZ: What . . . you think Mr. Garson had sexual designs on you?

AVERY: See? Even you don't believe me. Stupid little cheer girl thinks everyone wants her. She doesn't understand how counselors and coaches work.

But I do know. I know the line was crossed. The whole school convinced me I didn't.

GWEN: Lizzy never told me who her boyfriend was. She was all glowy and giggly, like you get when you start a new thing. Her smiles were brighter, her laugh louder. And she started dressing differently. She wore V-neck shirts and push-up bras. She wanted to be noticed by someone. She just wouldn't say who.

I didn't tell Mum and Dad. I thought I was being a good sister. And when I heard other students trying to figure out who it was, I told them to screw off.

But things started going downhill midsemester. I heard Lizzy crying in her room. She spent hours with concealer, erasing the hollow rings around her eyes. She disappeared from her after-school curriculars. Mum's phone started ringing at midnight, one, two a.m. Lizzy's voice slurred and fuzzed. School rumors got vicious. *Lizzy was getting blackout drunk every night. Lizzy would snort anything from crushed-up candy to cocaine. Lizzy was fucking a teacher, a parent, the entire lacrosse team.*

I don't know. Would you believe every rumor you heard?

And then.

The phone call.

The drive.

The empty car. The empty bottles.

The almost-empty police report.

None of it mattered to me. Lizzy was just . . . gone. An empty death, I thought. But that wasn't true.

MUÑEZ: You know what I think? I think you're trying to distract me from the real problem. The Emma problem. Some of your student colleagues suspected that you and Emma were an item.

AVERY: Yeah. I mean, yes, those were rumors. I guess I understand why. Boys like to, um. Imagine things. Be gross about it. And Emma was so hopeless at cheer, and I wanted to help her. I know people think a lot of things about bi girls, but I'm not into Emma just because I'm bi and we're friends.

MUÑEZ: Do you have proof that you and Emma weren't together? That you didn't want to be with her?

AVERY: Uh, no? We just hung out?

MUÑEZ: And what did you do when you "hung out"?

AVERY: We did cheer routines. *I* did cheer routines. She tried to follow. But honestly, she didn't really care, and she cared even less after Lizzy died. She was the first to notice that Garson was . . . interested in me. She asked if I thought it was creepy, the way he always asked how I was, put his hand on my shoulder, that kind of thing. And she started poking around, right? She said she was worried about Lizzy, but I didn't put the two things together until after Lizzy died. Long after.

The thing is, girls can tell. There's a little voice in our heads that says *get out*, *get out*, but men spend years convincing us to ignore it. To tell ourselves we're wrong. Women, too, like the teachers at JLH.

The first time I was called into Garson's office, that voice was screaming.

Garson called me in for a health check. It was announced at cheer practice and I was first, so instead of changing into my jeans I went to his office in my cheer uniform, sitting on his pleather couch and trying to tug the skirt as far down my thighs as it would go. As he flicked through my file, I kept my eyes on the office—tall chipboard shelves stuffed with medical and physiotherapy books, dotted with weights and exercise bands. Pictures of the lacrosse team, newspaper clippings of the trees he planted, the students he mentored, the ways he made Lorne love him.

I could feel my heel trying to bounce. I smoothed my skirt and pressed down on my legs, taking a deep breath. Garson's eyes flicked to my chest. "Avery Cross." He leaned back in his chair. He folded his arms, making his biceps bulge. I got the feeling he was doing it on purpose. "How are we doing today?"

"Fine," I said, because that's what I always am. Even though I wanted to run.

"You have a good form out there. I was watching your high kicks. You could make captain, if you practice."

I felt a surge of hope. I was angling for captain, but the position's more about social standing than ability, so I just shrugged and looked at my knees.

"Your mom says you take some medications. Mind telling me what you're on?"

My mouth fell open. *Get out.*

Garson seemed to read my mind. "If there's an accident at practice and we have to call an ambulance, then I need to know your medical history."

"Um." I closed my mouth. "Ketamine, vitamin C, vitamin B."

"Birth control?"

He asked it so casually, but I could see in the way his head tilted that he listened carefully to the answer. *Lie*, said the little voice inside me.

But Mom always said I should be honest with my teachers. She wouldn't want me getting caught in a lie and embarrassing myself, or the family. So I said, "Yeah. Yes. For, um. Period pain."

"Anything else?"

"Xenadrine," I whispered.

Garson gave me a sharp look, then examined his file. His pen tapped against the paper. "That's a weight-loss supplement," he said, as if I didn't know.

He put the paper down. His eyes moved to me—moved over me, caressing. My knees jerked together and stuck. "Adolescence is hard. Your body's changing, and you don't always like what you see. Maybe you think others don't like what *they* see. The cheer image puts pressure on your body. But, Avery, a weight loss pill isn't the answer. You need to appreciate yourself. You need to love yourself." His voice turned soft.

We sat like that, for a long minute. I was supposed to say something, but what? And Garson just looked at me. Looked at the cut of my shirt and the swell of my breasts, at my bouncing knees and skinny thighs. I stared at my knees, too, hoping that he'd just tell me to take care of myself and let me go.

Instead I heard the scrape of his chair on the linoleum floor. "Come here," he said.

Bile rose in my throat. My heart was a hummingbird, desperate to flee. But Good Avery knows that her teachers want the best for her. Good Avery does what she's told. I stood, letting my hands come down to the edge of my skirt, curling around the hem and pulling it as low as I could. My shoes tapped on the floor like hooves.

Garson pulled a scale out from under his desk. "I know my weight," I mumbled, too afraid to say it loudly in case he thought I was talking back.

"It's all right. Come." Garson put a hand on my shoulder and guided me onto the scale. The numbers flickered, ticking up. This is Avery Cross. I'm a number. And when my number doesn't look right anymore, I don't get to do the lifts in cheerleading. I don't get to be a perfect girlfriend. I don't get breakfast. I don't get to be anything.

"Avery, you're on the lower end of normal for your body mass index," Garson said. His arm slipped from one shoulder to the other, pulling me in toward his ribs. I couldn't move. "You're active. You've got perfect arms, perfect thighs, the perfect stomach. . . ." His hand drifted down my back, circling my rib cage, pausing at my waist as if to measure it. My breath had stopped and I couldn't make it start again. My lips, my thighs, my fingers—everything squeezed together, as tight as it could go. If I didn't keep it all in, I'd throw up or scream or fall completely apart.

"You're perfect," Garson whispered. His hands inched down to the sharp points at my hips.

Breath exploded in me and I vaulted off the scale. My face burned. The heat became tears behind my eyes as I tried to grab my backpack without bending over and giving him a look at my backside.

Garson was sitting in his chair by the time I turned back around. He held my file. His voice was casual. Normal Mr. G, who never had anything but support and encouragement for us, who was a good and responsible coach. "You need to talk to someone about this. I'm going to start you on counseling. Girls like you shouldn't be worrying about weight-loss supplements. You should be focusing on the positive power of your body."

He looked up at me then. "O-okay," I stammered past the choke point in my throat.

And all I could think as I fled the office was *No way. Not possible*. Mr. G couldn't have done . . . that. He was just trying to help. Be encouraging. I misinterpreted. I started it.

MUÑEZ: So . . . you're saying that Mr. Garson touched you inappropriately. And that Emma knew about it.

AVERY: You don't believe me. I shouldn't be surprised. Mrs. Willingham didn't believe me. Mr. Mendoza didn't believe me. I didn't even *tell* my parents; good girls don't spread rumors like that. And anyway, Avery's too stupid to know the difference between well-meaning and predatory.

MUÑEZ: I never said that.

AVERY: You don't have to. It's clear what you think.

MUÑEZ: I think you're a liar. I think you're concocting a story to hide the truth: that you were in on a plot to kill Emma Baines, and you killed Randy Silverman, too. Bitterness for an ex can cause a lot of heartache. Gwen would have done anything to help you get rid of her.

AVERY: That's not what happened.

MUÑEZ: Then why are your fingerprints on Randy's gun?

AVERY: *He* tried to kill Emma. We were fighting him. Someone kicked the gun and it hit a rock. It went off.

MUÑEZ: So you didn't mean to kill him.

AVERY: I didn't kill him at all.

CLAUDE: Lizzy got . . . problematic. She'd follow me around school until I gave her what she wanted. Teachers started to notice. It was difficult.

One day I ducked into an empty classroom and shut the door.

"What the hell, Liz?" I snapped. "Are you *trying* to get caught?"

Maybe she was. Maybe that's what I was missing.

"I know you have them," she said. The *them* was still Adderall. It was all I'd agree to get her anymore. It sounds weird, but I *wanted* her to ace the tests, grab the scholarship, and leave us all in the dust. I wanted her to get out of Lorne, away from whatever the hell was killing her, and get a new life at college.

Yeah, yeah. Pathetic excuse for dealing. I know.

I pulled the goods out of my bag. "Next time, we meet by the river—" I started.

The door behind Lizzy opened. Garson stood there. His eyes landed on the clear plastic bag.

Fuck, I thought. *Fuckshitshitshitshit—*

When he crossed his arms and said, "And what's happening here, girls?" I couldn't come up with a single fucking thing to say.

Lizzy lifted her chin. "Nothing. None of your business."

His eyes glinted. "That's no way to speak to a teacher, Miss Sayer. Please wait for me outside."

She straightened her shoulders. "What if I don't want to?" she said, tone sullen.

Garson's voice was colder than the top of the mountain. "I said go. Head out to the parking lot and I'll meet you there."

Parking lot, I thought. *Weird place for a counseling session.*

Lizzy stormed out. Garson watched her go, then carefully shut the door again, keeping us alone inside. "You're an interesting young woman, Claude," he said.

"Yeah." I shrugged. I don't usually have a problem being confrontational, but I was already in deep shit. And something bugged me. I didn't want to look him in the eye.

"You're a juvenile delinquent with a missing record. You've been caught truant, vandalizing Anna's Run . . . you've had so much time in detention, it's a wonder you weren't held back a grade. . . ." He stepped forward. "I've been wanting to get my hands on you."

Ew. Gross.

"Lawyer mommy protects her tough girl, doesn't she?"

Get out. The softness in his voice made my stomach churn. Like he was enjoying himself.

"You probably know what happens if I take this little bag to Principal Mendoza." Garson plucked it from my unresisting fingers. "Expulsion. No high school diploma. No future." He put a hand on my arm. I shoved it off, but it left a feeling like oil slicked across my skin. "Yes, you're a fine young woman. It would be a shame to cut that future short." The hand came back, landing fingertip by fingertip.

I tried to skip backward, but my thighs hit a desk. I was trapped. "What do you want?"

Wrong question. Garson's eyes glinted. "You don't need expulsion, Claude. You need counseling. Your sexual activities are infamous." The hand moved from my shoulder toward my collarbone, where the strap of my bag cut across my body. Garson's eyes fixed on the spot. Then he stuck his hand in his pocket. "You don't need to be kicked out of school. You need a . . . more well-rounded perspective." His breath hit my neck and chest and I jerked back. *Get out.*

"And if you don't come," he breathed, "we may have to revisit that expulsion, hm?"

BRYSON: You are involved in a sexual relationship with Avery Cross.

GWEN: I'd call it a romantic relationship.

BRYSON: Did your sister know about it?

GWEN: Avery started talking to me after Lizzy died. So

no. We texted after Avery came by with flowers, and then we started hanging out, and then . . . it happened.

BRYSON: Did Emma know?

GWEN: No. Avery kept our secret. But Emma was more like a girlfriend than I was. Emma was the one hanging out with my girlfriend all the time. She got to hear about Aves's day. She got to actually be a part of it.

BRYSON: You were jealous of her.

GWEN: First Emma took my sister, and then she took my girlfriend. She was angling to take everything away from me. Yeah, I was jealous. And one day she just . . . switched off. She stopped answering questions in class, even when Mrs. Willingham called on her. She'd say she didn't know.

She always knew.

Emma was friendly enough to most people, most people excluding me. I knew something was up when she screamed at Jamie Schill. He was only going in for a high five. Even then I thought it was stress. I didn't realize.

BRYSON: Didn't realize what?

GWEN: And then she stood up at the assembly and said, "Elizabeth Sayer didn't kill herself." After that, I didn't care what made her scream at Jamie or look like a rabbit that's about to be blown away. I just cared that she was hell-bent on ruining my life. And Avery *still* hung out with her, still tried to help her, still spent more time with her than she would with me. And Aves . . . well, she was already cheating on Michael, wasn't she? What was it to her if she cheated again?

I decided to end things. I went from yearbook to the

Morning House, where I knew Aves and her squad would be with fries and Coke. I sent her a message and hung behind the garbage until the rest of them had sauntered off to their cars, then slid into the still-warm booth and took a cold fry. "You can tell me," I said between bites.

"Tell you what?"

Avery has this thing where she pretends to be stupid. Her eyes go wide and her mouth softens. It makes students roll their eyes and teachers take pity. This time, though, she looked genuinely confused. It only made me angrier. "If you don't want to be *study buddies* anymore." Avery reddened and ducked her chin, taking a fry and tapping it on the table. Something hardened in me. "I get it," I said, though I sounded like I didn't. I tried to push some kindness into my stony words. But it was hard to be anything other than angry—at my situation, at Avery, at the fact that I had to deal with being in the closet, my first girlfriend maybe cheating and my sister killing herself. "I'm boring. I only ever study. I don't want to . . . you know." Come out. I couldn't help glancing around to see who was close enough to hear. "But I'm already a side piece, and I don't want to be. I'm not going to take third place."

"What're you—" Avery's eyes widened in panic as a shadow fell over our table.

The waitress scooped up half-empty baskets and cups of ice and backwash. "You need anything else?" she asked pointedly.

"Let me drive you home," Avery said.

I didn't want her to. But I said yes, because I'm a stupid sucker for Avery Cross.

I always feel prickly in Aves's car. The seats are real leather and the car still has that "new" smell, the smell of fancy cars that aren't bought at the friends-and-family rate. Dad's truck is legitimately older than me. I kept my thighs off the seat and squeezed my shoulders in so that I was touching as little as possible.

Avery looked at the clock on the dash. "Crap." Then she turned the wrong way out of the parking lot, away from my part of town. "I need to stop at school first."

"Why?"

Avery's leg started to bounce up and down. "I just have to do something real quick."

"With Emma?" I said before I thought about it.

"Gwen, no." And she sounded so earnest—so pained. I wanted to believe her. "Is that what this is about? Why you're talking about . . . breaking up?"

"You have to be together to break up," I muttered.

"Whatever. Stopping whatever we're doing."

"Well, why not? We never hang out." *Because you're always hanging out with her.*

"Gwen, people have been spreading rumors about me forever."

"Well, it feels different with her," I snapped. "Like there's something I don't know about you two."

For a long moment, she was silent. Then she said, almost too quiet for me to hear, "There's a lot you don't know."

"Then tell me," I said.

The silence built up as we drove, becoming thicker and thicker, a rising river. And the silence was worse than whatever she might have said. It was a rising tide and I was drowning.

Time after time I tried to say something, but choked on my own words.

We pulled into the empty parking lot of JLH and she turned off the car. She stared at the steering wheel. Her hands were shaking.

I had to say something. "Seriously, Avery. If you had to do this, any other person at JLH would've been better. Do you know what she's done to me? To my family?" My voice was rising but I didn't care. The drowning feeling had been replaced by a flood. "Why her? Why pick that freak over me?"

Avery's voice was a bobbing tremor. "I'm not picking her—"

"You spend all your extra time with Emma. You do homework with her instead of me. She's with you for cheer, math, history . . ." Things that I could be doing with her.

"She's going through something," Avery said.

My sob built in me. I tried to push it out as a sarcastic laugh. I could touch my rage. I could turn it into claws and tear off the roof of the car.

It took me two tries to unbuckle my seat belt with shaking fingers. "Thanks for the ride, but I'll walk from here." I jerked the car door open and fell onto the asphalt. Palming the tears from my eyes, I grabbed my backpack and set off toward the road.

I heard the scramble of Avery tumbling out of the car. "Gwen, wait! Just—just listen. . . ."

That was what hit me the hardest. *Just listen.* Unreasonable Gwendolyn just has to listen, and then she'll understand. Gwen's strong so she doesn't ever hurt. Gwen doesn't show pain, so she obviously doesn't feel it. Gwen's under control, so you can say or do whatever you want. I whirled around and let the rage overtake me like the tide. "*She's going through something?* I'm going through something. My sister died and no one gives a shit? My girlfriend goes out with two other people? What can *she* possibly be going through that's so bad?"

And Avery told me.

And it was that bad.

CLINE: So you planted a murder weapon at Ken Garson's house? Because you wanted him to take the fall? Because you *claim* he had a sexual interest in you?

CLAUDE: The Jefferson-Lorne police, ladies and gentlemen. Capable of being so right and *so wrong* at the same time.

I'm not surprised you don't register it as sexual interest. It's what happens to girls all the time, right? We should be used to it. We should take it as a compliment. We should wear something else or be something else. That's what I thought, too, when it all started.

I'd intended to stop dealing. Really, I wanted to. But then Mom lost out on a promotion to an idiot guy at work, and Janine's timing belt broke, and honestly? Once I moved my business off school property, it seemed to matter less. Who cared if I had to endure one old dude creeping on me? That's the life of a girl. We shrug off detailed questions about our sex lives and preferred positions. We don't tell them to go fuck themselves when they suggest a padded bra. When they touch us over our clothes, well, at least it's over the clothes.

We're women. We endure. And I thought, *Two more years.* Two more years and I'll be out of this mess.

Mandatory counseling involved massages. He tried to unbutton my jeans to "check for cutting marks" on my thighs. He accused me of stealing from his office and asked what I'd do to keep him quiet. I told him I'd tell Principal Mendoza what a perv he was, and he only laughed. "Principal Mendoza knows I'm trustworthy," he said. "He's been watching you be a slut for years. And sluts get what they beg for."

I don't beg, I wanted to snarl. But he was right, wasn't he? No one would believe me if I cried rape. If I complained now, they'd say, *Why didn't you complain earlier?* If it was so traumatic and horrible, why wasn't I screaming from the rooftops the moment he touched me?

CLINE: Well, why didn't you?

CLAUDE: If I scream without evidence, I'm the Girl Who Cried Rape. *"Men can't even give hugs anymore." "He was so misunderstood."*

Trust me. You think we haven't been here before?

CLINE: But if your whole objective was to get rid of Ken Garson, why did you wait until now? Why are two others dead while Mr. Garson is on a field trip with the cheer team?

CLAUDE: Because I thought I was free. Garson stopped calling me in for counseling last year. He left me alone. I didn't know why and I didn't care. I figured he got bored with me.

I didn't realize he'd found another target.

MUÑEZ: CCTV footage shows you with Emma behind the school on September 8. She's crying, you're angry. Eventually you hug and leave the scene together. You never mentioned that in any of your other interviews.

AVERY: It was a couple weeks after the assembly. Gwen kept texting me, things like **what the hell** and **you still friends with her?** Gwen wanted me to pick: Emma or her. And I was ready to pick her.

I took Emma out behind the school, so I could kick her off the cheer team. I didn't want to do it in front of the other girls, right?

Her face was blotchy, her mascara smeared. Her ice-blond hair stuck up in two-day tangles. She met my eye, just for a second, and within her I saw . . . emptiness. Not boredom, like she sometimes got on the squad. Not distraction, like when she was finishing an essay in her head. She'd been cleared out. Like she didn't care.

I took a deep breath. "Emma, you know the cheer squad has a code of conduct to uphold."

Emma didn't say anything.

"And, well . . . you broke it." I floundered. How do I sound like the eloquent and clever one when I'm talking to the smartest student at Lorne? "You shouldn't have done that."

"Done what?" Her voice was flat, like she wasn't really there.

"You shouldn't have brought up Lizzy," I said. "We're all trying to move on."

"I can't," she whispered, and she broke.

She bent at the middle as though I'd punched her. The air around us went dead. I leaned forward without thinking and grabbed her shoulders, watching her tears as they hit the ground in fat drops. Emma's face had twisted into an unrecognizable horror. It was a horror so deep I couldn't comprehend it. But the self-loathing that came with it was something I understood so well.

We'd talked about Lizzy before. This was more than Lizzy. This was something new.

Emma was trying to say something. I leaned in close. Her breath came in great gulps, a cycle of gasping and sobbing and gasping again.

"He—" she wheezed. She couldn't say anything more.

"He who?" My mind raced through possibilities. He, Michael. He, her dad.

He, Garson, who touched the tops of girls' bras and let his hands run down our backsides. He'd seen Emma for mandatory counseling. What had he done?

I put my arms around her and I lied to her. I said it was going to be okay, and I would drive her home now. She didn't tell me that day, but I found out. I talked to her and I sat with her and I helped her on our routines, and I kept Gwen off my back about her, until she was finally able to tell me.

Mr. Garson raped Emma Baines.

It sucks that I just look at you and know you don't believe me.

BAINES: That's a fucking lie.

GWEN: No it's not.

BAINES: You're trying to cover for yourself. You *killed my daughter* because you were jealous of her and your girlfriend.

BRYSON: Chief, I got this—

BAINES: No, you don't. You think I wouldn't know if my own child was raped?

GWEN: She didn't know how to tell you.

BAINES: Shut up—

GWEN: She'd gathered all this evidence—

BAINES: *I told you to shut up.*

BRYSON: Chief, can I talk to you for a sec?

BRYSON: It's Sunday, December 9th. The time is 12:14 a.m. Recommencing interview with Miss Gwendolyn Sayer, with Officer Bryson present. Gwen, would you continue please?

GWEN: Everything cracked. The buildup, the anger. My heart. I wanted to throw up. Avery's face was awash in tears. Her shoulders shook. I came forward slowly, like the air was water between us, and wrapped my arms around her. She fell against me.

I know what raw pain looks like. I've seen it in my mother's face every day for a year. When something happens to someone you love, and you can't understand why, the pain cuts deep and angry and over and over. As Avery sobbed on my shoulder, my first thought was: *She's definitely in love with Emma.*

My second thought was: *Someone raped Emma, and that's not okay.*

"What happened?" I said. "Who did it?" I was ready to report him to Principal Mendoza. To get him expelled and kicked out of Lorne at the very least.

"It was a teacher," Avery whispered against me. My blood turned to the ice of Anna's Run.

You can't tell the administration when the perpetrator is the administration.

"It's not just her," Aves said, and her shuddering gave way to trembling. To fear. I locked my arms around her and held her up. "He . . . touches me." Her entire body locked up. "He tried to kiss me." Her shoulders rippled as a fresh wave took over. "Gwen, don't be mad."

"I'm not mad," I said. I could've lit a match with the power of my fury. "Who did it?"

"Wait, Gwen." Avery's voice was so faint I almost couldn't hear it. She took a breath, then another. "Emma said . . ." She swallowed.

I took her face in my hands. Her skin was smooth, her cheeks rash red from the sting of the cold and from her tears. "You can tell me." I needed her to tell me. I needed her to trust me, like girlfriends trust each other.

"Emma said he did it to Lizzy, too." And the bottom dropped out of my world again.

CLAUDE: I started dealing to Avery last year. Valium, an easy pill. She was always skittish about getting it, so we worked after hours, usually meeting in the JLH parking lot after everyone else had gone home.

The day I found out, I was waiting for her. I sat in Janine, doing the required reading for English, when I heard an unexpected voice: Gwen Sayer, sounding *pissed*. "What could *she* possibly be going through that's so bad?"

"*She was raped*," Avery screamed back.

I don't care about JLH's gossip. I know better than anyone how rumors are manufactured. But this hit. I knew it wasn't rumor.

I eased open Janine's door. Gwen and Avery didn't notice. They were locked in a hug that looked a tad intimate.

"Who did it?" Gwen asked.

I didn't hear Avery's entire response. But I heard the word *teacher*, and I knew. I knew why Garson stopped bothering me.

I stood awkwardly, waiting for them to notice me. They didn't. So I cleared my throat and said, "Is now a bad time?"

They sprang apart. Avery booked it without giving me a second glance. Gwen gave me a serious *I'll kill you* glare and followed. And I stood alone in an empty parking lot, feeling like an asshole, wondering what I was supposed to do. I waited around for half an hour, but Avery never came back for her stash.

I took Janine over to her house later that night. I parked down the road and walked up the pristine white concrete drive, between pseudo Greek columns, to knock on her maple-and-gold door. The doorbell echoed inside with a Big Ben chime. A moment later I heard the light patter of Avery's feet. "I got it," she called as she opened the door.

Her eyes met mine. She turned pale. "Go away," she whispered, and tried to slam the door.

I caught it with the edge of my Doc. "Wait."

"Who is it?" a woman's voice yelled from inside. Avery's eyes widened. Her mouth twisted in panic. "Um."

"Salvation Army," I muttered.

"Salvation Army," she called back.

"We don't have any cash. We'll bring some stuff by on Sunday."

"I can't do this now," Avery said, bumping the door against my foot.

"I gotta ask you something." I put my hand on the doorframe, leaned in. Avery looked at it like it was an unexploded grenade. But I couldn't let her better-than-you attitude get in the way of this. This was important. I took a deep breath and pushed the words out with it. "Did Mr. Garson touch you, too?"

Silence. But her wide eyes seemed suddenly wet, and the breath she took shook like a rattling autumn wind. Her throat bobbed. "I can't . . ."

"Avery." That was presumably her mom. Footsteps thumped angrily down the hall. Avery pushed the door, and this time I was wise enough to move my foot.

I had the answer I was looking for. But I didn't have the solution I needed.

It was Gwen who gave it to me, ironically. It was hard to trust anyone about it, even another girl. But I talked, and then she talked. And I learned a lot more than I wished to learn. And we agreed: Garson was dangerous. And he was the most popular person at JLH. And if he knew that Emma planned to expose him . . .

Emma was dead.

Which was how we came to be sitting in an empty classroom, long after school was over and I was supposed to be at Jamie Schill's.

Emma burst in five minutes after three. She looked like a total mess—she always did, these days, and not the kind of mess I aspired to be—and she said, "Sorry I'm late, I had to drop off . . ." Then she recognized me. "What're you doing here?"

Avery sat on the floor next to me, legs crossed, looking down at her knees as they bounced. Behind Emma, Gwen closed the door. Emma whirled in time to see the lock click.

"We all have a problem," I said. "And we're going to kick his ass."

Part of me felt guilty for not realizing sooner. For being relieved that Garson had stopped bothering me rather than suspicious. To think I was the only one. To him, I wasn't some-one special. I wasn't even someone especially vulnerable. I was just a piece of the link. The long line of conquests, of victims.

But goddamn it, if we were going to be victims, we were going to be his last.

30
THE TRUTH

The river washes through Lorne and takes the truth with it. And the debris it leaves behind is picked through without understanding.

It is the night of December 5. Silence has fallen with evening, giving the town a sense of lifelessness, stillness. Everyone who still wants a life after dark is on Diamondback Ridge. Wind bends the evergreens and whips at the bare aspens. Tomorrow will bring snow, but now the sky is clear.

A charcoal-gray Honda pulls away from the gas station and winds along the road, following the flow of the river as it rushes toward the foothills. The inside of the car has books tossed every which way, a headrest on the back seat, french fries mummifying under the passenger side. A phone rings from the glove box, and nail-bitten fingers covered in chipped polychrome polish fumble at the latch.

Claude finally grabs the phone. "What?"

"You have to come now. The plan. We have to do it tonight."

"*What?*"

"Someone's following me. Him. Meet me at the Run."

Claude taps her fingers on the steering wheel. "Shit," she mutters. "Shit, shit *shit*." Then she hits the brakes, whips the car around, and speeds back toward Lorne.

The river churns, full of snowmelt, rising toward the bank. On the hill behind it, safe from flooding, the ring of mansions cut into the mountainside is a dark strip with one burst of light and laughter. The scent of expensive whiskey and sour craft beer lingers in the air.

Two houses down, a dark shape slips out the front door, tucking strands of an ice-blond wig under her knit hat. She opens the trunk of her car and tosses in a pair of Pine Nation boots and a big black coat. She slams the trunk and goes around to the driver's side, pulling out her phone. "Lyla? I need a massive favor." Her laugh is bright and fake as she turns the ignition. "I know it's super late, but Michael *just* called, and I'll be grounded for a *million years* if they catch me out with him." Her voice drops. "He really wants to see me, you know? You're the best. Talk to you tomorrow."

The smile slips off her face like rain as she cuts off the call. Checking the house behind her one more time, she pulls out of the driveway, heading for lower ground.

She drives through the dead center of Lorne, past the newly renovated downtown with its cookie-cutter cafés and taffy shops, past the Breakfast Club and the Eternal Christmas store, where Santa waves from the window, past the flickering light of the motel. The mountains rise like prison walls.

She parks at the edge of a crumbling drive, a few houses down from the yard with filthy windows and thorns tangling in the gutter. A window slides up with a sound like a guillotine and a shadow tumbles from the Sayer residence. Gwen noiselessly trots to the car.

"Thanks for picking me up," she mutters as she slides in, bringing a blast of cold air with her. Avery puts the car in drive and speeds away, moving her hand to Gwen's leg.

"Thanks for being ready so quick," she replies.

Gwen takes her hand in an iron grip. "I hate plans gone wrong," she says. Avery squeezes back, hard as she can.

Lorne is silent. It is the silence of a town that won't reveal its secrets. It is the silence of a town where silence is complicity, and driving here is like driving through an elaborate tomb. The trees move back and forth in the wind, but they don't even rustle. The only sound is out of town, where the river runs deceptive and deep. And under the churn of water, the sound of twigs snapping and the panting breath of someone utterly terrified.

There are no more phone calls. Emma Baines runs, open-mouthed, letting the cold Rockies air hit her teeth. She runs knowing someone is behind her. She runs like it's the last night of her life.

The ground is hard and slicked with frost. Her boots slide and stub against roots. Bare hands scrape against bark and come away bloody. She cuts across the land, aiming for the road, but he paces her, pushing her deeper into the wood. Toward Anna.

More noise penetrates the forest. *"Emma!"*

The feet behind her speed up.

Emma skids onto the bridge over Anna's Run, slipping on icy gray planks, slamming into the weathered railing with a *crack*. A glove closes around the hood of her parka and yanks. Her scream is cut short as he claps a hand over her mouth. Emma flails; her legs slide out from under her, and two bodies land hard on the bridge. She kicks, connects with the railing. *Crack*. The hand moves from her mouth to her throat. She tears at his arm, reaches up for his face. Her nails scrape the flesh on his cheeks and he grunts. His arm constricts. She kicks again. *Crack*.

The shouts draw closer, and as Emma's hearing fuzzes in and out, she can make out the crash of bodies through the underbrush. She kicks harder. An elbow to his stomach makes him loosen his arm a fraction; her head slides out and she rolls to the edge of the bridge. Her lungs are raw and cold. Black spots explode in her vision. Emma stumbles to her feet, but she can't run now.

She turns. He's nothing more than a smudge of shadow at the edge of the bridge. His arms are out, fingers closed around the grip of a gun.

"The others know I'm here," she blurts. "They're coming."

"I'm sorry," he says, and at his voice, confusion flashes on her face. He takes a breath, steadies the gun.

Something smashes into him. The gun goes off. Emma hears a scream that is not her own. She can't move. She can't even breathe. The shadow on the ground is a tangle of limbs.

Two more figures appear. The gun skitters over the earth and the man launches himself after it. "Move!" Gwen yells, and finally Emma moves. Her body's not entirely convinced that she's not dead. Shaking, she clings to the railing, using it to pull herself to the other side of the creaking bridge.

The man grabs the gun at the same time as Gwen. She grips the barrel, forcing it toward the sky. Her lips pull back in a determined snarl. He punches her hard in the abdomen, and she folds. Avery screams again and pounces on him. Claude grabs his feet. He kicks but she holds on. Their bodies smudge together until no one knows who has the gun.

It fires.

Claude scrambles away. Two figures lie prone on the ground. Then Avery gets up, her whole front covered in mud. Her blue eyes are wide, and twin tracks smear the dirt on her face.

"Avery!" Gwen rushes over. "Are you okay? Are you hurt?" She cups Avery's face.

"I'm fine, thanks," Emma mutters.

"I—I think—" Avery stammers. She's trembling. "I think he's dead."

The prone figure sucks a bubbling breath. He's not dead yet, but soon.

"It's okay," Gwen breathes. She tries to pull Avery in.

"I said *he's dead*!" Avery pushes away. Her voice rises. "Do you know what that means? What's going to happen to me?" She stumbles, and Gwen grabs her by the shoulders, steadying her. Avery's breath begins to hitch.

"Deep breaths. No one's going to do anything to any of us." Claude stands, brushes off her jeans, strides over. She's got her cool *fuck you* face on, though she's pale beyond pale and she clenches her fists to keep her hands from shaking. "This is what happened: He shot himself. *After* pushing Emma in the water." She looks from face to face, working her jaw. Gwen nods immediately. Emma, after only a moment. And Avery looks to each of them in turn, mouth gaping.

Claude crouches and puts her gloved hand on the body's shoulder, heaving it over. "We're still going through with the plan. Maybe it'll be easier with him gone. We're still— Who the fuck is this?"

Her phone flashlight flips on. Emma staggers forward, breath catching as she takes a step onto the groaning bridge. Gwen leans in but Avery turns away.

Three girls peer into the lifeless eyes of a man they've never met. Instead of smart winter clothes, he wears a tattered Salvation Army coat and shoes. Instead of a salt-and-pepper goatee, he has a dark three-day beard, interrupted by a scar that cuts from his nose to his lip. They exchange baffled looks. "I thought it'd be . . . ," Gwen says.

"Garson." Claude runs the light down his body, revealing his tattered jeans, his holed shoes. "Do you know him?" she asks Emma. Emma shakes her head. "Think he was trying to mug you, or . . . ?"

"He said he was sorry. Nothing else. I think . . . he was trying to kill me."

"Maybe Garson sent him," Gwen says. Avery finally turns

back, peering through wet eyelashes at the man on the ground. Gwen squeezes her shoulder.

"It doesn't matter. The plan is still the plan." Claude bends down and tugs at his gloves.

"You're taking the clothes off a dead person," Avery whispers.

Claude rolls her eyes. "Great observation, Einstein."

"You're not exactly in the running for valedictorian," Gwen snaps. Then she draws in a breath and turns to Emma. Her eyes are of a softer flint than they were a few weeks ago, but not totally devoid of coldness. "Claude's right. We have to see the plan through. This doesn't change anything."

"She's supposed to be Garson in the video," Emma says.

"Well, now she's this guy." Gwen's features twist in disgust. "We should've known he wouldn't do the dirty work himself. If Garson really sent him, the truth will come out anyway. We just have to do our parts. I'll get the phone and hack in." She looks at Avery one more time, hands tightening on the other girl's shoulder. Avery takes a deep breath, then nods. Their mouths meet lightly.

"Focus, guys," Claude says.

"I am focused." Avery says, though she shivers and doesn't look at the body. As Gwen goes over to set up the tripod, Avery hands Claude her father's hiking boots, dropped during the fight and now as muddy as the rest of them. She pulls off her hat and hands it to Emma. The ice-blond wig is lopsided on her head. She tugs on it.

"You're never . . . here." Emma shoves Avery's hat on her

head and comes forward to straighten the wig. Their eyes meet and hold, and a wistful smile tugs at Avery's mouth. Emma matches it with one of her own. "Think you could shrink a couple of inches?"

Gwen coughs from where she sets up the tripod. Emma rolls her eyes a fraction. Claude pulls on the dead man's coat. "We gonna get him out of the shot or what?"

Avery's shaking, and tears swim at the bottom of her eyes. She swallows hard.

"I'm adjusting the camera. Can't see him or anybody's feet," Gwen calls. "Emma, did you get the rope?"

Emma gets the rope from where she slung it around a low-hanging branch of Anna's tree. Claude trades her shoes for the Pine Nations. Then she picks up the gun and starts buffing it with the corner of the dead man's coat. "He should've sprung for a dry clean every once in a while," she mutters. Then, louder, "What're we going to do with this?"

"Ask baby cop," Gwen says.

"Gwen," Avery admonishes softly.

"What?" Gwen's tone is sharp, but her face softens as she comes over. "It's ready."

Emma returns a few moments later. The rope floats downstream, tied to a sturdy pine. Avery will grab it when she's pushed over the edge and use it to haul herself to shore. In theory. If Anna's feeling generous tonight. "And the gun?" Gwen says.

"Bury it," Emma decides.

"What if we plant it on him?" Claude says. "Garson."

"No." Emma blows out a puff of air through her nose. "We stick to the plan. Bury the gun and forget about it. As long as he goes far enough downstream, no one will suspect he had anything to do with me."

Avery straightens her coat and goes over to the side of the bridge, awaiting her cue. Claude slides the dead man's gloves over her hands.

"We're ready," Gwen repeats. She looks at Avery. "Are you sure—"

Avery nods.

Claude pulls her black scarf up over her mouth and nose, her black hat down. She rolls her shoulders. Gwen raises her hand. When it slices through the air, Avery stumbles onto the bridge. She turns, pale hair whipping into her eyes. Her mouth parts in a gasp. Her body stills, poised to flee. But it's too late for that now.

The river below roars for her sacrifice. Claude lunges, eyes wide with panic, slipping on the bridge as it creaks and grumbles. Her hand connects to Avery's sternum and she pushes as hard as she can.

Crack. The guardrail snaps one final time and breaks away. Avery tumbles back with a scream and the river swallows her up.

Claude freezes at the rail. "Do you have it?" she calls over the river.

Emma looks at the camera on its tripod. But Gwen's not there anymore. She's dashing along the riverbank, racing the water, looking for a dark shape and shouting Avery's name.

Emma joins Claude on the bridge, staring into the depths. "She shouldn't have done it."

"She's the strongest of all of us," Claude says, and there's something like admiration in her voice. "If anyone can beat Anna, it's her."

It's a big *if.* And suddenly, the noise seems to rush back into the wood, until Emma can hear nothing but the rattling of the trees and the chatter of the water, the screech of night things in the underbrush. They wait for one eternity, then another.

"Come on," Claude says at last, and goes over to the body. She starts to take off his coat and gloves.

"What about Aves?" Emma says.

Claude pulls the scarf down. Her eyes are hard, her mouth turned down. "By now, she's either out or we have major problems. Let's take care of this one before we freak out completely."

"Too late," Emma mutters, but she joins Claude and together they redress the limp figure and roll it to the busted rail of the bridge.

"Are you sure we can't plant the gun?" Claude puffs as they work.

"Yes," Emma replies shortly.

When they're done with the dead man, they dig at the ground around Anna's tree, scratching against roots until they've made the handgun a shallow grave. Claude wipes it down one more time and lays it to rest. And as they pat the dirt back into place, they finally hear the stumbling footsteps of Gwen and Avery.

Avery's wig is gone. Her hair hangs in wet strings around her face, and mud coats every part of her, slick from her forehead to her boots. She shivers in her soaking clothes, gasping every time the wind rustles the underbrush around them. She might be the only person to have swum Anna's Run and survived.

Gwen holds her tight, ignoring the way water seeps through her coat. "We have to get her out of here. Now."

Emma nods. Claude looks sidelong at her. "That means this is it," she says. She shakes a lock of dark hair out of her face. "Are you ready?"

Emma's gaze lingers on Gwen first, her angry determination bound with a softness wherever she and Avery touch. The one everyone at JLH calls the uncaring bitch. Then she looks to Avery, the airheaded, weak cheerleader. Then to Claude, the self-serving rebel. Three girls she'd never have expected to help her.

"I'm ready."

They head back to the road—Claude striding resolutely, Avery and Gwen stumbling behind, and Emma bringing up the rear. At the edge of the wood Emma stops, drifts back between the trunks. She cannot be in Lorne anymore.

Claude checks the dark road, then gets two bags out of Janine's trunk. She walks back to the trees and hands them over one at a time. "Tent and sleeping bag, fire starters. We haven't been camping in, like, five years, so there's probably a million dead spiders in there."

"Thanks," says Emma.

Claude hands her the other bag. "Laptop and backup battery. Who knows what you're going to get for internet out here, but maybe when I come by with food. I can set up a hot spot and we can mastermind posts."

Emma nods. She's ready to make her blog debut—she's even decided on her pen name. She thinks Adams West has a nice ring to it. "You know your jobs?"

"Get Lizzy's phone," Claude says.

"U-unlock it," Avery stammers.

"Find her secret account," Gwen finishes.

Emma nods. "I'll do the rest. Don't let him corner you. Don't let him catch on."

They fall silent. They don't know what to do. They're not friends, exactly; they're less and more. They're in this together. Three of them are risking it all, and one of them is dead.

She doesn't wave. She hefts her bags and takes one step back into the woods, then another. Then another. And then she turns, and the dappling moonlight turns her into an incomprehensible jumble of shadows, moving between tree trunks until the girls cannot see her at all.

31

THE LITTLE SISTER

BAINES: So Emma was the one in the woods? My daughter escaped my notice and evaded me?

GWEN: Maybe she had insider information on how to hide.

BRYSON: Chief—Miss Sayer, I'm going to continue with my original line of questioning, okay?

Who shot Randy Silverman?

GWEN: He shot himself. We told him what he was about to do, and he couldn't go through with it.

BRYSON: It'd be pretty difficult for him to shoot himself in the back of the head. Your fingerprints, however, are on the gun.

GWEN: I fought him for it. He was trying to kill someone.

BRYSON: Why did you kill him?

GWEN: I didn't.

BRYSON: Miss Cross and Miss Vanderly said it was you.

GWEN: No they didn't.

BRYSON: They said you thought it was Mr. Garson. You thought he'd come back to finish off Emma, the way he finished off Lizzy. It's an understandable point of view. You were acting out of self-defense. You wanted your sister back. He was trying to kill someone. One heated moment is all it'd take.

GWEN: Interesting. A few minutes ago, I shot him and killed Emma because I was a jealous lover. Now you understand my true motives? I don't think so. You don't even care about the truth, about how Emma and Lizzy were almost the same. You don't care how Lizzy connects to all this. I shouldn't be surprised. You never put much effort into her case in the first place. Even when we dropped the phone in your lap, you didn't care enough to investigate it—

Oh my god. Oh shit. I just realized. Where's the phone?

BRYSON: You can't have access to your phone.

GWEN: Not *my* phone, her phone! Lizzy's phone, that you confiscated from Claude! Give it to me. I know the password.

BRYSON: How about you tell us the password, and we unlock it for you?

GWEN: Fine. 74547252. My nickname. Pilipala. Butterfly.

BRYSON: Miss Sayer, if you're lying about this . . .

GWEN: Look in her notes. Try her diary app.

BRYSON: Uh, why . . . Oh.

Chief?

BAINES: This. . . isn't possible. This is a setup. This is a lie.

GWEN: Would you risk her life over it?

Again?

BAINES: If you're lying, I will try you for murder, and I'll try you as an adult.

<u>Lizzy's Diary</u>
<u>9/3/2015</u>

Mendoza saw me going into G's office today, fuck fuck fuck. He so knows. I told G about it, and he said I was freaking out, like normal, I needed to calm down. He said people go in and out of his office all the time, don't worry about it. I told him we should meet off school grounds, and he said if I thought he was going to pick me up from Mom and Dad's with a big bouquet I could go fuck myself. I cried in the bathroom. G hates it when I cry.

<u>9/27/2015</u>

Tried whiskey for the first time today. Whiskey is good. Whiskey-flavored kisses are better. Mmmm.

<u>10/15/2015</u>

I flunked the calc test. I know I didn't study enough, but G kept me behind every day this week. He says it doesn't matter if I fail one test. He doesn't get it. If I don't get the scholarship, I can't get out.

<u>11/6/2015</u>

G wants to break up with me. I'm ugly and fat and my boobs are too big and I'm not smart enough and I want to fucking die and he said we'd be together forever and now I'm too fucking fat and I'm not even smart enough to get the scholarship and I don't even get why I'm alive anymore.

<u>12/12/2015</u>

Holy shit how much did I drink last night. I went to G's house and blacked out and I have no idea what happened but I couldn't find my

320

underwear and G told me to pick up a morning-after pill on my way in? So I guess we had sex??? I thought we were waiting til I was 18? G says it always hurts the first time so maybe it's good I don't remember, like the next time will be better? I feel sick.

2/5/2016

What the actual fuck claude fucking vanderly. <u>What is she doing in his office?</u> G says it's normal but if he's fucking claude we're done. We're done and I'm going to Mendoza and spilling everything. I put my whole future in this, my scholarship is gone and my parents hate me and I need a drink halfway through first period, I am NOT going to end up some shitty side piece in the Mr. G show. He has to put as much on the line as I have.

2/7/2016

Fuck I feel awful. G's done so much for me. He puts himself on the line every day, for us. He could go to prison if the wrong people knew about us. . . . I want to tell Gwen, but I can't. I want to tell Mum and Dad that I'm ok but I can't. I can't fight with him. Life is hard but we can be strong. When I graduate, we'll skip over to Utah or Wyoming or wherever, G can teach at a new school and I'll work until I can go to college. It's going to be ok. I just have to trust him.

3/20/2016

Who even fucking am I anymore

3/25/2016

G wants to go for a drive tonight fuck fuck he wants to break up with me I fucking know it wtf am I going to do

THE GHOST

Emma Baines unclips her tentpoles from the body and folds them neatly, sliding them into their bag before rolling up the tent. Ms. Vanderly's old MacBook sits on a tree stump; she checks the time on it before shutting it and sticking it in the second duffle. Her breath puffs in the night air. There's nothing for her in Lorne now. The best she can do is move away, move on, forget what happened and what she left behind and what she gave up.

Something snaps behind her. Her hands freeze on the bag. Her brain hopes that it is Claude or Gwen or Avery coming to tell her that everything's fine.

Her body knows it's a lie.

She turns, slowly, ready to run. She keeps her eyes on the ground until she sees the Pine Nation boots. Then she can't pretend anymore.

Garson doesn't look out of his mind with rage. He doesn't even look like he lost a night's sleep. Light from her flashlight bounces off the snow to illuminate the sharp edges of his nose and cheek. It deepens the shadows beneath his eyes, turning them into wells.

"I really thought you'd just die," he says. His voice doesn't shake. "You didn't strike me as the survive-at-all-costs type. Certainly not the type to kill a man." His hand comes up. It's wrapped around a gun. "Claude Vanderly did that part, didn't she?"

She doesn't say a word. One foot slides back.

"Don't," he snarls, and Emma freezes. "Don't fucking move. You think you're smarter than me? All four of you working together weren't smarter than me."

Emma tries to suck enough air into her lungs. The world tilts. "They're going to catch you," she says. "It doesn't matter what you do now. They know what you did to Lizzy. And me. And everyone."

Garson laughs harshly, an animal, barking sound. "With what evidence? I took your notebooks. I erased your files. There's nothing linking Lizzy to me." His expression shifts almost imperceptible in the darkness.

"You didn't even care about her."

"Don't be stupid," Garson says softly. "I loved Lizzy. She was the one who didn't love me. She wanted to leave me in Lorne and fuck the professors at Harvard. She was the one who said she'd tell. She was the one who ruined everything."

He speaks with real pain in his voice. He speaks with earnestness. He really believes it. "I've spent my life helping kids be their best. I give them good advice, good educations, good scholarships . . . This town needs me." His voice rings with self-righteousness. "I couldn't let Lizzy destroy that, not when she was going to leave anyway. And I won't let you destroy it, either." He raises the gun.

Run. Hide. Fight. Emma dives to the side. The gun goes off and she screams. She digs her boots into the ground and launches, praying that her cheer training has given her the speed and strength she needs. And even then, she wonders: Can she really outrun him? She has nothing to run *to*. She's just a dead girl who chose the forest as her grave.

Her boot catches on a hidden root and she falls through the blanket of snow. Lightning flashes through her head as her temple strikes something hard and her teeth slam together. Something hot trickles down the side of her face.

She hears a shout. It doesn't sound like him but he's getting closer, his rubber-soled boots thundering on the ground. She has nothing, she grabs for the nearest thing she can find, her hand closes around a rock—

A boot hits her shoulder and flips her over. Her spine thwacks against the tree root. Mr. Garson pushes down with his foot, trapping her arm on the ground. She screams again. Close up, she can see how his hand shakes.

That doesn't really matter when he's aiming point-blank.

"You did this to yourself," he breathes. "You bitch."

And then there's the crack of the gun.

Emma Baines is no longer considered deceased, but a missing person, according to testimony and evidence provided late last night, Saturday, December 8.

A warrant was obtained to search the house of Kenneth Garson, lacrosse coach and counselor at Jefferson-Lorne High School, after new evidence was secured. Mr. Garson was not at home, but his car was located at the side of County Road 43, near the site popularly known as Anna's Run. It is believed that Garson was searching for Emma Baines with the intent to kill; he fired on officers in the woods and died in the resulting cross fire. Near Garson was a laptop bag and a fire pit, and food waste was found in a container nearby. It will be tested for a DNA match with Emma.

"This is a difficult day," said Police Chief Baines, the man who fired the killing shot. "The police are still conducting their investigation, but there's no doubt in my mind that Ken Garson went into these woods with the plan to murder Emma, and he has possibly killed before. We want to stress that we're working through this, that the threat is neutralized, and that no one else is currently a suspect in any crime involving students at Jefferson-Lorne High school. Emma, if you hear this, if you read this: Please come home. It's safe now. You don't have to hide in the woods or behind Adams West on the internet. Just come home."

The three former suspects, friends of Emma's from high school, could not be reached for comment.

33

THE UNCARING BITCH

Officer Muñez takes her home in a squad car, but she doesn't make Gwen sit in the back. It's after two in the morning.

"We'll release the truck in the morning. We're sorry it can't be sooner." Muñez does sound sorry. But Gwen doesn't particularly care.

The squad car crunches over the snow and stops outside her house. The light in the kitchen's still on, fluttering weakly with a poor connection that they've needed to fix for years.

Muñez escorts her to the front door, knocking stiffly once they get there. Gwen hears Mum moving around inside, slowly, as though she's been replaced by a stringless mario-nette. After a few moments the swollen wooden door shudders open and Mum's face peers out. Her eyes flick between Muñez and Gwen.

"Officer, you want a cup of tea?" she says in the coldest voice Gwen has ever heard.

Muñez wisely declines. She mumbles something about Gwen getting a good night's sleep and retreats to the car. Gwen slides inside and takes off her boots. The air here feels colder than outside, for all that her breath doesn't puff out in a cloud.

The plastic Christmas tree droops with cardboard and paper ornaments, candy-cane reindeer and hand turkeys. The house smells stale. Nobody ate tonight. Mum and Dad stare as Gwen shrugs out of her coat, unties her shoes, does whatever she can to not look at them.

But then she's standing in her socks and sweater and she can't put it off anymore. "Um. So." What next? *So I deliberately framed myself for attention. So Lizzy got sexually assaulted by a teacher and I knew months ago. So I didn't have dinner—is there anything in the fridge?*

"I'm gay," she blurts.

They stare at her, unblinking. This is it. Mum's going to ask, *Are you sure?* Dad's going to say, *Don't be ridiculous, Gwen.* Maybe one of them will change the subject without addressing it at all.

"Is that why they arrested you?" Mum says.

"What? No." Gwen tries to wind up this new thread. "They thought I had something to do with Emma—they thought a lot of things. But, um. I'm innocent, and they know that now. And also I'm gay." And the police know *that*, too, for all the good it will do them.

Mum and Dad look at each other. "Okay," Dad says uncertainly.

"That's not what we need to talk about—" Mum says.

"I just—" Gwen starts at the same time. They stop. Mum nods for Gwen to speak, tears brimming at the bottom of her eyes.

She just wanted them to know. She wanted to get it out of the way and tell them what she should have told them years ago, with Lizzy holding her hand. She wanted to be out to them before the paper outs her to the world. She wants control over her story.

She wants Lizzy there.

She doesn't realize she's crying until the first tears drip onto her hand. She looks down blankly. The tear shimmers in the white lights of the tree. A moment later Mum's arms come around her.

"It's okay," she whispers. "Don't be upset."

"I'm not upset about that." She's overwhelmed with the simplicity of it. That she waited years for this. That she feared loud declarations, protestations, Mum wondering if she should ever have left her cult church. That she was so afraid of "okay."

The couch creaks as Dad gets up. He comes over and joins in, wrapping his arms so carefully around his wife and daughter. His bristly mustache presses against the top of her head. "We love you, Pilipala," he says. "We're proud of you. Nothing's ever going to change that."

"But we have to know the truth," Mum says.

The truth. "It's about Lizzy," Gwen says. Mum's grip around her hand tightens. Dad nods. They need to know.

Telling them is harder than telling the police. She wants to leave out bits she knows will hurt them. But that story is the story they need to hear the most. Even when she has to admit that she snuck out of the house twice—and once to get rid of a stupid wig.

* * *

The water roared. A branch snapped wetly behind her. And though Gwen always thought of herself as the girl in control, she couldn't control the scream that slipped out.

"Chill! Calm down!" Emma sounded like she didn't know whether to laugh or shout. Gwen whirled around.

"You chill," she snapped. "I thought—"

"There's no reason for him to come out here," Emma said.

Gwen folded her arms, hugging herself. "Maybe he wanted to see if his hired gun finished the job."

Emma cocked her head. "The police would already know if he hadn't. And since they're sniffing around after *you* . . ." She shrugged. "Bring me anything? I could kill for a burrito."

Gwen blushed. The friend thing with Emma was hard in a way it wasn't with other people. Memories sliced at her, all the ways in which Emma was more deserving of love, of scholarships, of Lizzy's help.

She quashed them. She wasn't here to snipe at Emma. "I came looking for the wig," she said.

"What . . . ?" Emma's frown cleared. "Aves was supposed to get rid of the wig."

"Yeah, but I realized." Gwen looked down at the water. Anna seemed sated, but it was just a ruse. The current tugged from beneath, dragging everything from stray branches to stray people under. "She came out of the river without it."

Emma stared at her. "They can't find it downstream. They'll know." Panic tinged her voice.

"That's why we're going to look for it, isn't it?" Gwen snapped back. "I have an idea."

They walked in silence, using Gwen's phone as a flashlight. After a few moments, Emma said, hesitantly, "I'm straight, you know."

"So?" Gwen bit out.

"So . . . I know Aves and I are close. And maybe that was weird for you. But she's a really good friend, and . . ." Emma took a deep breath. "She likes you a lot. She admires you."

"Um, okay. I'll call you the next time I need relationship advice," Gwen said, but her skin warmed and a smile tugged at her mouth.

They came to the tree with the rope still hanging, soggy, around the middle. "You didn't haul it in?" Emma said with a touch of incredulity.

"She was getting hypothermia," Gwen protested.

"I can't believe you're going to win the scholarship," Emma grumbled, and pulled on the rope.

Branches and other flotsam made a tangle of it, and the heavy weave of it scraped their hands. It reminded Gwen of trying to climb rope in PE, pulling and pulling and getting nowhere. She ignored the burn in her arms, heaving until the rope finally flopped free and they could bring the end to shore.

They untangled branches and rotting prairie grass and roots until Emma held a muddy mess up to the light of the flashlight. "Is this it?" She tried to wipe a clump of wig clean but only succeeded in smearing mud onto her gloves

Gwen huffed in relief. "Thank you. I owe you a hot chocolate for that."

"Good. Let's take this back to my place. We can burn it—and the rope."

They trooped back, sticking to the far side of the bridge and ducking under the police tape. Emma led Gwen another half mile into the wood. "You trying to get me lost?" Gwen said.

Emma snorted. "You were part of the Lorne Outdoor initiative." They both were. JLH gave extra credit for it. "Not my fault if you can't remember how to use a compass."

At last they found the dark lump of Emma's tent. Gwen waited outside while Emma rummaged around, coming out at last with a granola bar and a fire starter. A few minutes later the fire was crackling, covering their silence with something a little friendlier. Emma coiled the rope around the edge of the fire and tossed the wig on top.

"I guess this is what the police mean when they say vagrants in the woods," Gwen said, stretching her boots toward the fire.

"I have to move a lot. Doesn't give me much time to write the West posts and keep up on your scintillating activities," Emma replied. "At least I have service, though. Mostly."

They fell silent again. The fire snapped and smoked. Finally Emma said, "You know I'm sorry about Lizzy, right?"

Gwen rolled her shoulders. "Why should I know that? It's not like you ever told me."

"I didn't know how," Emma said softly.

Gwen snorted at that. Her dark eyes reflected the red-orange of the fire. "It's not hard. 'Hey, Gwen. I'm sorry your sister died.' See?"

"I just—couldn't believe she was gone. Like that."

Gwen opened her mouth as if to argue, then closed it again.

Then she said, "Neither could I." She took a stick and poked at the soggy rope. "You sure this is worth giving up your shot at the scholarship?"

"You're risking it, too. The Devino Scholarship gets revoked if you have a record," Emma said.

Gwen leaned forward to warm her hands, tugging off her gloves and stretching her fingers toward the fire. "Lizzy's worth it to me."

"Me too," Emma said. At Gwen's sidelong glance she flushed. "She is. All the girls who got . . . destroyed by him. They deserve justice. And hey, if I'm smart enough to pull this off, maybe I'm smart enough to get to college another way. Or maybe I don't need college at all." Her white teeth flashed as she smiled humorlessly. "When you're the head of your own company, maybe you'll remember who helped you get there, and I can be your secretary. Then I'd get a good job and you could boss me around all day. Win-win."

Gwen rolled her eyes. "You'd make a terrible secretary."

"Why do you think I offered?" Emma countered.

They grinned at each other, and the ice between them cracked a little.

Gwen's phone chimed as it connected to Emma's hot spot. She pulled it out and squinted at the screen, then hit the CALL BACK button, bringing the phone slowly to her ear. "I thought we agreed, no contact."

"It's about Lizzy's phone." Claude's voice was tinny but clear on the other end. "I've been calling you. What are you doing?"

"Tying up loose ends in the woods," Gwen replied. "What'd you do, lose it?"

"No." Claude's tone was frosty enough to sound like Mum's. "The police have it. It's still in custody. But they can't open it. So unless we have the password, *we* can't open it."

And any evidence inside was useless.

"Don't worry. Emma and I will talk about it. I'll tell you the revised plan tomorrow," she said.

"You and Emma are going to buddy-buddy it?" Claude was clearly skeptical.

"Best young minds in Lorne," Gwen replied, and hung up.

The woodsmoke had taken on a dark tint, and an acrid stench rose from the fire. Emma leaned away, wrinkling her nose, and Gwen coughed as a stinging tendril invaded her throat.

"It's the wig," Emma wheezed, fumbling for a stick to pull the polyester wig out of the fire. The best young minds in Lorne apparently forgot that polyester doesn't burn.

Gwen talks until she's hoarse. She forgets the way the couch springs dig into the backs of her thighs, the way the duct tape squeaks every time she shifts. Her parents go pale and silent, and they make no effort to get rid of their tears.

Talking is like drawing out a poison. When Gwen's finally finished, she feels like someone has tapped into her and pulled all the anger out, all the sorrow and disappointment and bitterness. She feels empty, but ready to be filled with something better.

"You'll probably have to go to court," Dad says. "Even if it's just to testify."

Gwen nods. She's known that from the beginning. She's known the scholarship might get revoked because of her arrests, or her cheating, or because she's gay, or just because she attracted too much attention in this screwed-up world. But she's also proved she can *change* the world, and she doesn't need any scholarship to do that.

Mum pulls Gwen in, until her head is resting on her shoulder. "This place . . . likes to dwell on things. Your father and I think it's time to move on." She squeezes. "When you go away to college, we're moving, too."

Gwen's breath hitches. If they move, she'll never have to see Lorne again. She'll probably never see Avery again, either, but that thought is a fleeting one, eclipsed by a strange rootlessness. She's never wanted to live here, but she's never lived anywhere else, either.

"Moving's expensive." Especially in Colorado now. "And you'll have to start over. . . ."

Dad makes a noise in the back of his throat. "They always need construction workers. And that's why I've been working late—studying at the office. I'm getting certified in accounting and in operating heavy machinery. Mr. Mecklin says that'll open managerial positions." He reaches over and squeezes her hand.

Maybe, Gwen lets herself think. *Maybe things will be all right.*

34

THE SELF-SERVING REBEL

Claude's mom picks her up at the station. She's led out and handed over with cold politeness; it seems the good officers of Lorne aren't pleased she won't be staying overnight. After all, the sexually active girl is usually either dead or ruined by the end of the story.

Mom puts an arm around her shoulders and doesn't let go until they've trooped down the treacherous icy steps outside the police station and over to the car. Claude can feel her shaking with the effort to keep it together in front of the cops. The Vanderly women have always maintained their public image.

They get in the car. Mom's fingers drum on the steering wheel. She looks straight ahead. "Claude, I need to know now. That man who got shot—Silverman."

Claude knows what's coming. "What about him?"

"Did you do that?" Mom takes a deep breath. "I'm not trying to judge you or trick you or turn you in. But I need to know. If you shot him in self-defense, we'll get a good lawyer—"

"Mom, I didn't," Claude says.

She half expects Mom to ignore her. No one else is going to believe she didn't do it. But Mom stops saying anything at all.

Claude focuses on the upholstery of her seat, the cold take-out coffee in the cup holder between them, the dirt-rimmed piles of snow at the edge of the parking lot. Heat prickles at the corners of her eyes. She feels small, exposed. She kept the mask on for the cops, but she can't do that now.

At first Mom doesn't even breathe. Then she takes a desperate, shuddering gasp, and props her elbows on the steering wheel. Her shoulders shake. She sits like that for a long time, and Claude doesn't know what to do besides lay her head on her mother's shoulder.

"Fuck," Mom whispers. She grabs a paper napkin and noisily blows her nose. "Claude, why didn't you tell me?"

"I couldn't." Claude's voice cracks. She can't be strong anymore. She still feels the sinking, twisting shame of dealing pills even though she knew she shouldn't, of being powerless under someone else's probing fingers. She wanted to cut out all the places he touched, but the best she could get was cheap liquor to numb it. She thought she could define her own sex life, but she could never control how others define it. And then she started to let them define it for her.

"I failed you," Mom says.

"No," Claude begins, but Mom pulls back.

"I did." Mom wipes under her eyes and sniffs. "If I'd been a better mom, we'd have talked about this. I was so busy showing you how far single moms could go, I couldn't see what was happening right in front of my eyes." Another tear slips out. She dabs at it with her finger.

"Mom, stop." Now she's crying. "You're the strongest person I know, and I . . . wasn't. You would've kicked him in the balls or something." And she'd been so shocked, so scared, she'd just let it happen. "And who was going to believe me?" she asks bleakly. Guys hit on her all the time, and she enjoys it. She's encouraged it before, too. Maybe she's so used to it, she doesn't know when she's *not* encouraging it. Maybe she was asking for it, like everyone says. She never said no before, they whisper. She just regrets it now.

Mom turns so that she can take Claude by the shoulder. Claude can see her drawing on that strength, using it to straighten her spine and fill her face with fire. "Claude, you *are* strong. Strength isn't just kicking a guy in the balls. Sometimes it's persevering through hell. Sometimes it's maintaining your self-respect. And *nothing* you do ever means you deserve to be assaulted." She squeezes.

Claude draws her knees up to her chin. "I know," she whispers. It's just, there's only one Mom to tell her that she has a right to her body. And there are millions of boys ready to tell her that their sexuality is all her fault.

"Sex isn't wrong. I've told you that your whole life, and I still believe it." Mom's hand moves up to smooth Claude's hair. "Predation *is* wrong. Ken Garson is wrong. And you dealing pills was wrong, but that's not a valid excuse for what he did. You don't ever have to be someone else's excuse."

You don't ever have to be someone else's excuse. Claude wonders how the world would be if everyone thought that.

They drive home in the snow, taking it slow, not really talking. There will be time enough to talk, and right now Claude feels like her eyelids are turning inside out every time she blinks. The world shifts in and out of double vision, hazing over in a picture of white and neon. She wants to sleep and then go for a drive. She's been trapped in Lorne for the past three days, and the only break she got was breakfast burritos in the forest.

"Thank god it's you." She offered the burrito. "Hungry?"

"Yes." Emma snatched it, fumbling at the aluminum foil with her gloves. "Still warm," she groaned.

They sat by the fire. Emma ate her entire burrito in less than a minute, so Claude gave up the other half of hers. "Missing real food?"

"You have no idea." Emma smiled down at the burrito half. A lump of avocado stuck out on one side.

"People, find yourselves a love who looks at you the way Emma Baines looks at her burrito," Claude quipped.

Emma rolled her eyes and took another bite.

"Snow called for tomorrow," Claude said. "And Mom says the police have asked for a canine search team."

Emma finished the second burrito and put a hand over her stomach, sighing. "Bring me another tomorrow," she said.

"You should be on the other side of the mountain tomorrow," Claude replied. "If the police show up with dogs, you're not going to get away."

Emma shook her head. "I have to finish the blog. And we've already had screw-ups. If you need me . . ."

"Aren't you afraid of getting caught?" The blog was a provocation, not worth blowing Emma's cover.

"Of course I'm afraid. Mostly I'm afraid that *he'll* figure it out." *He* wasn't her dad. "So keep him distracted for me. And the police, if you can."

"It's still a bad idea for you to stay in Lorne," Claude said.

"I've done without a mom for seven years. You don't have to step in now," Emma snapped.

They were silent for a moment. Then Claude laughed. "You think your mom would help you fake your death and frame a pedophile? I'm so much worse than a mom. So when even I say you have to get out—"

"I know what I have to do." Emma crumpled the aluminum foil into a ball. "Believe me, getting out of Lorne has always been at the top of my bucket list. And I want to do it soon. It's just . . . hard. I always knew I'd be leaving, but I sort of thought I'd be leaving under different circumstances." As valedictorian with a full scholarship.

Claude looked over at her, sitting on her overturned log, staring at the cold firepit. Even in the dark her eyes shone with a hunger—a hunger to succeed, a hunger to destroy everything that ever hurt her. A hunger to be validated. Unease spread up Claude's back like a chill. "Just be careful, all right?"

"I'm always careful," Emma said. "Don't worry about me."

"Jesus," Mom mutters as they pull up to the house, bringing Claude back to the here and now. "How long has *he* been here?"

Mrs. Schill's mom van is parked in the slope of the drive-way. As they pull up, the door opens and Jamie hops out.

"I'll tell him to go," Claude says. "Just give us a minute?"

Mom sighs. "All right. A minute. But I don't want him coming in tonight, not even for a cup of coffee."

"Got it." Claude leans across the stick shift and throws her arms around Mom. Mom hugs back, squeezing tight, like she wasn't sure she'd ever be able to hug Claude again.

Jamie's self-consciously studying the ground when Claude gets out of the car. "Um," he says.

"I'm going inside," Mom says pointedly. *One minute*, she mouths at Claude before stomping up to the front door.

"Hi," says Claude. She leans against Mom's car. A little curl of brown hair sticks out from under Jamie's cap, and she wants to tuck it back under. So she does. He inhales sharply as her fingers brush his forehead.

"I'm really glad you didn't do it," he blurts. Red flushes over his cheeks and down his throat.

"Thanks." Claude waits a moment, but he doesn't seem keen on saying anything more. "Me too."

Maybe this is a bad idea. She never wanted a relation-ship, and this is why—the constant fumbling and stuttering, wondering if everything she's said is the wrong thing. She's confident when she knows where she stands, one way or another. Right now, things are just . . . awkward. She never had a problem talking to Jamie before.

But her hand is still on his forehead, and instead of dropping it, she brings it around to cup his cheek. And she thinks about what she'd normally say, and what she might say instead. . . . "You can't come in." His face falls, just a fraction. "Tonight. But I'll ask my mom if you can come over tomorrow."

"Or . . . you could come to my place," he says. "In the daytime. I'll teach you how to play *Gotham City*, aka the greatest Batman game of all time. Or I'll show you my spreadsheet comparing the teachers of Jefferson Lorne to prime numbers." Claude raises an eyebrow and Jamie goes even redder, but he seems determined to keep talking now. "You said when all this was over you might be . . . um."

"Interested?" Claude supplies.

"Yeah. Wait. Hang on." He fumbles with the door to his car. Easing it open, he turns. Claude hears a faint rustling.

When he turns back, she bursts into laughter. Jamie holds a mock bouquet of striped lollipops, Jolly Ranchers, Snickers bars, and a packet of M&Ms. He wrapped it with a carefully cut and taped Cheetos bag.

"I thought you'd freak out if I brought you real flowers," he says, and she laughs again.

Her laughter seems to encourage him. "Claude Vanderly," he says formally, clearing his throat, "will you be my girlfriend? Will you sit next to me at lunch and steal my fries? Will you make me watch all the bad movies you like?"

"They're not bad," she murmurs.

He ignores that. "Will you walk into my house through the front door? Will you try going out with me?"

It's not giving up her independence. It's not chaining herself to the patriarchy. It's taking a step. Hell, the step probably

341

won't last till prom. Who knows? She wraps her hands around the junk and leans in. "Okay," she says.

"You're beautiful," he breathes, and kisses her.

It's a gentle kiss—maybe it will be good to take things slow, for once. And she promised Mom she wouldn't invite him in, anyway. She can feel his smile against her mouth, breaking wide open, and she smiles, too.

35

THE AIRHEAD CHEERLEADER

The holiday market buzzes, still busy despite the fact that it's a Sunday evening and Lorne hasn't exactly been in a holiday mood. Avery's family goes every year, and this year is no exception. It will take bigger problems than a murder-assault case to keep the Crosses from showing their faces at a community event.

Avery's not sorry. She's desperate for fresh air. The minute she got home this morning, her phone was confiscated and she was installed on the couch with a cup of hot cocoa and the promise that she's grounded for the rest of her life. She can't tell if her parents are proud of her. It's like they want to pretend nothing happened.

The press came this morning. The Crosses said that Avery needs rest. That she was a little angel and they never lost faith. They sat in the living room, keeping the bay windows clear, the room brightly lit, so that the photographers could get their shots of the family united. Healing.

When they were alone again, Avery's dad looked at his lap,

jaw clenched. Her mom traced little circles on the quilt over her chair and finally broke the silence. "Aves . . . why didn't you tell us?"

Because they would have told her to do what made her look good, not what would have helped her. She thought of the way her father dismissed Lily Fransen and said, "It was hard."

Mrs. Cross put a hand on her leg. "I know you're at an age when you think you have the solution to every problem."

Avery stared into her cocoa. *No one else had one.*

"But sometimes you need help, okay?" Mr. and Mrs. Cross exchanged a look. "We're going to withdraw you from school."

Avery blinked. "Okay." She wasn't sure how she felt about that—but maybe she felt good. She wouldn't have to walk the whispering halls. She wouldn't have to hear people wonder aloud if she got raped, if she did it in a classroom, if she was less unwilling than she claimed. . . . She wouldn't have to pretend that it didn't bother her.

"And we think you should take some time off from the dating scene."

That stung, enough for Avery to jerk her head. "Why?"

"You need to process."

"You wouldn't say that if I were still with Michael."

"That's not true," Mrs. Cross started.

"I won't stop being bi just because you tell me to." Avery glared into the cocoa. She took a sip that congealed on her tongue, and her stomach clenched like a fist.

Mrs. Cross sighed. "We're trying to do what's best for you. Okay?" *And they don't want to be seen with a daughter who dates girls.* "Your father's going to talk to some schools, see if this changes any minds about you being on a college cheer team." More like see if they had to give bigger donations to get her on one.

Mrs. Cross took a deep breath and pasted on a smile. Clearly this conversation was over. "Now, do you want to go to the fair? Your dad will stay home with you if you don't."

Avery has learned to be tired of being a people pleaser, but the fair is her one shot at freedom. So she said, "Of course I'm going," in her best good-girl voice and slipped into her coat.

Avery carefully helps her mom set her plate of gingerbread cookies on the judges' table at the winter fair. Mrs. Cross keeps one arm wrapped around Avery, holding tight and kissing the top of her head for the judges and effectively preventing Avery from sneaking off.

"Can I go to the skating rink?" Avery says.

Mrs. Cross purses her lips. "I don't think that's safe right now."

"Why wouldn't it be safe?" Avery asks.

"They still don't know who shot the maniac," Mrs. Cross says. "There's a killer out here, and you're going to be careful. This is what I mean when I say you don't know everything you think you do, Aves. Claude Vanderly could've aimed that gun at *you*."

"Claude didn't do it, Mom," Avery mutters.

Mrs. Cross isn't listening. She fishes around in her purse. "But you can have this. For an *hour*. No more." She holds out Avery's phone. Avery barely contains her squeak of excitement.

The sky is clear, the twinkling lights of the market dimming the pinprick stars. The market is full of kids who don't care who Avery Cross is. They play tag in the stalls, get yelled at for throwing snowballs, barter for candy, and line up to rent ice skates. Avery can focus on them and ignore the whispers that circulate among the older ones. Every so often she glimpses a face from the halls of JLH, but no one comes to say hi. So she wanders, between Lincoln Log stalls filled with candles and little ceramic elves and things that everyone thinks they want but no one actually needs, and she thinks about how she's free. She'll never run into him at the grocery store. She'll never catch his eye at a school dance. She'll never change into jeans halfway through the day again because she's more likely to see him after lunch. She doesn't have to worry about him lurking places like the winter fair. She can go where she wants without having to think about where he isn't.

Something touches her arm and she turns. It's Michael, with two hot chocolates. Blood pools in her belly, then rushes back to her face, making her hot and cold at once.

"Hey," Michael says.

"Um." Avery glances around. Mrs. Cross is talking to a judge, Mr. Cross is smiling at Heather Halifax. "Hey." She gestures at the two cups of chocolate. "Got a date?"

It's supposed to be a joke. It falls flat. "Actually, I bought it for you."

Poor, sweet Michael. He didn't deserve her. She takes the hot chocolate and glances back at her mom. Still occupied. Together she and Michael walk to the edge of the ice rink and sit on a bench. In the rink, groups of shrieking tweens and teens falter on their skates. A guy tries to impress his girlfriend by skating backward. It makes Avery think of Gwen. She imagines stumbling together on the ice, giggling at their own clumsiness until they can't feel their toes. She thinks about buying Gwen a hot chocolate and sharing it in her car. She wonders what it would be like just . . . walking with her. In the market, through the halls at school, down Lorne's empty little main street.

"It was fun when we did that," Michael says, and Avery comes to herself with a jolt.

"Hm?" He's looking at the skaters. "Oh. Yeah." They'd clung to each other until Kyle Landry, the only decent skater in Lorne, had torn between them shouting, *"Get a room!"*

Even now, she's thinking about Gwen when she's with Michael. "Though it was more fun when you lost the ball toss."

"I did not lose the ball toss. The ball toss cheated." Michael laughs.

"We had some good memories together," says Avery, and Michael turns toward her with a serious face. *Had.*

"Did we? All this stuff with Mr. G . . . Look, maybe you don't want to talk about it, but it was going on at the same time, wasn't it?"

She pauses, then nods. Michael's hand balls into a fist. "There's nothing you can do about it now," she says quickly.

"I can still be pissed," he snaps.

True enough.

"Was he . . . doing something the other day? When I walked in on you two at the gym?"

"Um." That's a little harder to explain. "Yeah. But I was

kind of angling for it." Michael's face screws up in confusion and the beginnings of anger, so Avery goes on. "We were looking for evidence. Gwen and me. She was supposed to break into his computer, I was supposed to keep him away from the room."

"By letting him molest you?" Michael says.

"By faking my ankle so he'd look at it." By letting him touch her. For Emma, for Lizzy, for the girls he wouldn't ever get the chance to hurt. The understanding makes her feel lighter, even as she feels a crawling on her legs that she won't ever be able to itch away. "I'm glad you came in when you did, though."

"I wish you'd told me." Michael's face is hard, but he's not angry at her. "I'd have chopped that asshole's dick off."

"Yeah," Avery says, and she thinks, *Maybe*. Maybe he'd do it. Or maybe so many people would have accused her of lying first that he'd struggle to believe her. She's not sure her own parents believe her even now. She's heard the words *pillar of the community* more than once where Garson is concerned.

"I mean it, Aves," Michael says. "I would have believed you, and I would have done something. I'll always believe you."

"Not just me, Michael. Every woman who tells you something. Promise?"

Michael smiles over his cup. "Promise."

They finish their chocolate without speaking, watch a bunch of four-year-olds spend more time on their butts than their skates.

"Weird that they didn't arrest anyone for killing Adams West," Michael muses.

"What?"

"The hobo guy. Adams West."

"He wasn't . . ." Avery stops. She has to be careful with what she says. "Maybe it was unrelated."

He shrugs. "My money's on Vanderly." Avery smacks him. "What? She's a cold lady. She's got the chops for it."

Yes. Claude fits the profile of a stone-cold high school killer. In a way that sweet, sweet Avery never will. Maybe, Avery thinks, all a person needs to plan a perfect murder is a bunch of friends who are all willing to believe she's stupid.

Luckily, she doesn't intend to commit murder again any time soon.

They hug and he walks away. The scent of his aftershave reminds her of safety and comfort, and she feels a pang at the loss of it. But while she misses it, she doesn't really *want* it.

She pulls out her phone. I think we're in the clear, she texts to Claude. Then she erases it. She also erases everyone thinks u killed him and lucky u taking the blame. She wouldn't be surprised if the police monitor their phones for months to come. She settles for, u ok? If Claude hadn't gone after the gun, she might not have been arrested last night. And if Avery hadn't called her on Friday, she wouldn't have gone after the gun.

"We have a huge problem." Avery stood in front of Gwen's window, feeling a little foolish, like she was about to serenade her love from beneath.

She couldn't think about these things now. "They found a body in the river."

Gwen's face drained of blood. "Shit—"

"It's not her," Avery said quickly. She levered herself up on the windowsill. "Can I come in?"

"Be quiet," Gwen whispered, and smoothed over her bed-covers. Avery slipped her shoes off and landed lightly on the bed. She'd never been in a bedroom with Gwen before. "It's him."

Him. The man they didn't know, the man who'd attacked them.

"Oh." Gwen frowned. Then realization hit her. "Oh. Oh shit. Garson's going to know she's not dead, isn't it?" The Welsh expression slipped out. She sounded just like her mum as she started to pace, still whispering furiously. Avery watched her and tried to focus, even though her heart constricted every time a lock of hair fell in Gwen's face, every time she took a deep breath and bit her lip, thinking. Did Gwen know she took on her mother's Welsh accent whenever she was upset? "Okay. Okay. Is Garson going to the competition tomorrow?"

She looked expectantly at Avery, catching the other girl staring. "I hope not. But I think so," Avery said.

"So we're going to have to get evidence while he's gone. But we can't break into his office. Shit. But maybe he stores his stuff on the cloud, so we can break into his house computer." She snapped her fingers. "Does he have a home security system?"

"I've never been to his house," Avery said, horrified.

"And I won't have a car, so I can't get over there. . . ." Gwen picked up her phone. "We're going to have to ask Claude." She flopped down beside Avery on the bed. The gentle brush of their arms made Avery shiver in a way that had nothing to do with the cold.

"Do you think she'll do it?" Avery said.

"Will she be mad? Yes. Will she do it? Also yes." Gwen punched the call button and they leaned over the phone together, hair and breath intermingling. Waiting.

Her phone buzzes. Avery expects Claude, or maybe a text from Mrs. Cross saying, Get back here now. But her sender is one Study Buddy: Look behind you.

She turns.

Gwen leans against a booth selling reusable hand warmers, arms folded, smiling. Her dark hair is tucked under a winter hat. Slowly she approaches, and though Avery sees the same weight in her eyes, Gwen seems to have a measure of hope, too. "This seat taken?"

"Actually, I was thinking of going for a walk." Avery shivers. Her butt is numb from the bench.

"Cool." Gwen holds out a hand.

Clasping it feels strange, somehow. More intimate than when they made out in the back of Avery's car. Everyone can see the linked hands, and everybody knows what they mean. It feels like she's being performative again. But at least this time, she's performing for herself.

"Your mom let you come out tonight?" Avery says.

"We agreed we didn't want to just stay home," Gwen says.

"And I knew you'd be here, you keep going on about that gingerbread competition like your mom's baking for Jesus—"

Avery laughs, drawing a few looks from vendors. The glances they throw her are almost disapproving, like she's supposed to be tragic and traumatized now that they know what she's been through. But she doesn't have to pretend for anyone anymore. She wants to ignore her mom's no-being-bi rule, especially while Mrs. Cross is distracted.

"Aves?" Gwen seems nervous.

Her stomach jolts unpleasantly. She's had enough breakup conversations to be worried when she hears this tone. "Yes?"

"You know I'm going to leave Lorne when I graduate." Crap. "And my parents have decided to move away, too." Double crap.

"Uh, yeah." She wishes she hadn't drunk her hot chocolate so fast. She could use something to hide behind.

Gwen stops and turns. Takes Avery's other hand and looks her in the eye. "Okay, we all know Lorne is a shithole. And if you want to get out, even if *we* don't work out too well—you can be my roommate. You can work or go to school or something. But you'll have a place that's not here."

Avery's mouth falls open.

"What?" Gwen says.

She wants to lean forward and kiss Gwen, under the twinkle lights of the winter fair, with cheesy Christmas music playing around them. But Lorne's not ready to see two girls kiss in public. So Avery turns her answer over, carefully, before replying. "I think that's the nicest thing anyone's ever said to me." Not many people believe in the future of Avery Cross.

"We're all going to get out of here. You, me, Claude," Gwen says as they start to walk again.

"Adams West?" Avery suggests.

They stop at a shop selling snow globes. The vendor takes her time talking to a hetero couple at the other end of the stall, but Avery doesn't care. She can watch the snow swirl in a little snowglobe with a bridge and a stream and a troll inside.

"Hopefully already gone," Gwen says quietly. "But I guess we'll just have to see about that."

THE GOOD GIRL

On the night of March 25, 2016, a body was found at the bottom of a ravine in Jefferson National Forest. The body was one Elizabeth Sayer, resident troubled teen of the nearby town of Lorne. The death shook the town and served as a cautionary tale: good girls didn't do what Elizabeth Sayer did. She partied too hard and had too many boyfriends. She slept through class and ignored the advice of her teachers and friends. But not one year before, Elizabeth Sayer was the top of her year, beloved by students and administration alike. She was a heavy contender for the most prestigious scholarship in Colorado. She'd never been caught with a drink or with a boy. Lizzy Sayer was the textbook example of the good girl. What happened?

Lizzy Sayer was always precocious. She wanted to be the best at everything she tried, and she was—whether it was a spelling bee or a musical performance or an Advanced Placement Calculus exam. She still had time for her friends, her sister, and the younger students, who looked up to her as a mentor. And she had big plans—to win a full scholarship to a college on the East Coast, to major in business with a minor in biology or physics, to start a company that would change the world.

The broken body found near Anna's Run tells a different story: a girl overcome by addiction, in great distress, her future in shambles. When her body was found, police ruled the case a suicide. They determined that fresh boot prints on the scene had belonged to a hiker and not to a companion. Their redacted report concluded that Lizzy, overwhelmed by her stress and distraught at ruining her own life, made the choice to end it.

The police have done what so many men and women do constantly: they assigned Lizzy a label that made them comfortable, that explained her life the way they saw it, and not the way it was. They placed the blame on her, so that they didn't have to go looking for who might be responsible.

Lizzy Sayer was a thorough young woman who documented everything. She wrote about the first time she was approached, after school, by lacrosse coach and school counselor Kenneth Garson. According to her diaries, he asked how the scholarship applications were going. He offered to give her some help and they made plans to meet in his office. Lizzy thought Ken Garson was funny and handsome, too sharp-witted and interesting for Lorne. She recounts his stories of adventure in his days before Lorne, and she writes with compassion about his mother's long illness, the move home to take care of her, the ultimate heartbreak when the elderly Mrs. Garson passed away from lung cancer.

Records show that Ken Garson moved to Lorne in 2012 from Arizona. Census information reveals that Mrs. Garson is alive and a retired nurse in Phoenix.

Lizzy also described the first day she was alone and unsupervised with Garson: he invited her on a hike. She was excited at the prospect of climbing a fourteener, something she'd never done before, and was under the impression that others would be joining them. In her diary she notes her surprise when she discovered they were alone. But she wasn't worried. She was comfortable around Mr. Garson. He felt she was the only one mature enough for a venture like this, she writes. She was the only one who wouldn't balk at taking a sip from his flask when they finally reached the top of the mountain.

They stopped for lunch on the way home. Garson paid. Lizzy, who had never been on a date before, wondered if this was what dates were like. She jokingly asked if they could go hang gliding next time.

Mr. Garson said yes.

Receipts from office administration show funds going to Garson for "field trips" that take place outside Lorne: hiking, ziplining, a bear-watching tour in Rocky Mountain National Park. Despite administration rules, he never provided a list of students who partook in these excursions, nor any permission slips obtained from parents. Announcements for these trips could not be found in physical form or on the school website. No student has claimed to have gone on one aside from Lizzy. But the money disappeared.

At the same time, Lizzy began to experiment. She stayed

up later and complained of fatigue, writing eventually in her diary that she'd "fixed the problem." She also started alluding to a new boyfriend. Though she never mentioned him by name, her references to the age difference made it clear: she was seeing an adult. He pushed her boundaries—she drank a beer, even though she'd always thought her first beer would be with her dad. She skipped a class to go see him. When her grades dipped, he was there to console her. He encouraged her to forget about her extracurriculars and the classes she once prized. As her old life slipped away from her, she clung to the idea of this wise older man who got her drunk or high for her own spiritual enlightenment or for her own maturation. She became obsessed with keeping her lover, and just as obsessed with keeping this lover a secret.

Since he began working for the Jefferson-Lorne school district, Ken Garson has received seventeen complaints about his behavior from female students or their parents. Most of these complaints concern an unwanted touch or remark. They are mentioned in passing in his teacher file; the complaints themselves are locked in a file cabinet inaccessible to student workers. One former student, Melody Lankhe, alleged that he kissed her. Evidence suggests that no action was taken against Garson regarding the incident; Melody transferred to Empire High School.

But is it all a lie? Are the allegations a result of overactive imaginations, of girls who like drama and trouble? Is it simply because Ken Garson is the best-looking single teacher at school?

Lizzy was seen going in and out of Garson's office regularly in the last six months of her life. This surprised no one—she was a troubled teen, a falling star, and Garson was the school counselor. His counseling sessions had little effect, however. Lizzy descended, fighting with her parents, her sister, anyone who used to know her. Until the night she died.

At eleven p.m. on the twenty-fifth of March, Lizzy went to the Circle K gas station at the edge of town. Videos of her interaction with the attendant show a sober girl buying a quart of milk and a bag of Doritos. She left from there and hit up the ATM—several ATMs, in fact. She went to every cash machine in town, withdrawing $200 from each until her savings account was dry. At each one her PIN was correctly entered on the first try. It's easy to speculate that she was preparing to run away; it's not so easy to know whether she intended to take Garson with her, or whether he called and convinced her to see him one last time.

There is no record of her stopping at a liquor store that night.

At midnight, she rang her sister's phone. Gwen Sayer did not pick up. Around one a.m., Mrs. Sayer's phone rang. It was the police.

"Suicide," they told the Sayer family, without showing them pictures of the body and the boot prints. They pointed to the bottles and pill bags in the car. They never ran a check on the boots. They never found out that the prints come from a Pine Nation Overland in a size eight and a half. They never considered the teaching body, all of whom had Overland hiking boots courtesy of a parent donation. They never looked at Garson's feet, which are often clad in Pine Nations and in a surprisingly small size for a man. Perhaps it wouldn't have been enough evidence to charge him. But they didn't even try.

Lizzy's story fits a classic cautionary tale: girls can be one thing or the other. We are good, or we are bad. We are smart, or we are stupid. We are the Madonna, or we are the whore.

You call me many things: A slut. A nerd. A liar. You have the power to call me everything and nothing. You told the world all the things I did wrong, and all the things I didn't do right enough. You told my story . . . but it wasn't really mine. It was the story we all shared—the liars, the bad girls, the good. The nerds and the cheerleaders. The tragic, heartbreaking, conveniently dead girls. The silenced.

The silenced. So many of us are. You don't see it, because we talk, but we make sure to talk only about the things that make you comfortable. The things that *won't* make you uncomfortable. We wouldn't want that.

Only, I do want that. I want to talk not just for me, but for all of us. For all of us who were told to keep our mouths shut, or else. My name is Emma Baines, and I wanted to tell Lizzy's story.

This is the end of Adams West. I hope you enjoyed the ride. . . . Well, that's not entirely true. I hope you learned something, but I kind of think you didn't. Please, Lorne. Prove me wrong. Please.

And Lizzy, I know it's too late for you. I don't know if you can see this, but we did it all for you. More than anyone else, maybe.

I hope our truths bring you justice.

ACKNOWLEDGMENTS

It is always exciting to reach into new territory with a book, and my first foray into the thriller genre would not be possible without the support and guidance of many wonderful people. First, thank you to my agent, Kurestin Armada, who helps me dream big and plan practically, and who nudges me into new genres and experiences. I look forward to many more journeys into the unknown with you.

The Glasstown team has been incredible every step of the way. Lexa Hillyer, Alexa Wejko, Deeba Zargarpur, and Brandie Coonis: thank you for this project, for your enthusiasm, your invaluable insight, and your knowledge of craft. Working with you has been a wonderful process.

Elizabeth Lynch, my fabulous editor, sharpened all the edges of *The Good Girls* and had great insight into the project from the very first phone call. Thank you for believing in us.

Thank you so much to Diana Sousa, who designed the cover of *The Good Girls*, and to Kaethe Butcher for the cover art. It's stunning, thrilling, chilling, and everything I want the book to be.

This writer works best when she can bounce ideas off other authors, bemoan bouts of writer's block, pick through problems, and be a part of a writerly cheerleading team. Much love for the Armada, who make great work-from-home colleagues, and to my team in the greater Copenhagen area: Kitty, Crystal, Helene, Anja, Skjalm, and Marie.

And shamelessly saving the best for last: my beautiful family. Thank you for a literal lifetime of support, love, enthusiasm, and hope for my writing. To Mom, Dad, Liz, Elias, and Baby—I couldn't ask for better.

It's time to acknowledge something unpleasant: According to RAINN, one in six women in the United States has been a victim of rape or attempted rape. Every seventy-three seconds, someone in the country is sexually assaulted—and every nine minutes, that victim is under the age of eighteen. Both high-profile cases and statistics support the same conclusion: The vast majority of abusers are not punished. Cases that do end up in the public eye place the victim under close scrutiny, pick apart their lives, accuse them of being too drunk, too loose, too confused or confusing. It's easier to say nothing than get destroyed, discredited, and denied justice. Many great people are working to change that, and things have improved, but we still have a long way to go.

If you or someone you know needs help, please get in touch with RAINN, the Rape, Abuse & Incest National Network, at www.rainn.org, or by telephone at 800-656-4673.